Act I

The Crimson Mask

Joel Doyle

Act I

Yes. I wrote a book

Act I

October

A warm coffee sits on an old diner table. The early morning sunlight seeps through windows that have seen decades of patrons coming and going down the main vein of the city. The sunlight is a welcome change, the rain hadn't stopped for what felt like weeks. Cold was setting in as the days got shorter. The city braced itself for a change.

"Any breakfast to go with that coffee?" asked the server. The question brought Detective Sam Cole out of his blank stare through the window "um, no, thanks, I'm just waiting for someone" The diner door chimed with a bell just as he spoke. Another man entered. He wore a long coat draped over a wrinkled button-up shirt. The man slid into the booth across from Sam. Neither made eye contact, they weren't much for greetings. "Coffee?" asked the server "yes, all of it, in a large jug please" responded Detective Christopher Davis. That response drew a slight smile from the server. He settled into the booth and pulled his long coat off and set it beside him. His wrinkled unkept shirt showed signs of someone getting dressed in the dark, or someone who slept in their clothes from the previous night. Detective Cole pulled the coffee from his mouth "did you even sleep?". They finally made eye contact, "Took off my shoes, hit the bed and bounced back

Act I

into my shoes and out the door." responded Davis with a grin as he went back to staring out the window. The Crimson Bay Chronicle, the last of the printed newspapers, sat on the table. The paper had been laid to keep the headlines face down.

The server brought detective Davis his coffee. "Anything else for you?" she asked. "No, just this, and maybe ten more" As the detective tried to revive himself with caffeine, Cole nudged the paper slightly, this caught Davis's eye. "Have you seen it yet?" questioned Cole, the steam off the coffee clouded Davis's face "yeah, yeah on the way over. How could something like this leak to the press so fast? It just doesn't make sense"

Cole agreed with a subtle head nod, "we should probably go" detective Cole finished his coffee and placed money on the table. This caught Davis off guard, "But I'm not, oh come on" as he downs the rest of his coffee. Both men head for the door, the server (Grace, according to her name tag) notices the newspaper they left behind. Voices travel in a small diner, she was already curious to see what was on the other side of the paper. As she approached, she felt a slight twinge of anxiety. What could rattle two detectives and cause them to pull an all nighter. As the paper turned over, the headline caused an audible gasp from Grace. DE LUCA FOUND DEAD it read in block letters.

The chill of the late October air hit both men as the started down the sidewalk. Even with the sun finally out, the city still felt damp from the rain. There was no warmth to be felt that morning. "Mine or yours?" asked Cole, knowing the answer before his partner even responded. "It's a twenty-minute drive through the city, there is no way that I am not napping" Detective Cole sarcastically scoffed at his partner as

Act I

he climbed into his rebuilt '66 Mustang. He took a lot of pride in that car; it was his dream car as a child.

"Why didn't you get the coffee to go?" asked Cole as he fired up the engine. "I Panicked, I'm tired, everything hurts" said Davis as he clipped his seatbelt. "Well get it together, because this is going to be a rat's nest with the press and the crowds" Warned Cole. They pulled out onto the street; it would be a slow crawl through the city with everyone else on their way to work. "How bad do you think the bridge is?" asked Davis as he fought the urge to nod off. Crimson Bay was a city divided; the bridge connected both sides of town and was the only way over the water. The city was a mix of gritty, industrial sections full of factories and power plants. On the other side, wealthy high rises lining the downtown core. That morning the city welcomed the sunshine; it bounced off the tall buildings and lit up the darkened alleyways.

'It'll be bad, but it gives us time to figure out how to approach this" responded Cole. They both had experienced their fair share of mind haunting crime scenes; this one would be no different. Eight years of chasing leads and diving deep into the criminal mind had molded Sam into a sharp, detailed detective with little patience for people wasting his time.

Detective Davis on the other hand was still relatively new to the job and some might say he drew the short straw when it came to partners. Everyone considered Sam Cole a lone wolf, the fact that the detective agreed to the partnership caught everyone off guard. It had only been six months, which is six months longer than anyone had in the office pool.

Act I

Davis found himself staring out the window at the skyline slowly passing by as they moved towards the bridge. "This could be anyone" he exclaimed.

Cole let the comment hang there and only gave it a subtle head shift in Davis's direction. "Victor De Luca is connected to everyone who is anyone in this city. The list of people who would want him dead is a mile long. This is going to take forever to figure out" Davis almost had an air of complaint in his voice.

Victor De Luca was a real estate mogul and developer that had deep ties to the city. All the politicians, the judges, the mayor, everyone was on his contact list. Detective Davis did have a glimmer of truth in his exhausted synopsis. This would take a while to figure out.

"The team has been there all night; we will see if they have anything for us to look at. Theres an answer in that house, and we are going to find it" Cole was always collected, he had a process, he was calm but had an intensity about him that always garnered attention when he entered a room." Don't talk to the press" warned Cole. "This is a powder keg, and the match is already lit. It's very likely they have people on the inside leaking information; we have to play this one very close to the chest. It's our case and I won't have them turn this into a circus"

The morning traffic was heavy as expected. The bridge was full of cars; the smell of exhaust filled the air. Beyond the bridge, the cityscape grew along the water, it was expansive and a sight to behold. It was a view that sold anyone when they first experienced it. This was the other side of the city, away from its gritty industrial counterpart. This was the part of town that everyone dreamed of living in. But for all its beauty and

Act I

endless opportunities, it had a past that stained it to its very core and only certain people could see it for what it really was.

Sam Cole was one of those people.

The other side of the bridge had that bright lights, big city feel. The towering skyscrapers lining the enormous grid of streets with many small pockets of villages and shops. Each section had its own identity. Once you finally make it to the outskirts of the city, the gated communities take over. Massive trees cover the streets and keep the mansions in a mystery state.

Detective Davis looks on in awe as they wind through the gated community. Mansion upon mansion as far as the eye could see "I need to move to this side" he said. Only

a slight eye roll and on observation from detective Cole "This side is much more dangerous than ours my friend, much more"

The press had already made a crowd outside the gates of De Luca's Victorian style mansion. It had a very gothic look to it; painted all black with large torches outside the main entrance. The tree-lined driveway climbed the large hill the mansion sat on. Detective Cole approached the crowd. His black Mustang drawing everyone's eye with a microphone and notepad. "Are they going to move?" asked Davis. "I doubt it, they're vultures" said Cole as he put the car in park and rolled down the window. An officer approached the car from the crowd and spotted Cole and Davis. He immediately turned and started removing people from the gate.

"Alright! Everyone clear out. Make room!" he shouted at the crowd. This vehicle had left before the press arrived, so they hadn't seen it yet that day. Everyone became curious of who these two men could be. Sam recognized a few

Act I

faces from the local news stations and previous dealings on high profile cases. Laura Snow from channel 5 news is one that always stands out in the crowd. She was on the tv in the diner that morning, likely a sleepless night for her as well.

The gate finally swung open to let the detectives drive in. The shouting from the reporters drowned out the news broadcast on the radio. Everything was about the murder. "Who killed Victor!? Do you have any leads!?" was a repeated cry as the car drove away from the crowd. "Vultures" said Sam almost under his breath. All they want is information to be the first one to break any story. Sam had dealt with them for years and in this city, they pushed hard for information. They neared the house; the full scene coming into view. Police Vans, Ambulances, squad cars and even the Police Chief. Oscar Freeman didn't make many appearances unless he knew it would be high profile.

Stepping out of the car, they could both feel the pressure of the situation. There was almost fear amongst the team as they approached the steps. Walking through the crime scene tape, showing their credentials to officers, they didn't recognize. "I thought this was ours" said Davis in a hushed tone. Cole quickly responded "It is, those are Freemans guys. Special investigators. Stooges." They walked through the very tall, wooden front doors. It felt like a castle inside. The main entry was a cathedral with a giant double staircase. The architecture was some of the most impressive works they had ever seen. Even though they had been there hours prior, they hadn't got the chance to take in the full effect of the house.

The forensic team in charge of mapping out the crime scene were standing at the foot of the stairwell. "James, what do we have so far?" asked Cole to the lead of the team. James White

Act I

turned to Detective Cole, "Well Sam, why don't we go upstairs, and I can walk you through it?"

The three men headed upstairs, as they reached the top James stopped them. "You can see the first signs of struggle here" as he pointed to the blood-stained railing. "The trail continues down this hall towards the bedroom" blood was splattered on the walls and the floor, very much like a horror movie. The two detectives had already been through the initial shock of this hallway earlier that morning, this time it didn't even register. "There are bloody handprints on the door and the wall, almost like he was walking away from someone. Like he was hunted." They slowly pushed the door open to Victor's room. The body of the victim was still laid out on his stomach on the bed. A pool of blood covered the sheets. "Yeah, I don't know if I can look at this again," said Davis. "I plan on trying to sleep at some point in my life"

Detective Cole turned to his partner "What? you've never seen a guy with his head chopped off before?" This stuff didn't bother Sam Cole. It was the job. He was more than desensitized, but Davis, he wasn't ready for a beheaded body so early in the morning.

"No." mouthed Davis. Barely getting any sound out.
"Even on patrol? Really? Nothing this bad?" questioned Sam.

Davis was slightly squeamish. Sam knew it, so he tested the limits of his partner. "So, no addicts under the bridge eating each other? No homeless people in the tunnels doing the unimaginable? You must have seen something on this level?" Cole pushed, and Davis wilted." I'm going to get some air" said Davis as he backed out of the room. Detective Cole was comfortable in the uncomfortable. That's what made him so good at the job.

Act I

Victor De Luca had been decapitated by a sword. His own sword. They knew this because the killer left it laying on the floor. There was no attempt to hide it, almost left like a trophy. Victor's head had rolled into the corner. "How do you think it got all the way over there?" asked Cole.

"He kicked it. A last act of rage perhaps."

"Makes Sense" agreed Cole.

"Anything else I should know?" asked Cole. His forensic colleague turned to him and posed an interesting question. "How well do you know Victor?"

"Honestly, only surface level. I've seen his commercials; I've heard the rumors, but this is the first time he has crossed our path" stated Cole. "Well, he wasn't his father as they say. But he definitely died the exact same way" These words from James hit the detective like a brick.

"What did you say?" he asked. "You mean, his father was also decapitated?"

James tried to fill the detective in on the history, "You don't know the story of his father? The crimson mask killer from the nineties? Victor Sr was one of the victims." This was long before Sam Cole even lived in Crimson Bay. He grew up two hours north of the city. Moved here for school and never left. This little history lesson somehow escaped him in his past eight years. " How have I never heard this story?" questioned Cole. James tried to keep his description as straight forward as possible. "We had a serial killer in this city in the nineties. I was only a kid, but I remember my parents talking about it. But now no one talks about it, it's

like a dark family secret that everyone keeps hidden." The thought occurred to Cole that maybe there was even more to this city than he imagined.

Act I

His almost perplexed stare prompted James to give even more detail "It was major. The old crime families were involved, the mayor, everyone." Crimson Bay in its current state was a big city with a lot of history but the old days of it being run by the crime families were behind it. Detective Cole had always assumed that there was still a tie back to the old days when the mob's payroll included every major player in the city. But he had yet to witness anything that would prove it. "Did they catch the killer?" asked Cole.

"No. It's cold case now" answered James.

Cole pondered for a moment. "Has anyone else mentioned the connection of this murder and his fathers?"

"Forensics, Davis and you are the only ones who have seen this. Well, the housekeeper too." Said James. The similarity theory had completely distracted Sam Cole, you would never know both men were having this conversation next to a severed head. "Not even Freeman?" asked

Cole. "Hasn't been upstairs yet, I figured he would be all over this but he's a ghost" responded James. Cole nodded and put his notepad away. He motioned to James that he was going to leave, and James acknowledged. Sam's Mind was starting to race, why hadn't he heard of a serial killer? What else didn't he know about this city?

Cole found Davis downstairs with what seemed to be the rest of the precinct. "Feeling better?" he asked.

"I may never recover. I'm going to need a few weeks off" joked Davis. Cole did not crack a smile. "I'm going to see Freeman and then we are out of here" stated Cole as he walked away.

Detective Cole made his way outside. He located Chief Freeman near his car. Their relationship wasn't anything

Act I

special, no lunches or drinks after work. Just one detective doing his job and his boss. "What do you think, kid?" asked Freeman. Neither man made eye contact.

"Did you go upstairs at all?"

"Don't need to. That's what I have you for"

Detective Cole leaned in and lowered his voice. "His fucking head was cut off. Does that mean anything to you?"

Chief Oscar Freeman shot a look mixed of confusion and fear. Like he had stumbled upon something he shouldn't have. He immediately took out his cigarettes and lit one.

"Not here kid, not here. Find me after the press conference" he said as he walked back toward the house. The response from the Chief told Sam that there was more to this story than meets the eye.

The circus show was about to begin. The press conference had been called for eleven o'clock in the morning. Freeman would address the murder and take questions from the Vultures

for a few minutes and then turn the whole thing over to the press director Travis Robinson. That's when Detective Cole would have to make his move to get some answers from Freeman. But for now, he would just have to wait.

"Let's go" motioned Cole to Davis as he opened the door to his Mustang. "What did Freeman say?" asked Davis as he climbed in the passenger seat. "It's not the first time he's seen the headless horseman, let's just say that" said Cole. A confused look upon Davis's face was the proper reaction to that line. "I don't know if you notice back there but I turned six shades of green so I'm clearly not at my best, so could you

Act I

explain that one to me like I'm a five-year-old?" asked Davis. The side eye shift from Cole again followed by "De Luca's father was decapitated too. Do you think that's just an unlucky family coincidence?"

The Detective fired up the engine and pulled down the driveway. "What do you know about the Crimson Mask Killer?" questioned Cole. "Because I have never heard that name until today and apparently it was a serial killer that got away, and he killed Victor's father the same way." Davis had heard the name but not much of the detail. He was only a baby when it

happened. Most of the details were kept tight lipped. "I haven't heard that name since the nineties, when I was a little kid."

"Watch out!" yelled Davis. Cole was becoming increasingly frustrated with the thought of this serial killer and the lack of information. This was causing him to speed up going down the driveway. The gate was open, and the crowd of reporters were in the line of fire. Davis grabbed

the dash as Cole hit the brakes. The crowd of reporters ran for cover and the car came screeching to a halt only a few feet from disaster. The usually calm and collected Detective Cole had to take a deep breath and try to reset himself. He knew this level of frustration would only hurt his investigation. Cole could only give a half-hearted wave of apology as he pulled out onto the road. He wasn't sorry, they were lucky to get the wave.

The drive back to the station was quiet. On the outside. On the inside Cole's mind was still racing through all the possibilities that could arise from this case. Meanwhile Davis was flipping through radio stations, trying to avoid a news brief but with no such luck.

Act I

"Wealthy Real Estate Mogul Victor De Luca II was found dead in his north side mansion earlier this morning. Police are suspecting foul play. They plan to brief the public at eleven. Keep it locked on Q97 for the updates as they come available."

"Great" said Cole.

He turned off the radio.

"Are you thinking it's a copycat?" asked Davis. He couldn't take the silence. Cole knew he had to keep Davis on a short leash. "I don't know yet. But Freemans reaction is telling me he knows a lot more about this. Keep this in the car. This has shit show written all over it."

Detective Davis was still green, but he could read a room and going around asking too many questions would stir up the masses and kill the investigation. He knew how Detective Cole worked and tried to walk step for step. Learn as much as he can and try not to get in the way.

They crossed the bridge to their side of the water "We have an hour before the press conference. I need food," said Cole. Davis was waiting for this; he was running on fumes. "Finally, I had a deep breath for breakfast. Diner?" The city had every type of food you could think of, and it was available at any time of day. So, they obviously ate at the most old school diner in town. It also helped that it was nowhere near the precinct. No officers, no other detectives hanging around, just coffee and hot food.

Grace Alexander was only halfway through her shift when the same two detectives from earlier came walking back through the door. The first one through the door was taller, thin with short dark hair and a very defined jaw covered in stubble from a very late night. (Sam Cole) The second man was

Act I

younger and a bit shorter. He had more of a muscular build, wavy hair, a slight deer in the headlights look on his face (Chris Davis). They sat down in the same booth as that morning, only they looked even more disheveled this time. "More coffee, gentlemen?" she asked with a bit of a sarcastic tone. She followed up with "Maybe an IV drip?"

A grin came across both men's faces. The reality that they looked horrible wasn't lost on them. "We'll add some food to the order this time. Two Breakfast Specials please." Said Cole as he rubbed his eyes, trying to keep himself awake. Davis looked at Cole with a quizzical face. "I'm an adult, I can order my own food"

"You take too much time thinking about what you want. Now you don't have to think, just eat." Replied Cole. This was a very true statement, even with the short amount of time spent together, Detective Cole had picked up on all of Detective Davis's quirks.

The ticking from the clock on the wall seemed to be louder this morning. Maybe it was the lack of sleep, maybe it was the pounding of blood rushing to his ears from the anxiety of what was to come. Whatever it was, time was seemingly against them.

"This is really getting to you, isn't it? I have never seen you this out of character before." Questioned Davis, he was very intrigued by a case that finally got detective Cole rattled. Cole was brought back to reality with Davis's question. He snapped out of it and looked at Davis and said "I've always had this feeling that everyone was lying about something. It's almost impossible to prove. It just always felt like there had to be something else behind the curtain. That there was more to the story and only a few people really had all the answers. This city gives off the working class feel on one side and the rich

Act I

elite on the other. Almost taunting everyone. Look what you could have. But it's a façade, a rouse, it's all smoke and mirrors. This could be the first crack in the armor." Davis's eyes had grown wide listening to Cole's diatribe about the city. Cole continued as their food arrived "Freeman saw ghosts out there. Ghosts that just came back to haunt him"

Act I

Old Dog. New Tricks

The crowds grew outside the Crimson Bay Police Department headquarters. They filled the large steps at the front entrance. A podium stood atop the stairs between the tall concrete pillars that lined the building. An architectural wonder that stole everything from the roman empire. The city was full of these buildings. Pillars and statues faced all the major buildings. Lions and Gargoyles defended the bank, the courthouse and City Hall. The jaded locals let the city's stunning views fade into obscurity, while tourists clamored for photos of the architectural marvels that built the landscape of Crimson Bay.

The eleven O'clock hour struck. The cameras and microphones pointed toward the podium as Police Chief Freeman walked out into the chilly morning air. A hush fell over the crowd. The whole city knew what was coming, but the verbal confirmation would sign off on everyone's suspicions. Freeman stepped to the microphone; he shuffled his notes and cleared his throat. He had given this briefing a few times before but nothing of this magnitude. A very prominent figure in the city had been murdered. Crime in the

Act I

city had been down for years, the days of shoot outs on the street were past. The city still had its problems, but everything was smaller scale and seemed manageable. "Good morning" the speaker echoed the sound down the street. "As you may have already heard, our city has lost one its most beloved residents. In the early hours of the day, we received a phone call that Victor De Luca had been found deceased. We can confirm that Mr. De Luca was found deceased in his home. There is an ongoing investigation as to cause of death and if foul play may have been involved. Until we have completed our investigation, no further comments will be made by our department. An update will be issued when we deem it appropriate. I will at this time open the floor for a few brief questions but that will be it for comments."

"Foul play, the guy's head was cut off with a sword. Yeah, I'd say it was foul play" These words came from under the breath of a shadowy figure behind one of the pillars. A figure that blended into the background of the other police officers and Investigators. Davis looked over at his partner. "Are you hiding back there? you're the lead on this; shouldn't we be out front?" Detective Cole stepped out from the shadow of the pillar. No one had heard his comment; his frustration was becoming an internal struggle. The chief knows more and is just standing out front lying in plain sight.

The crowd erupted into chaos as everyone tried to get their question out. This was a huge story, and they all wanted to be the one to break it wide open. The overwhelming response caused Freeman to pause and collect himself. He rubbed his police issued moustache, removed his hat and ran his hand through his greying hair. He had been doing this job for a very long time and was nearing retirement. This would likely be his last big case to oversee, and he knew it. He wanted

Act I

his last time to burn bright in the spotlight, one that he would be remembered for.

As Chief Freeman collected himself and motioned for the crowd to calm down, he was shot twice in the chest.

Killing him instantly.

He fell backwards amidst the screams and hysteria. Gunshots rang out, the sound bouncing off buildings. The scene almost seemed to play out in slow motion. Bystanders fleeing the steps, people diving for cover. Horrifying screams of fear as everyone ran for their lives. Officers drawing their weapons, scrambling to find where the shot came from. Blood started to slowly pour down the steps around the podium. A horrific scene captured on video in front of every member of the press. The press conference was live on every news channel in the city. Everyone had just witnessed the murder of the city's Police Chief in broad daylight.

Detective Cole stood on the stairs with his gun drawn. As did the rest of the police force. No one knew which direction to aim, let alone shoot. The pillars became cover for everyone else, the sound of blood curdling screams reached an ear-piercing level. Cole's ears were ringing as everything played out in front of him. A group of officers seemed to move across the street to one of the buildings. Another group rounded up bystanders and tried to get them to safety. A small group had created a wall around the Chief as the emergency responders arrived. A shockwave rippled through the city. It took mere seconds for everyone's outlook to change from intrigue and sympathy to unbridled fear and panic. Detective Davis landed in that group as well, "What the hell is happening?!" he yelled to Cole. But it was so chaotic that his partner could not hear him. Davis hid behind a pillar but kept Cole in sight. After what felt like an eternity, he finally managed to get Detective

Act I

Coles' attention. He motioned to the doors at the front of the building and Cole nodded, they both took off running.

The heavy doors swung open to reveal a large crowd mixed of officers and reporters. Everyone was trembling in fear, rightfully so. The detectives cut through the crowd and made their way to the back stairwell, one flight of stairs away from their office. Everyone working there had made their way to the main floor for the press conference. The office was empty, glass walls everywhere surrounding the bullpen, lined with whiteboards with pictures of all the criminals in Crimson Bay. The detectives both stood in the middle of the office, trying to process what they had just endured. Sam walked to his desk and sat down. His mind was racing, he couldn't stop thinking about how Freeman knew more and never told him and now he was gone. It was a selfish moment, and it bothered Sam that he even thought it. It was at that moment; he knew this was bad.

The rest of the day was a blur of witness statements and trying to find any surveillance footage that could help them try to pinpoint where the shot came from. A perimeter was set up to shield the crime scene from the public. The same team from earlier that morning arrived to analyze the mess. Cole and Davis made their way outside to meet them, this one would have every eye on it. "Twice in one day, that's new" the voice was emotionless and flat. The voice of

someone who sees crime scenes every day and sleeps easy at night. "Really, James?" scoffed Cole.

"Yeah, sorry, this isn't the right place for my standup routine," said James. His lack of empathy shocked Cole and Davis. "You really don't care, do you?" asked Cole.

Act I

James turned slightly, "It's the job, I don't feel things. If I did, I would have jumped off the bridge by now" Both detectives made a face that said, "that's a good point". James started to unpack his gear, "let me get set up and I'll call you when I have anything good"

The detectives started to walk down the steps as Cole's phone rang "It's Taylor." Said Cole.

"Bill?" answered Cole.

"Are you still local?" asked Lieutenant Bill Taylor.

"On the steps with forensic. Why?' responded Cole.

"We need to talk, grab Davis and meet me at the crown" suggested Taylor.

"On the way". Cole hung up his cell phone. "Lieutenant wants to meet" said Cole to Davis. "In his office? asked Davis.

"Nope, the Crown"

The Crown was the pub that almost every deal in the city took place at. Bill Taylor was in that circle and only met there if he wanted to keep things quiet. Everyone knew what the crown

meant. An invite was a big deal, it could push your career if it went well. Bill and Victor De Luca were friends, so Detective Cole anticipated Taylor reaching out.

"Do I talk in this meeting? asked Davis.

"What do you think?"

Davis just shook his head. "no, definitely not"

Bill was no nonsense and a very intimidating figure. He was taller than most and used that to his advantage, he also had the blessing (or curse) of having gravel in his throat. His voice cut through every room.

Act I

      The Crown was only a block away. The detectives got there first, the doorman motioned them to the back corner "Back booth, he'll be here shortly". Cole nodded and kept moving past the bar, Davis followed while he tried to figure out how the lieutenant tipped off the doorman so fast, and why did this pub have a doorman? The pub was an alleyway style room. Bar on one side, booths on the other. This opened to the back room, where the upper echelon met to conduct business

The Pub was empty, everyone in the city had recoiled into hiding. Davis tapped his fingers anxiously on the table, this meeting made him more nervous than having someone shoot at them. "Calm down, have a drink" said Cole, he knew a nervous partner would ruin this meeting. "Maybe six cups of coffee is too many" said Davis.

"That can't be healthy" responded Cole as he stared at the door. Just then, Bill Taylor came through the door. He whispered something to the doorman and ordered a drink with one wave of his hand.

He got to the table, "Gentleman, good to see you're in one piece"

"Thanks Bill"

He sat down, "Let's just get to this because we don't have a lot of time. What do you guys have on Vic?"

"Didn't Freeman tell you when they got back?" asked Cole. "Didn't even see him this morning, too busy." Responded Taylor.

"Vic had his head cut off, sir"

The lieutenant paused. He looked at both men and made a face of someone who really didn't want to be sitting there. "With

Act I

the sword?" This was starting to give Detective Cole that feeling in his gut.

He slowly said "Yeah, with the sword, how did you know that?"

"Same as his father. God Damnit, if I knew that I wouldn't have let Freeman do that press conference". Detective Cole's entire body filled with an anxious energy. There was something more to this. He couldn't hold it in anymore "Once Freeman found out, he asked me to find him after the press conference, like he had something important to tell me. Almost like we had stumbled upon something." The lieutenant scoffed at the remark, "Yeah….something like that."

Cole couldn't make eye contact with the lieutenant. The city was burying a serial killer deep in its memory. The fact that was hidden from him almost felt personal, even though that would be ridiculous. He didn't expect it to be on the front page of the welcome brochure, but it at least could have been mentioned over the inaugural welcome to the Crimson Bay Police Department pancake breakfast. (neither of which actually existed)

"So, what now?" asked Cole. The department had devolved into a frenzy. The city felt like it was on lockdown. The streets were empty.

Taylor took another drink, but there was no plan. "Honestly, it's a mess. We've never had a police chief killed on live television before. Welcome to uncharted territory."

"If the details of Vics murder come out, the city will implode. Anyone who lived through the Crimson Mask has buried those feelings down deep and we don't want those coming back." Lectured Taylor. He wanted this to be dealt with quietly.

Act I

"How bad was it?" asked Cole. He needed to know the real truth behind the darkest secret in the city. It would confirm that gut feeling he got every time he crossed the bridge and took in the huge skyline. How would he be able to get into the mind of a serial killer without the real story. "We don't have time for all the details. Just know we can't relive it" The lieutenant brushed him off.

"Do you think it's a copycat or maybe someone is finishing the job?" asked Cole, he was persistent on the subject.

Taylor started to stand up from his chair, "Look detective, maybe it's time for you to do some actual detective work on this one. And do it fast. At this rate we will be burying half the

department by next week." Bill Taylor was an asshole. Everyone knew it. He turned to leave without giving any more thought to even helping the two detectives. It was their job, not his.

The frustration inside Sam had boiled. It was too much to take, he needed answers "How the fuck can I find the killer if everyone who has information either won't talk (Taylor) or is dead (Freeman)!" Cole was standing at this point; Davis had never seen his partner explode this way.

The lieutenant had made it to the door. He pulled his hat out from under his arm and placed it on his head. A smirk crossed his face. "Go ask Finn, then" replied Taylor as he pushed through the door.

A confused look appeared on both detectives' faces, who was Finn?

The Days that followed were a blur between the visits to the De Luca Mansion and the meetings with the team to share findings on Freemans Murder. Cole's phone and email were

Act I

full of messages. Tips from every corner of the city. All of it garbage. Panic stricken mumblings of people seeing ghosts.

The stack of job folders piled up on the corner of Coles desk. He sat tapping his pen, staring off into the abyss. His mind raced; he was waiting for the office to calm down before he started his search for someone named Finn.

Freeman and Taylor were the only officers left from the team during the old days. This Finn character must be listed in their database somewhere. Cole shot to his feet and made his way across the room "Sawyer!", he said. Erin Sawyer turned to see who was calling her name. She was easily the most senior detective in the force, with an impressive list of criminals put away. She wasn't physically imposing, but her sailor's mouth and death stare kept everyone in check. "What is it, Cole?" She turned back to her computer. "This better be good" Cole slid into the chair across from her, he looked around to make sure no one else could hear what he was about to ask. "Finn?" no response. "Sawyer, what does the name Finn mean to you?" still no response. Cole stared at the side of her head. Burning a hole through her with his eyes. "Erin….?"

"Not here, dipshit, give me five minutes, meet me downstairs." She didn't even turn to acknowledge them.

A cold wind blew the flags that stood in front of the Police headquarters. Cole and Davis stood just outside the doors of which they crashed through days earlier. A much different scene was painted on the stone steps as the crime scene had been cleaned up, leaving only leaves and garbage to blow in the wind. "It's freezing out here, why can't we do this inside" whined Davis. "Can't you see? They want this buried for some reason. Taylor was right, no one wants to talk about it" replied Cole, as Detective Sawyer stepped out to meet them.

Act I

She had a file folder tucked under her arm. "This didn't come from me" she said as she handed the folder to Detective Cole.

"Cold case?" questioned Cole.

"Everything's in there. His notes, paperwork, photos and a few cards."

"His notes?"

Erin stared at Sam, "Finn? Jack Finn. The lead on the crimson mask case. Isn't that what you were looking for?"

Sam stood, almost speechless as his mind started to put the pieces together.

"Freeman told me all about the case, years ago. This folder was the black eye for everyone back then. Once I heard about De Luca, I pulled this out and set it aside. I asked Taylor for the case, but he wants you to do it. Don't fuck it up Cole."

"I still don't understand why everyone keeps this quiet, especially since there's likely a copycat or the same guy still out there" exclaimed Cole. "If you can find Jack, he can fill you in. It might make more sense coming from him," said Erin as she he started to pull away. "Also, good luck finding him. After that he basically disappeared. He's a ghost."

"Great" muttered Cole. "Just Great"

"So, Freeman, Taylor and Sawyer are the only ones who really know anything about the case. And they don't want to talk about it. Or can't. And now there's a mystery fourth person who may or may not be alive or even in the country? Welcome to a needle in a haystack" said Davis as he finally chimed in.

"You're such a good detective" said Cole as he sifted through the folder. The sarcasm was dually noted.

Act I

The pressure was on the two detectives. They had to find Jack Finn, if he still existed, before anyone else got hurt. The city stayed on high alert for the following days, the police presence on the streets was noticeably higher than usual. The youth still flooded the streets at night, nothing stopped them. Not even a serial killer.

The loud siren of an alarm clock rang through Coles' ears as he tried to find his bedside radio. He didn't use his phone alarm; he still had the old clock by his bed. He managed to hit the snooze button but accidentally turned on the radio. The 6am news report blasted out of the speaker. "Good morning, Crimson Bay! You've got it dialed on Q97, it's six o'clock and here are your headlines for this chilly October morning; The city is still in mourning after the tragic murder of our beloved Police Chief Oscar freeman. This coming on the heels of the suspicious death of Real Estate Mogul Victor De Luca, has the city on high alert as the police try to restore some order to our streets. Long serving Lieutenant Bill Taylor has been named deputy Chief in the wake of the tragedy. He will give an update on this case later this morning. In other news…"

The Radio magically landed on the floor. "Taylor? Fuck sakes"

It was a great early wake-up call for Cole as he pulled himself together. His old farmhouse on the outskirts of the city felt colder than usual. It needed a bit of work when he bought it years ago, and it still needed the same work all these years later. Signs of a true workaholic. The house was three levels, bedrooms upstairs, kitchen and living room on the main and a scary damp basement that came directly from every Halloween movie. Davis always joked about the bodies that are hiding down there.

This was the furthest south the city touched before it turned into the next town. It had an easy commute to the

Act I

office. It was almost a straight shot; it didn't feel like the outskirts to him. Everyone always questioned why the police department was on this side of the bridge. The rich elite wanted protection close by but the city wanted its police force away from the bright lights and closer to the grit and grime.

Cole's coffee warmed his hand as he stepped out into the brisk chilly morning air. He kept the Mustang in the garage, out of sight. His driveway was long and treelined, it created a nice escape and some shelter. He could disappear off the main road and lose anyone who may have followed him. It had never happened, but that's just how his mind worked. As he stepped into the garage, his phone buzzed, Davis had heard the news too. "Morning sunshine" Chimed Davis. Even under the dark cloud, he was always cheery in the morning (if he slept). "Did you hear?"

"Yeah, the board must have called an emergency meeting last night"

The Board of Commissioners. Headed by Mayor Michael Gray. The District Attorney, Carson Hill. Chief Justice, Oliver Reeves. Financial Director, Charlie Banks (yes, that's his last name). Housing authority head, John Oak, and Infrastructure director Rory Mann. The police chief held the final seat. Six seats, with the mayor having final say in any decision, or the tie break, depending on what was tabled. Taylor would now hold that seat, which didn't sit well with either detective. Freeman stayed out of their business for the most part, but Taylor always had something to say.

John Oak knew Victor De Luca well. They had a weekly lunch that usually extended into supper and beyond. Their friendship and, as some would say, partnership allowed De Luca to acquire land and properties at an accelerated pace. Everything was above board; they were good at paperwork and

Act I

loopholes just seemed to find them frequently. Or so it appeared. Detective Cole always thought that there was likely more to their partnership. It just felt that Oak was feeding information to De Luca and orchestrating everything from afar. Likely a kickback program in there as well, but so far, no trace of evidence.

Cole fired up his car's engine and let it idle, it's older, you can't just jump in and drive away first thing in the morning. "It might be good. He will be too occupied with the cult leaders to even bother checking on us." Said Cole, his voice echoed his untrusting views of the board. They both knew that time was ticking on this one, the lieutenant was not a patient human and even with his new role, when he checked in, they better have something for him to chew on. "I hope you're right. Which you usually are, but this one feels different" replied Davis. "Oh, I have a feeling this one is going to push us to the limit, I'll see you at the diner" Cole hung up as he pulled out of his garage. No radio news briefs, no music, just the engine. Like a psycho.

That same bell chimed as it did days earlier. The same long coat, the same booth, the same order. It was rinse and repeat for these two detectives. They met here most mornings to start the day. Cole and Davis both functioned on caffeine and greasy Diner breakfast. Somedays this was all they would get to eat. Cases can take you all over the city at all hours and they usually don't get to eat.

"Gentleman" They were greeted by Grace. This was her regular shift, and they were secretly her favorite customers. The mystery and intrigue that hung over them was almost intoxicating. She loved true crime novels and podcasts, so having real detectives around gave her a chance to live vicariously through their stories. "Are you drinking back-to-

Act I

back coffees?" exclaimed Davis as Grace placed two cups in front of them. "I didn't sleep. I just read the file over and over." Both men knew today was going to be difficult. They were heading to Jack Finn's listed address in the file. They both doubted he still lived there. The address was on the south side of the bridge. The heights, which was a rough neighborhood on a good day. "We are going to get shot aren't we" joked Davis. A slight grin crossed Cole's mouth. "All in a day's work. Might get some vacation time out of it"

"A hospital stay isn't exactly my ideal vacation," said Davis

Cole pulled the cup from his face, "In this line of work, it's the only vacation you get"

Davis didn't laugh. He made a face that said "oh, great" He was trying to keep up with the workaholic tendencies that his partner exuded but it was wearing on him.

"Should we tell Taylor that the last time we had a morning press conference, it didn't go so well?" questioned Davis. It was dripping in sarcasm. Neither of them understood why they would call this address only a week after Freeman's death and a day before his funeral. Just put out a notice in the news and the papers and be done with it. "Taylors baiting the killer. Try it again, lure him out. It's a bad play. This guy isn't that dumb."

"We know he's a good shot though" Davis was insinuating that Taylor would meet the same tragic fate as Freeman. Davis stared at Cole to see his reaction. Was it too far? Too much? He didn't really mean it, but he did. Cole stood to put his jacket on and place his money on the table, he rolled his eyes ever so slightly. "We won't get that lucky"

Davis felt his anxiety disappear. That could have gone bad. He smiled at Grace as they both pushed through the door, into the cold again.

Act I

The same drive they made almost every morning from the diner wouldn't cut it today. They pulled on to a different street. The buildings got smaller; the air seemed to get heavier with smoke from the factories. This part of town was where dreams went to die. It was a depressing area that should have a much-needed facelift. It was like the city had forgotten about it. Everyone just referred to it as the Heights. The street corners filled with trash. Garbage cans were on fire, the streetlights seemed to stay on all day under the heavy fog. "It's....cozy here" said Davis. He paused, "where is everyone?" They hadn't seen a person for blocks.

"It's too early for the junkies. They don't start crawling out until after lunch, or later." Replied Cole. He was scanning the building numbers. A row of old townhouses came into view. "I think this is it" Cole pulled the mustang over across the street. They sat there for a few minutes, scanning the scene. A brick townhouse sat across from them, it had a three step walk up and Victorian style windows and doors. If it was kept up, it would almost look like someplace a normal person would want to live. But who fits the bill of a normal person these days anyway?

Davis couldn't handle the silence any longer "are we just going to knock on his door and say, "Hey it looks like that serial killer is back, want another shot at it?"

"Maybe,...maybe you don't talk for this one. Just observe, quietly."

Davis nodded. The neighborhood made him nervous as it was.

Cole pushed open the car door and tucked his gun behind him. Davis caught a glimpse of this move as he made his way around the car. "What's that for?"

Act I

"If it's on my hip it might spook him. If I look unarmed, it might get me through the door. And if shit goes sideways, which it might. Then I'm ready" explained Cole.

"I thought we were just coming to talk to the guy?" asked Davis, his nervous system started to kick into overdrive.

"I'm guessing you didn't do any research on Mr. Finn did you?"

"I didn't think I had to? Retired Detective took his leave early. Probably stressed out from the case. Tucked his tail and called it a career?" They landed on the front step. A gunshot blew the screen door of its hinges above them. Both men dove to either side of the step. Cole and Davis drew their guns and tucked themselves against the wall. Cole looked at Davis "Not Exactly"

"What the fuck!" Yelled Davis

Another gunshot rang out through the wooden door. Splinters dropped on them from above.

A deep voice bellowed from the other side "You're wasting your time boys"

"We just want to talk, Jack!" yelled Cole. He had read a few notes on Jack being slightly volatile back in the day. The years obviously had not softened him.

"A heads up would have been nice!" said Davis as he tried to keep it together.

"I thought you knew. You said we were going to get shot"

"Very funny, asshole" Davis was struggling to see the humor in their current situation. Unlike his partner who seemed to welcome the confrontation.

Act I

"Are you going to keep shooting or can we come in now?" asked Cole in a sarcastic but respectful way.

The wooden door swung open, "I've got nothing to say to you two or anybody. Take off your fucking shoes"

Davis was still shaking in his stylish leather boots. He looked at Cole, who had a smile on his face. Cole had met his match, and he seemed to like it. "I knew we were going to get shot at down here" said Davis under his breath. They collected themselves and made their way up the steps, guns still drawn. "Come on in, I'm not going to fucking shoot you" came the voice of retired Detective Jack Finn.

The house was nicer than what they expected. Jack hadn't been heard from in years, almost like he had been banished to this part of town. Hardwood floors, impressive trim work that dated back a hundred years. Big wooden doors with curved tops. It was a big open feeling space that definitely didn't match the rest of town. Jack sat at the end of his large wooden table in the dining room, smoking a cigar, a glass with just a small amount of brown liquor in it. Revolver sitting beside the glass.

Jack was in his late fifties. Still had great hair, it was dark and full. He was a large human, even sitting down you could tell he was big. Wide shoulders, and hands that could break every bone you had in a handshake. Just an intimidating man.

He kicked a chair away from the table." Give it your best shot detective" he said. "What gave it away?" replied Cole. Both men still stood in the hallway just inside the door, the wood chips still scattered around them. The tension was starting to subside. "If you're showing up at my door, then you've read my file, and probably talked to Bill Taylor, cause

Act I

Oscar ain't talking" This made Jack chuckle to himself as he hauled back on his cigar. He blew out the smoke, "It doesn't take a genius to figure out who you two are" Cole and Davis both approached the table, they pulled out the chairs and sat down. Neither man took their eyes off Jack. For good reason, being shot at usually garners someone's attention.

Cole sat closest to Jack. He needed to get this right if they had any shot of figuring this case out. "Look Jack, I have read the file. I just need you to fill in a few gaps and then we will be on our way"

"A few gaps?...what do you have so far?" questioned Jack.

"Vic De Luca was found decapitated, just like his father and now Oscar is dead. Now the rumors of a serial killer are making their way around, and somehow that story has eluded me all these years."

"They buried that story deep in the back of cemetery where everyone is too afraid to walk at night. (he wasn't wrong, the Crimson Bay Cemetery was terrifying even in the middle of the day) I've never seen anything like it. Case closed, no arrests, just funerals."

"It was your case though, wasn't it?" asked Cole, cautiously

Jack reached behind him to the China cabinet with several bottles on it. He grabbed the closest one and set it on the table. "Where are my manners, boys, want a drink?" asks Jack as he pours more into his glass. "No, thank you Jack; we are on the clock," said Cole. This brought a grin to Jacks face. "Fucking times have changed, a good detective should be able to do this sober, hammered and everywhere in between."

"It's mostly coffee for us these days," said Cole

Act I

Jack laughed at the comment "Coffee doesn't help with the stress and nerves, just makes it worse. Enjoy the ulcers, boys"

"My liver appreciates it" Cole was quick with his response. Jack was getting off topic. "So, it was your case? The Crimson Mask Killer?" Cole had to push back and try to get any bit of information.

Jack nodded and learned forward. Almost preparing himself to finally give them something they could use.

Jack blew more smoke; he paused and watched it fill the room. "Get the fuck out of my house."

Act I

November Rain

Davis's teeth started to chatter as the wind whipped through his coat. He sat under a streetlamp on a city bench. He was dressed for a night on the town. Big coat, scarf, his nicest shirt and pants combo and shined up dress shoes. A perfect outfit to bring down the low life's in these cases they were assigned to.

The courtyard behind City Hall was a main pass through for shoppers on foot. The downtown shops lined both sides of the street, the grass was beaten down, it looked like a university lawn in some ways. People everywhere at all times of day, further down the street had bars and restaurants, most of them open late into the night. His pocket buzzed. A text from Cole. "5 minutes" it read.

It had been a week since their abrupt removal from Jack Finns House. They hadn't been back yet and had no communication with him. It was their only shot, and neither detective had taken their foot off the gas. But they still had other cases. Everyone assumed their case load would drop with the current investigation being top of the list, but Taylor was a dick and vetoed the dropping of cases. This left both detectives

Act I

confused, what is his motive for this? Doesn't he want the killer caught?

"4 Minutes" Davis's phone lit up his face.

The dampness from the bench was really starting to get into his bones. Hurry Up Cole. Davis scanned the courtyard for any signs of his partner. Shoppers filled the pathways under the trees. The lampposts created a very storybook feel to the park. Nothing out of the ordinary for a Friday night. The city was easing back into its normal ways after a period of fear and uncertainty. Two weeks in this city can feel like a lifetime to some.

"3 Minutes"

Detective Davis's anxiety started to build. His scanning of the scene became more frantic. Faces blurred in the streetlights. Laughing and conversation filled the air, the anticipation was almost overwhelming. "Why are we even out here" muttered Davis to himself. He stood up to try and stay warm. Partnering with Cole had been an adventure, this was par for the course. Detective Cole liked to do most of the dirty work and use Davis as the finisher. Wait outside and tackle the guy as he ran out. Wait outside and call for a bus when things went sideways. Wait outside and….

"Runner. North side"

Davis looked down at his phone. North side? He spun around expecting to see a commotion. Nothing there. He turned back around, "Which way… is .. North? Fuck". He finally locked in when he heard the screams of patrons as the were crashed into by a man in a dark grey hoodie, torn up jeans and work boots. He landed on one of the lawns and bounced back up in full sprint. Detective Cole was steps behind; he jumped over a

Act I

downed shopper. "Davis!" he yelled. An outstretched arm came from behind one of the big oak trees in the park. A beautiful diving clothesline to the chest. The perp dropped to the ground and groaned in pain. Detective Cole put his knee on the guy's back and held his arms. "Absolutely textbook" he said as he pulled out his cuffs. "Who taught you that?" asked Cole as he almost broke out in laughter. A few cheers from the gathering crowd took Davis by surprise. He had blacked out and just did whatever he thought he had to. And it worked. "I thought you were just going to ask him a few questions?" said Davis. "Oh, I asked a few questions. He didn't like them and bolted out the door" "I know it's a Friday night Davis, but why are you all dressed up?" question Cole as he lifted the runner up to his feet. This was the first time the partners had seen each other all day. Davis got a text from Cole telling him where to be and at what time. Cole was going to see an informant and get some intel on another small case they had. Davis was going to wait outside.

"I'm meeting a friend later for drinks" replied Davis as they walked their new friend over to Coles Mustang. "How am I under arrest? I didn't do anything?" cried the sprinter. "It's bad enough I'm a rat, if you put me in Ravenwood, I'm dead." He was referencing Ravenwood Penitentiary, the final stop for criminals in Crimson Bay. Cole ignored the man's plea as he opened the car door "Which friend? You have friends?" asked Cole, this news came as a shock.

Davis kept his cool, "It's nothing, just some drinks with officer Frost."

"Allison Frost? As in the one from Freeman's funeral?"

"Yeah, that was the first time I really got to talk to her"

Act I

A voice from the backseat interjected "Hey guys, I hate to interrupt but am I actually under arrest? It's freezing back here….." The car door slammed shut. The voice trailed off.

Cole Smiled "Picking up women at a funeral. You're something Davis". The Funeral for Oscar Freeman happened one week earlier. The day after, the detectives met with Jack Finn. The turnout in the cemetery was immense. Uniforms and unmarked SUV's for miles. A full parade of vehicles, horses, politicians, and every figurehead in the city. The sun broke through the clouds that morning just before the ceremony, it cast shadows from the thin spindly trees over the casket. The mountain of flowers at the foot of the grave stood to eye level. The city had come out to show its respect.

    The tension in the air was still palpable. The security detail for the funeral took days to set up. Nothing was to happen to anyone during this day. Snipers lined the rooftops across the street. High alert didn't even begin to describe this day. A high-profile funeral could bring out all the crazies.

    Even during the day, the Crimson Bay cemetery could give anyone the chills. It was something about the trees that looked dead, but they continued to grow taller, the old headstones that towered over everyone as you entered through the enormous gate. Two pillars with gargoyles guard the main entrance. Torches behind the gargoyles were lit at night. The shadows from the flames played with anyone who entered.

    "I hate this place," said Davis. This brought a wry smile to Detective Coles' face. He turned slightly to his partner and leaned closer "it's ten in the morning, the ghosts are still asleep" Cole was amused by himself, Davis was not.

"Now I hate you too" said Davis, only half joking.

"Just now?" asked Cole.

Act I

"It changes day to day. It's a weekly rollercoaster"

"Fair enough"

The Detectives were plain clothed for the funeral. Taylor had pulled them aside and stressed that the killer would likely be in the crowd to enjoy his handy work. Detective Cole disagreed but he respected the order to stay out of any uniform and blend in with eyes peeled.

The crowd outside the gates lined the block and more. Traffic was backed up for miles. Main streets were shut down for the procession. The bells in the tower above City Hall rang out as the time struck ten o'clock, the city was silent.

Everyone stood on edge until they lowered Oscar Freeman into the ground. No security breaches, no issues, just tears and sorrow. He was a friend to all who knew him, he would be missed greatly.

"Taylors such a prick" said Davis as the detectives stood off to the side of the crowd as they made their way toward the gates. A voice came from their left that startled them "You can say that again"

Allison Frost.

In her uniform, hat tucked under her arm. "Officer Frost" greeted Cole, "Didn't see you there"

"I should look around a bit before I badmouth the chief of police, at the former chief's funeral"

Said Davis, this garnered a brief smile from Officer Frost. "I doubt anyone here would disagree, you're probably fine" she added. "How's the case coming? Any leads? She inquired. Cole knew this question wasn't for him, she had directed it at detective Davis, "I'll meet you at the diner" said Cole as he pulled away and headed for the sidewalk. Officer Frost and

Act I

detective Davis continued their conversation for a few minutes before officer Frost got called away by her lieutenant. Davis couldn't remember anything that was said, very professional.

"Let me out of here! I did nothing wrong! Fuck This! Fuck you!" yelled the track star from the back of Coles Mustang. "Are you going to cut him loose?" asked Davis. "Yeah, in a bit, he's got information to spill, it'll happen." A string of break ins in the area all had similar patterns and the screaming baby in the backseat knew what crew had taken the job, but it wasn't about them, it was about who hired them. "Someone's trying to capitalize on the city being distracted, got to nip that one before it blows up" said Cole, the criminals must be seething with excitement, the whole police force is focused on the biggest case in years, easy pickings for petty crime.

"We shouldn't even be out here; this is wasting time and resources from the real issues" griped Davis as he leaned on the car. He checked his phone; he was cutting it close. "Get out of here Romeo, I'll look after the flash" said Cole, Davis had served his purpose for the night, time to cut him loose.

Davis disappeared into the crowd as he made his way to meet Officer Frost. Cole shut his car door and waited for the complaints to start from his informant, but nothing came. He backed out and pulled away, still nothing. Cole checked his mirror, "are you going to give up the names or am I going to beat them out of you?"

"You're not gonna touch me, and you're never gonna find out who set up the break ins either"

Detective Cole peered into his rearview mirror, "You sure about that?" he asked.

Spit caught the side of Cole's ear. "Fuck you cop, let me out of here"

Act I

Detective Cole stomped his foot on the gas, the car pulled sideways. Both men pinned back in their seats. They cut across two lanes and Cole took an alleyway between two smaller buildings.

Sounds of screeching brakes and horns trailed off in the distance. The headlights illuminated the small parking lot behind the building. A storage building with an open overhead door became the target. Screams from the backseat landed on deaf ears, Cole wasn't hearing any complaints. He pulled the Mustang into the empty garage, he looked around quickly, no cameras.

The pressure had finally pushed Sam Cole to the edge, he was used to being comfortable in the uncomfortable, the gunslinger, but he knew there was something big waiting around the corner and the fact that he couldn't figure it out was eating at him.

The garage looked abandoned, a couple old cars in the neighboring bays looked rusted and beat down. The doors were broken and barely hanging on. They were in the heights again, the place that the city forgot about. Once Cole realized where they were at, his mind drifted back to Jack Finn. What was he hiding? What could they do to get him to talk? Coles Suspicions about the city needed to be brought to light. Fuel to the fire, it was starting to creep into the deep parts of his brain. The parts we don't talk about.

A boot kicking his car's rear window brought him back to reality. Enough of this shit, he thought. He opened the door, reached in and grabbed his informant. He only knew him as Junior.

"If you break my window Junior, I'm breaking your legs." Another spit take but this time it landed. One swift pull on

Act I

Junior's shirt and he was sent rolling to the concrete floor. "Who paid for the job?" asked Cole.

"I told you; I'm not talking!" Suddenly, the rat had a code.

"and I told you….." Sam's foot landed squarely in Junior's chest. A gasp of air shot out of his body. It was a hard kick. There was heavy intent behind it.

"I!" He kicked him again.

"Will!" another kick

"Beat!" another one

"It!" now a stomp to the chest

"Out!" he stepped on Junior's neck.

Cole leaned down, "of you! Remember? Junior? I keep my promises" Junior was in a lot of pain; he was wheezing trying to catch his breath. He finally composed himself enough to squeak out a response "I'm done being a rat, no more, send me back to Ravenwood."

"You'll be dead the first night"

"If I rat, I'm dead, If I don't, you'll kill me anyway, two dead ends" coughed Junior "I'm not going to kill you Junior, you've helped me before, and you're going to help again. Plus, the paperwork for killing an informant is never ending, the interviews, the evaluation, they take your gun, it's not worth it. I don't have time for it." Said Cole, he wasn't normally violent, but he needed cooperation, and words don't always guarantee that.

"So, I'll ask again. Who paid for the job?" This time Cole pulled out his Gun. Junior had his hands cuffed behind his back. He laid on the concrete expecting the worst. "I can't. They'll skin me alive."

Act I

"Who? Just say it Junior, end this nonsense" Cole pointed his gun right between his informants' eyes, Junior started to shake, and tears welled up in his eyes. "You said you weren't going to kill me" begged Junior.

"Close your fucking eyes."

"You said you keep your promises!" yelled Junior, his voice cracking with fear. He started to squirm, kicking his legs.

Junior closed his eyes, tears streamed down his face. Snot ran from his nose; he was a mess.

He felt the cold sensation of the gun against his brow, the pressure pushing down on him. The gun suddenly pulled back; a gunshot rang out through the abandoned garage.

Junior Screamed for his life. Was he dead? "It was Donnie's crew" he spewed through the tears.

"Did you piss your pants?" asked Cole. He was almost humored by the whole situation. Detective Cole had fired a round through the open door into the alley. His tactics had finally worked. Everyone's tough until you beat the shit out of them and stick a gun in their face.

Donnie Bruno was bad news. This shouldn't have come as a surprise to Detective Cole. The city didn't have organized crime anymore, but it didn't mean that people hadn't tried. Donnie was one of the guys trying to bring it all back. "So, Donnie paid for the job, who did the work?" asked Cole. "I don't know which crew; I just know Donnie put out the job. The city is ripe for picking No one is watching" Junior had heard that sentence, it didn't come from his half working brain. "You're sure its him?" asked Cole "Not the time to lie to me"

Act I

"He said that every cop is out looking for some guy who killed the police chief, now it's time for them to rise up and take over"

      Cole stood there, letting that last sentence sink in. Is this a copycat from years ago or is it someone making it look like a copycat, just to capitalize on the distraction? Almost genius when you think about it.

      The steel roof of the garage started to echo as the rain began to come down. Cole reached down and took the handcuffs off Junior. "Have fun walking home. Stay close to your phone"

"You can't just leave me here! I don't even know where we are?" said Junior as he tried to gather himself. "Remember this the next time you want to act tough" said Cole as he opened his door. "Donnie is going to kill me!" Yelled Junior. Cole fired up the engine and threw it in reverse. He slammed on the brakes and rolled down his window "You died ten minutes ago kid, consider this as extra time. Enjoy it" Cole peeled out into the rain.

Act I

A Murder of Crows

The landscape of the city had shifted. Everyone had started to get back to normal. Or what felt like normal. On the surface it looked fine. Underneath, the criminals smelled blood in the water. The Bruno crew had strung together an impressive list of break-ins and came out with cash, guns and anything they could fit in their vans.

The department was swamped with calls. Cases started adding up quickly. Detective Cole needed to meet with Donnie Bruno to put a pin in this, but he had to give his old friend Jack Finn one more shot.

The newspaper headlines changed every day, but the theme remained the same. Fear and uncertainty jumped off the page every morning as the innocent sipped coffee and tried to get going for the day. Cole set his newspaper down on the diner table. The usual morning routine, except this one, was to lead them back to the heights for a final shot at Jack Finn.

"Got your vest on?" asked Cole. Davis grinned as he sat down in the booth across from his partner. "I'm not scared. I don't need a vest, Jack doesn't scare me, you're scared." Davis half-heartedly attempted some humor. Cole only raised one brow at him. "Yeah, I have it on"

"Good, He won't be nearly as happy this time"

"We're calling that happy?"

Act I

"Look, if we can get him to talk, then we have a real shot at this. This new crime wave is going to overwhelm the department. It already has. This needs to be the plug in the dam. If Jack doesn't cooperate, then we are back at square one. Theres nothing in the De Luca house to pin on anyone. No surveillance footage, DNA, footprints, Anything. And the search for Freeman's shooter is stalling out by the day. The sheer number of resources they have assigned to this case is causing a blind spot in the field. Petty crime is increasing into violent crime, it won't take long until it becomes organized crime" Cole's monologue had captivated his partner. "What happens if it does become organized crime?" asked Davis. "Just hope it doesn't get to that point; you've seen the talent in our department. We don't have the players for that fight" replied Cole. Davis put his cup on the table, he waited to voice his reply. "So how do we get Jack Finn to talk about the case?" he asked. He needed to know just as badly as his partner. He knew that the city had come a long way from the days of the crime bosses that haunted the stories of his parents and their friends.

"He needs to see that we aren't hunting him. He needs to see that we need him to help us. I am sure he sees everyone pointing the finger at him and it eats at him. He's hidden himself away and become a recluse with anger issues. He likely hates Taylor and maybe even Freeman. He was the scapegoat, and they didn't step in to back him up. They threw him to the wolves." Said Cole, he had thought long and hard about how to get inside Jacks Head. "You don't know that they didn't back him up or threw him to the wolves" countered Davis. "Maybe he really did mess the whole thing up? Maybe innocent people were murdered because he couldn't do his job" he was pushing the issue at an early hour, uncharacteristic of him as well. This slight outburst struck Detective

Act I

Cole as intriguing, and a bit odd. This wasn't the rookie speaking, this came from somewhere else. "If he smells even a whiff of this bias on you, we aren't walking out of there. What's got you all wound up kid?" questioned Cole.

Davis had a stern look across his face, as if he had suddenly become a seasoned vet in a short time, he stared at his partner, the tension between them started to grow.

"Well? What is it, spit it out" Cole doubled down.

Davis's face cracked "My dad told me about what went on back then, he said the detective in charge blew it" Davis pointed his finger into the table to make his point.

Cole sat in comic disbelief. "Your dad? All of that was from his view thirty years ago. Was your dad a cop? Did he have an inside view of what went on?"

The answer to this question was going to arguably create a divide in their partnership. If Davis knew more about the case than he had let on, then Cole would be livid.

Davis hung his head, "No, he's an accountant"

Cole stood up and started to slide his black peacoat on. He didn't know whether to laugh or scold his young partner on being able to think for himself. "Please don't say a word when we get there. I don't want to have to tell your accountant father why we can't have an open casket" Davis

made a face of slight embarrassment. "Yeah, that's probably for the best" he slid out of the booth and followed his partner to the door.

The front door of Jack Finn's house sat ajar. The driving rain against the door was pooling on the floor. This wasn't the neighborhood to leave your door unlocked or a window open. Detective Cole slowly pushed open the door with his foot.

Act I

Davis followed, both men had guns drawn. They had seen the door as they parked the car. Something wasn't right. "Jack!" called Cole. "It's Detective Cole and Davis. Are you alright?" No response. "Shit. Alright let's go" Cole shouldered the door open, they both spilled into the entrance way. Jack's house was dark, difficult to see at the best of times through cigar smoke mostly. This time there was no smoke, just fear. They made it to the kitchen, the table they had sat at previously had been tipped over, chairs thrown around the room. A wave of desperation came over Detective Cole. He needed Jack alive, but it looked like someone else needed him dead.

They cleared the house, no signs of Jack. The selfish feeling weighed Cole down. He didn't care about the human; he cared about the information inside. Both men stood in the kitchen, this wasn't how today was supposed to go. "What do we do now?" asked Davis as he tucked his gun away. "He's our last link. This all goes back to square one and Taylor is going to lose his mind"

"Maybe we need to start over. Maybe we need a fresh perspective. Are we coming at this all wrong?" Question Cole. He had never felt like this. He was always calculated in his attack.

"We've got a real estate mogul with no head. A police chief murdered on live television. A copycat killer who is reliving a time that no one in this fucking city wants to talk about for some

reason. And the only person who can point us in the right direction is now missing. How do I explain all of this to Taylor. You're right, he is going to lose it." Proclaimed Cole, he was starting to accept defeat on this case.

"Fuck Bill Taylor and the horse he rode in on"

Act I

Both men turned and drew their guns.

Jack Finn emerged from the darkness, house coat swinging, and fuzzy slippers. A disheveled painting of a human being. Still had great hair though.

Neither of them knew what to say. They cased the entire house. Where was he hiding?

"I'm guessing from the dumb looks on your faces that you assumed I got kidnapped."

Cole nodded; gun still drawn.

"Do you really think I would live in this neighborhood without a secret room to hide in when idiots break in? Help me put this table back. Put your guns down," said Jack. Both detectives were stunned.

They set the table upright and put the chairs around it. All three men took a seat. Just as they had before. This time Jack was slightly more hospitable. But only slightly.

"I was expecting you sooner. Taylor must have you guys run ragged. Sounds like him, lazy asshole. Delegates to everyone else and then goes to jerk off in his office. Fucking coward"

Jack grabbed a bottle of rum and poured a glass for himself. "You guys still scared of being a man?" he cracked as he offered the detectives the breakfast of champions. Cole smirked, "No, Jack, we are still just kids sipping on our coffees"

"Figures" said Jack.

Cole finally got himself together to get his questions out. "Who broke in?"

"Didn't see. I was downstairs, heard the noise and hit the secret room. I heard them trashing the kitchen and running

Act I

upstairs. I haven't even been up there to see the damage." Replied Jack.

"They flipped your bed and ripped your closet apart. Looking for something?"

Jack took another sip of rum. "Theres nothing in that closet. Or my bed, or anywhere in this house, I'm not fucking stupid. Anything that has value is long gone. If I'm on that list of people that are getting paid a visit, then this is round two for this city. Good fucking luck gentlemen."

Jack finished his drink and went for an encore. He was clearly bothered by the whole situation, but he wasn't going to budge on just giving everything up to these two kids. "I think you know that you're our only real shot at this, right?" asked Cole. Only the sound of rum pouring into a glass could be heard. Jack stared through Sam Cole. The thousand-yard stare that looked as though the person was looking through the top of the eye lids. Menacing. This visit could end abruptly, or maybe put them in a place to finally get some real work done.

"I guess if they kill me then it's game over for the both of you. There's no one left to tell the story. The real story, not some bullshit lies that Bill Taylor spins to the newspaper, or the

evening news. I have never seen someone fail upwards that much in my life. Just a coward. When things got tough back then, we were up against it way worse than you guys are now. Freeman wanted Taylor to look over my shoulder and I told him to fuck off and leave me alone. He would just get in the way."

"How bad did it get?" asked Cole, prodding where he could. This was his shot.

Jack finished drink number two and went for the trifecta. "You kids wouldn't even know what hit you back in those days.

Act I

Everyone was on the payroll, cops, judges, the mayor! They ran everything and then every one of them got cut down in their prime. It was a bloodbath. You guys don't even know the half of it, no one does, it's been buried so long. If the public really knew we, we would have a camera crew in here making the documentary."

"Who…ran everything, Jack?" Cole's question wasn't smoke and mirrors, this one was real.

A half smile crept across Jack's face; he scoffed at the question. Maybe it was time. He looked at the two detectives. His house had just been ransacked. His old friend had been murdered, and he was the only one left. It was time to pull back the curtain.

"Alright Kids, buckle up" he pulled out a cigar and lighter from his robe. He lit it and filled the room with smoke. "It's showtime"

Act II

1994

Fingers tapped on a large oak desk. Stained dark brown. Two lions carved into either end. A gift from years before. There were always gifts coming through the door. The sunlight crept through a drawn blind into the large home office. The room almost resembled an old library with bookshelves on every wall. A room full of leather chairs and sofas. And the overwhelming smell of cigar smoke stained the carpet and drapes. Bottles of liquor lined the shelf behind the large desk. Meetings and celebrations must always start or end with a drink. A happy new years 1994 sticker found itself left over on the mirror behind the bottles. It had been a week since the turn of the year. A new year, with the same goals.

The phone on the desk rang. This call had built anticipation in the room. The receiver tied with an old cord barely made it to the man's ear. The voice on the other end came through "it is done"

"Good. Tell Nicholas to proceed" instructed the man.

"Yes Sir."

Both men hung up. The man pulled back on his cigar.

A voice from across the room cut through "I am assuming everything went smoothly"

Act II

"We are set up now. Nicholas will take it from here. He knows the job. His men are skilled"

"Your son has many talents. But can he handle moving that much money?" asked the shadowed figure. The job they spoke of was moving two million dollars' worth of cash from the Crimson Bay Bank and dividing it up between the smaller banks to clean it and then running it back through a few of their more recent acquisitions.

"I trust them with this one. Even if they have to shoot their way out"

The man nodded "Understood Angie"

Angie. As in Angelo De Luca. The head of the De Luca Crime Family. The family that ran the city. A black book of names that the federal government would love to have a look at, while envelopes full of cold hard cash distracted anyone who came sniffing around. And if that didn't work, then those people disappeared. Or took an extended vacation.

Angie had grown up in one of the wealthier families in the city. His parents were both in politics in some form or another. But neither were involved in the world of organized crime. Angie used his wealth, power and connections to build his empire from the underground. No one saw it coming, including his family. By his early twenties he owned multiple companies, that he used to launder stolen money. The excess of cash he built allowed him to pay off law enforcement and other authority figures to keep his path clear. By thirty he controlled the labor union, which gave him the ultimate upper hand over any businessman in the city. He had all the schemes in place. Kickbacks from the concrete business he owned. Skimming from his construction company. Extortion and

Act II

protecting rackets. All of it. Any construction project paid a percentage to him. His wealth grew to enormous heights.

The dockyard was the next takeover. He now controlled everything coming in and out and took his cut from it all. He paid his crew well and treated them fairly, so no one would ever think of double crossing him. But every now and then someone would get the nerve to make a run at it and then Angie would show his teeth. A sight that no man could erase from his memory.

"Why would you make me do this?" he would ask. He always made it their fault for what was about to happen. "I pay you; I give you a job and you disrespect me and the rest.? That will forever be unacceptable" this was the line that anyone from inside that crossed the line would hear before they disappeared. Angie was fond of burning them alive, in front of everyone. The screams haunted the rest, it was an effective tool. Fear.

Angie was a figure in the city. He stood six feet tall, with wide shoulders but a slender build overall. He had dark curly hair that he kept short and full of product. And a jawline that turned heads. His eyes were menacing. His stare could freeze time. There was a cold psychopath behind those eyes, but one that was in full control. It made any negotiation go in his favor, whether the opposition approved or not. When you are sat across the table from a man who you know will go to any length to procure what he desires, you have already lost. He was handsome, charming and terrifying, all wrapped into one, he didn't seem human.

As the head of a crime family, you had to look the part. Angie always had his tailor on call. Growing up rich had that effect on him. And as the money grew, the expenses came with it. The boats, the buildings, the cars, the houses, anything.

Act II

And anyone. The highest city officials all secretly answered to Angie. He was their best friend, he filled their pockets, and deep down they were all scared of him.

No one opposed the De Luca family. They were the only show in town. Neighboring cities had similar families but none on the grand scale as Angie. Corruption personified. As he aged on, he knew that he needed a succession plan. This is where the family part really kicks in. He met his wife Rebecca in their late twenties as he was rising to power. She was a nurse at Crimson General. One of Angie's men needed to be looked after, and normally a crime family would never go to a hospital. The cops would be called immediately. But if you have half of the department on your payroll, you can do what you wish. Rebecca was the attending, and Angie almost fell off his chair when she entered the room. She immediately hated him.

Too handsome, too confident, too rich, too fake. That was Rebecca Morris's first opinion of her now husband Angelo De Luca. With the suit and the hair and everything else, he would have been anyone's choice, man or woman. She saw right through it and assumed he was just like all the other suits in this city. She didn't have time for it. Unbeknownst to her, that man would put her name on a new wing of that hospital years later.

Rebecca was the only person who could take any focus from Angie. It was all business until she walked in. But Angie wouldn't let the two cross paths. She was separated from the life. The early seventies made it easy. No technology to track anyone. He would work all hours in his office at the house, but she wasn't allowed in that room. She knew why but never made a fuss about it. Deep down she loved the life, the danger of walking that line kept her interested.

Act II

The late sixties, into the early seventies were prime years for the uprising of organized crime in Crimson Bay. Small scale crimes had evolved into a full-scale operation that touched every corner of the city. On the street level, all the crews had their sections. How they made their money was mostly up to them. Protection was an easy one, extortion for hire. They protect your business for a cut of the profits. The drug trade was on its way up as well. Anything you wanted, they had. Guys on corners making drops and the cash just rolled in, because most of the police force were on the payroll. Easy to look the other way. Stolen goods were another easy one. They knew every route and every shipment. It was like clockwork, a very well-oiled machine. But Angie wanted more.

The union takeover was what really set the empire off. Angie took the operation from street level to pulling the strings on a larger stage. Union President Frank Dawson fell under Angie's spell as soon as they met. Frank all of a sudden had a new car, bills paid, booze and cigarettes at an unlimited supply, anything he wanted. Once Frank was onside, the money started to pour in exponentially. You needed a concrete truck; De Luca got a cut. You needed workers, you paid Angie too, it just became the way everything went. For years. The dockyards were the only thing left untouched. They would control the flow of goods coming into town, the drugs would be easier to import, it was the ultimate move. That takeover took a lot out of the crews. Bloodshed from the remaining police department, the feds, and the port authority covered the city blocks. Angie was left standing and assumed control over everything, but the damage was done to the city. It would take 5 years to come out on the other side. But it was worth it.

Act II

The bakery on seventeenth. The pub on main street. The drycleaners on fifth. Just small examples of business who paid to the family. Almost every street had at least one business that paid dues. If they missed a payment, then a new business would pick up the pieces after it was burned to the ground. The cycle of life continues.

A 1986 Buick Grand national pulled off the bridge and headed downtown. The city was still divided back then as well. But the rich answered to the family. The clouds threatened rain, it would only be a matter of time. Detective Jack Finn rolled through the city, his typical route, after a morning meeting at the department. Stale coffee in the cupholder, window down, cigarette smoke blowing out. A smart detective with a keen eye and no patience. Which put him in some interesting situations at times. He was still new to the job but all his life he lived vicariously through his father, Officer John Finn. The work always got brought home and Jack ate it all up. His age became a constant point of contention in the ranks, it's an old boys club and heavy emphasis on old. Experience was twenty years minimum before anyone would really take you seriously. A shit disturbers paradise, Jack loved it.

The car slowly pulled up to the edge of City Park. A young man in his early twenties, in a grey suit jacket and slacks, sat on a bench against the brick wall that provided the exterior of the park. Finn approached the young man and sat down beside him. Both men took out cigarettes and lighters.

"Morning Gio" said Finn. They both sat staring straight ahead. Gio Ricci, an associate of Mario Bruno, the right hand of Angelo De Luca. And a childhood Friend of Jack Finn.

Act II

"Jackie boy, how's it hanging?" replied Gio.

"Just sat through an hour of how you guys are moving big money around and we have to pinch it and take down Nicky. They want his head to bait Angie."

Gio grinned and leaned back on the bench. "Well, good luck with that. Nicky might be crazier than the old man, you know he will come out shooting." Gio paused, "wasn't that move signed off on? Aren't we in the clear for this one?" he questioned.

"Could have fooled me with that meeting. Freeman wants blood." Said Finn.

"Nicky is the wrong one Jack, cause if Freeman wants blood he's going to get it, and it'll be pouring out of your officers. Not smart on his end, maybe you should remind him who runs this city." Stated Gio, both men knew the family ran everything, nothing new there. Jack chuckled a bit, "yeah I'll run right in there and tell him to play nice" Both men laughed at the thought.

"When was the last time you talked to Nicky?" asked Gio. All three men were friends in school, obviously taking different paths. "Not since they gave him his own crew, it looks like I'm on Bruno for the foreseeable future. Maybe someday down the line our paths will cross" replied Finn.

"Well, from what I'm hearing, old man is heading toward retirement, and Nicky might be getting the nod" Gio flicked his cigarette and pulled out another one. "Don't you know those things are bad for you?" joked Finn. "It's only bad for everyone else if I don't smoke two packs" laughed Gio.

Act II

"Nicky could do big things, but those are huge shoes to fill, and at his age, will everyone buy in the same way? The old man is ruthless. Now Nicky is crazy, don't get me wrong, but is he calculated and able to control himself? That, I don't know" said Finn, finishing his cigarette as well. Gio silently agreed with a head nod.

"What's the plan today?" asked Finn. The two young guns met on this bench each week to talk business and a little bit about life. They tipped each other off on things hear and there, not too much, but just enough for both men to move up the ranks quicker. On the surface, Jack was still Gios friend, but inside he was pushing for Gio to slip up and give away something real. The more he gave Gio, the more he may get back. The deeper he could get himself into the maze. Jack wasn't concerned with the small-time stuff, but that was mostly what Gio would give him. In return, Gio was provided information on what the next steps the department was taking with the family and if they were getting raided. It was a long play for Jack but so far it had been working. It also helped that Gio wasn't the sharpest and loved to tell stories.

"Couple trucks tonight, me and Big Kev are on that one, and we've got some pickups over on Penny Lane (cleaning district, laundromats and drycleaners). Nothing flashy, nothing like the boys on the docks, boats coming in loaded with our new guns" Gio realized his slip up and waited for the next round of questions.

Jack smirked at Gio, "Well, c'mon, out with it"

"No, I can't, it's a Union job. Franks guys, we are just running protection."

Frank Dawson, Union President and best friend to Angie. The puppeteers of the underworld. He moonlighted as a captain for

Act II

Angie as well. Between Nicky, Bruno, Frank and their consultant Martin Wolfe, the family had crews working everywhere.

"You can't Jack, that's not the deal. That's a big one" pleaded Gio. He knew he messed up.

"I'm just going to observe, Gio, don't worry. They won't see me," said Jack.

Gio just let it go, "it's your funeral" he sighed. Gio stood up and stretched his arms, "well old boy, time to go run the city. You have fun hunting the boogeyman" he started to walk away, stopped and turned to Jack. "But seriously, don't go to the docks"

"No promises" said Jack as Gio turned and walked away. Jack stayed on the bench for a few minutes. The wind picked up and the rain started, a typical fall day. The dockyards were calling Jacks name, but so was the news that his childhood friend Nicholas De Luca would become King. That could really change how he approached this detective stuff. He could have an inside track to the Boss, this would push him very far up the ladder if done right. Or it could get him killed. But jack needed to find out.

Act II

A Long Night

The dockyard stakeout came on the same night that Nicky's crew were to move the money from the CB Bank. Keep the eyes off the shipment and focused on the money. Freeman didn't know anything about the guns. He hated that there was such a long list of law enforcement, politicians and very influential individuals on the payroll for the De Luca's. He couldn't prove anything about his own men, even though he tried. They would deny it to their grave, or else they would meet that grave very fast. Angie dropped crumbs to appease his opposition, but it was all smoke and mirrors. I give you an inch, but I've taken a mile, and you have no idea about it. It was cat and mouse, except the cat is a lion and the mouse is blind.

Angie held court at the Crown. They owned the bar, and pretty much the whole street it operated on. There was a back room that was invite only, even getting a table at this place was near impossible. Angie sat in is booth in the back corner with Mario Bruno, Frank Dawson, Martin Wolfe and his son Nicholas.

"It would seem that Mr. Freeman has woken up on the wrong side of the bed again and wants to step in on our money management" said Angie has he cut through his lunchtime steak. The family would meet at the crown to discuss the ongoing jobs, they kept the conversations vague though. Even though they owned the bar, you just never know.

Act II

"Got good word that Oscar is wound," said Mario. Gio hadn't wasted any time reporting the news.

"He's always wound, it's nothing new. If he wants to send someone to babysit then we will double the babysitters' wages, easy enough" This was Nicky's outlook. You just couldn't stand in his way. Supreme confidence in his abilities.

The other four men chuckled at the response. "It's just that easy isn't it, Nicky?" said Mario.

Nicky took a sip of his drink, "Theres always going to be wolves outside our doors.... But they'll never knock... because what answers scares them more than anything in the world."

The icy cryptic response sent a chill down Marios spine. "Goddamn psycho" he muttered as he returned to his meal. The rest of the table grinned. Angie nodded to his son, "Well said"

"Besides, if this one goes sideways then we wait for Frankie to come pay us a visit with his new toys" The gun shipment made everyone happy, it meant more muscle to impose their will. More power.

"I do love my toys," said Frank. "If the bluebirds get a little loud Nicky, just wait for me, they won't sing for long."

"Thanks Frankie, hopefully I won't but I would love to make that call"

The men finished their lunch and drinks and went on their separate ways. Angie would return to his home where he did most of his work, Martin Wolfe would accompany him as the family

Act II

consultant. Frank had plans to finalize for that night on the docks, Nicky and Mario had to meet up with their crews to set up the rest of the day.

All these cars had security following them. The family always had security cars out in public. They were easily a monopoly in the city, but they never wanted to get caught with their guard down. Angie usually had two cars watching him at any time. Sometimes three if they were being investigated. Which was always, it seemed, but that just kept the family lawyer busy.

Angie climbed into the back of his black Mercedes. Martin Wolfe followed, with his notebook and bag in tow. Everyone knew that car as it rolled through the streets. "Is This Freeman issue going to continue?" asked Martin.

"If tonight has any issues, then we will be meeting with our friend. It wouldn't be smart business on his end to interrupt anything we have going on. Frost will have him shipped out." Explained Angie. Frost as in Arthur Frost. As in The Mayor of the city. The man had sat in Angie's back pocket for years now. He got reelected because of him, and his approval ratings always soared, or so the news would have everyone believe.

"I believe everything is in order and will run without interruption. Your boy is coming along nicely" added Martin. Nicholas had stepped up and took on his new role in the previous months and had become a major earner for the family.

"He's a fast learner. Just has to keep that temper under control. He get's that from his mother"

Act II

Grinned Angie as he sipped on his glass. Martin returned the grin in acknowledgement. Both men knew who the real psychopath was in the family. Definitely not Rebecca.

Jack pulled into the parking lot at the main entrance to the Docks. Later that night he would return, but it was easier to case the place out in the light. It was built like a fortress, for good reason. The fences were high with barbed wire wrapped at the top. The flood lights covered every corner, and the only way in was the security gate that had round-the-clock surveillance. Not exactly a walk in the park. Jack noticed a neighboring building that might garner him a better view of the festivities. A mid-sized apartment building, likely the home to most of the dock workers. They wouldn't let just anyone overlook the bay.

  Jack waited around for the right opportunity to sneak into the building. He luckily caught someone coming out and grabbed the door before it locked him out. He figured the roof was the best place to set up shop. It was much easier to access than expected. The mechanical room was on the roof so he could just walk right out. The full operation of the docks was in view. He could see every gate; this would be perfect. He could come back tonight and watch everything unfold.

  "Jackie Boy" came a gravel voice from across the parking lot. Jack had just stepped out of the building to hear his name being called. Standing next to his car, Mario Bruno.

A scary human to say the least. He was tall and broad and had a big beard with some grey creeping in. Always dressed to the nines, as usual. This time he chose a purple suit, because why not stand out.

Act II

"Mario"

"Jackie don't tell me you're snooping around down here. You know Ang isn't gonna like that"

Mario had a playful feel about his banter, until he felt that it was time to flex his muscles.

"Just dropping a few things off to a friend, I'm heading to Sal's for lunch (Their hangout on 5th street) you and the boys wanna free lunch on your old pal Oscar?"

Mario scoffed "Haven't paid for food at Sal's in years buddy boy. Nice try though"

Mario hauled on his cigar and stared at Jack. "But seriously, go fuck off down the road. I don't wanna see you around here. You got a problem, call Oscar and tell him Mario sent you home. We own his ass."

"Will do, Mario" said Jack as he opened his door.

"I'll put two in your fucking chest you ugly fuck. Don't mess around down here"

"I hear you loud and clear. Take it easy Mario" Jack closed his door

"Yeah, you too you fucking useless cop"

"Fuck that guy" mouthed Jack as he pulled away. Leaving Mario standing there. Tonight, might be a bit more difficult if they knew people were watching.

    Sal's Diner was the home base for Marios Crew. Every crew had their own spot, a diner, A coffee shop, a strip club, anything they wanted really. The crews rarely met in full force; the

Act II

captains would meet at Angelos on the rich side of the bridge. He had a place downtown, as well as his big house in the gated community.

The door to Sal's swung open and no one lifted their head, it was bustling at the lunch rush, even lined up out the door into the cold. The left side of the diner sat completely empty; it was only three booths anyway. But these were always reserved for the family. No one else. Jack walked through the door and took a hard left turn and sat down in the first empty booth. This caught the eye of the staff and some patrons. He didn't look like one of the crew. A waitress rushed over to him, she didn't get two words out when he pulled his badge that hung around his neck and let it drop to the table. She stopped in her tracks. "oh, umm.. what can I get for you officer?" she finally blurted out. Jack smiled, "Detective, just a coffee and clubhouse with fries darling. Thanks" She turned on her heel and disappeared to the back. She returned shortly with Jack's coffee but had a troublesome look on her face. "Sir, umm, Detective? My manager says that you really can't sit in this section. These are reserved seats, so if you would like we can move you into a different booth and the sandwich is on the house" jack took a sip of his coffee, he pondered the offer. "How about I sit in this booth, and If anyone comes along that may want to sit here, you just let me deal with them" a smirk came across his face as he watched the waitresses process that information. She turned away again and disappeared to the back. A minute later she returned with another woman who he assumed was her manager, as she had previously explained. The manager leaned over the table to put her face close to Jacks. She kept her voice low to not draw attention. "Detective Finn, respectfully, please remove yourself from

this section before I throw you out that fucking glass window." The first waitress had a very shocked look on her face. They

Act II

weren't allowed to say those things to customers. Jack set his coffee cup down, grinned again and looked up, "I've missed you, Marilyn. You haven't changed a bit."

"Oh, piss off Jack, you were here last week, get out of the booth"

"They're all busy Marilyn, trust me, no one's going to know"

"Well, it's your funeral Jackie" she replied. "Leave him be, bring him his food. Avoid the area" and she walked away. Jack grinned "bye, Marilyn"

Jack finished his lunch and put the cash on the table, a small tip for the waitress who had to deal with that mess from earlier. No issues at all, no family members came by nothing. Jack turned to walk out and sure enough, Abel (Mario's hitman) came walking through the door.

They locked eyes and Jack didn't even have a chance to explain or plead his case. Abel was average height but insanely above average strength. He grabbed Jack by the coat and picked him up, walked him to the counter and dumped him over it, knocking everything down in his path. Patrons ran in the other direction, as well as staff. Plates and glasses crashed around Jack as he hit the floor on his back. Abel walked over to the table and pocketed the money. He sat down and opened the paper he found sitting beside him. "If I wasn't so hungry Jackie, I'd break your legs for coming in here. So, it's your lucky day." Said Abel, straight-faced, no emotion. Another voice came from over the counter, it was Gio. "Jackie! Whatcha have?"

Act II

A muffled voice came from the pile of plates behind the counter "Clubhouse"

"Yeah, nice, I'll have that. Good choice Jackie" said Gio as he sat across from Abel.

"Hey Jackie?"

"Yeah, Gio?"

"Mario's on his way over, so I'd get lost. You know what he's like when he's hungry"

Jack climbed back over the counter and shook the broken plates off his coat. "Yeah, yeah, I guess he's always hungry then"

Gio smirked, "Yeah something like that"

Jack turned to Marilyn as he opened the door "sorry about the mess Marilyn, just put it on their tab" Abel shot up out of his seat and Jack exited quickly. Gio grabbed Abel to settle him down "Easy big guy, he aint worth the trouble" said Gio as he ushered his very strong friend back into the booth.

Jack checked his face in the rear-view mirror as he pulled into his parking spot at the precinct. No blood, perfect. He was a little banged up from being thrown over a diner counter, but he had been through worse. He had already brushed the broken plates from his hair, which he always kept near perfect. He didn't need anyone questioning him or paying him any extra attention today. He walked through the front doors and into the usual chaos of the precinct. A bench full of the most innocent men in the city (just ask them) and a plume of cigarette smoke

Act II

welcomed anyone who stepped in. Jack nodded at the guys behind the main desk, no need for conversation, everyone is too busy. He rounded the corner to the bullpen, he was in the back

right corner, which meant he passed by everyone and usually had to face a barrage of questions and comments, but that was a morning thing, today everyone was at full speed. Jack thought this was perfect for him. If anyone on Angie's payroll caught wind of his plan, he would be toast. And there were a lot of people on that payroll, even though no one would admit it. The wall behind his desk had all the notes from the morning where Freeman laid out how they would intercept the money transfer from Nicky's crew. It was going to be in full force. A bloodbath loomed.

      Jack had been at his desk for all of two minutes when a tap on the shoulder came and a voice: "Freeman's office, Finn."

"He isn't wasting any time is he" said Jack as he got up. He crossed the floor and pushed open the heavy wood door of the chief's office.

"You wanted to see me, Chief? Asked jack as he closed the door.

"Have a seat Finn" Oscar was busy writing in a notebook. He hadn't even looked up. His office was a mess. Books, papers, boxes, furniture, probably food under there somewhere, all covered an enormous old desk. A Gothic Library style room. It was impressive. Minus the mess.

Jack sat and waited for his boss to finally look up. It never came.

"You're putting the cuffs on Nicky."

Act II

Shock was a feeling that Jack had only dealt with during his first few months on the job. He had been desensitized fast by this city. But he felt it today.

"Are you serious?" he asked.

"No, I just wanted to say words out loud and see what came out. Of course I'm fucking serious Finn. You're his buddy, and this sends a message to The De Lucas that we can't be bought."

Jack had gone to school with Nicholas De Luca. They were friends, even good friends. But life takes everyone down different paths and being a friend to the son of the most notorious crime boss on the east coast, while your father was also a cop, became a bit difficult. Nicky stepped into the dark shadows of the family, and Jack enrolled in the academy. Both kids followed in their family lineage, Jack knew his path and Nickys would cross at some point, but he figured they would be older and maybe had a better understanding of how each other worked. This was early, and he hadn't talked to Nicky in months. Plus, how could he be at the dockyard and the bank job at the same time. Freeman didn't know about the docks, and Jack wasn't going to tell him until he had concrete evidence of what was happening. This one was going to be tricky, if not impossible.

Jack sighed, "Yeah, that will send a message. Are we prepared for the blowback?"

"If it gets messy, then we are prepared for the aftermath, yes."

"Even if it doesn't get messy, their will be a retaliation, or worse"

"Worse?" asked Freeman, he finally lifted his head.

Act II

"These guys are psychos. They think they own the city. Anyone who stands up to them either goes missing or gets made into a public display." Said Jack, he wasn't going to leave out the fact that this was incredibly dangerous.

Freeman stopped writing and stood up. He placed both hands palms down on his desk and stared at Jack. "Finn…we are the motherfucking police! You're telling me that doing our job is dangerous? Like we shouldn't do it? We all signed up for this. I'm so fucking tired of these guys walking around assuming they can get away with anything and we just smile and like it. Well, that shit is done, Finn. Tonight, we will make a statement. We aren't backing down anymore."

Chief Freeman never broke eye contact. He burned a hole in Jack while he waited for the response.

"Yes Sir. Understood." Nodded Jack.

"Leave" stated Freeman.

The bank was only a few blocks up from the dockyard. Just enough distance to keep everyone looking away from the guns being delivered. Almost like they picked this area on purpose (they did. It was obvious). The troops all gathered as the sun dropped below the skyline. Darkness provided cover lit by the gas lamps that lined the city. A perfect setting for good and evil.

The bullet proof vest gives a false sense of security. Pulling it on meant you were walking into the lion's den. Blue jackets, vests, guns, armored vehicles filled the street outside the precinct. Jack pulled his gear on and joined the rest. He would follow in his own car. Park far away and

Act II

make it on foot to his mark. But he needed to get away from the group long enough to get eyes on the docks. That would be his test tonight.

"Your old pal Nicky give you any sense of what we're walking into tonight?"

Jack looked over to see Danny Flores standing beside his car. Full riot gear strapped to him. SWAT across his chest.

"You guys are here too? Jesus, Freeman isn't fucking around this time," said Finn.

"We make the mess and you guys come behind with the mop and bucket, teamwork Jackie boy"

Jack lit up a cigarette while they waited for the call to hit the road. "Leave a couple smoke bombs for me so I can slip out the back"

Danny laughed and leaned against the car "They almost brought the tank for this, you know"

"You guys have a tank?"

"We do. Call her Big Bertha. She will fuck anything up, figured it might be overkill for a money pinch."

Jack scanned the scene of police vehicles and cops as far as he could see. "Umm..you think? This is overkill, I could pick this myself."

The radio hit with the all units call. Danny and Jack straightened up "Go time"

Act II

They knew what time the transfer would take place. Everyone got in their cars and headed toward their positions. They would wait for the signal and jump in. If anything went sideways, the backup was ready, and the backups back up were ready too.

  Three masked men walked through the front door of the Crimson Bay Bank. The clock above the teller's desk read Six Forty-Five. Fifteen minutes to close. Only two people stood in line. Two tellers waited behind the desk. A security guard stood in the corner by the window. No one even so much as flinched. Sid Carpino, Bugsy and Tommy Brains, the members of Nicholas De Lucas Crew, walked past the teller counter and down the hall toward the vault. Everything and everyone were bought and paid for, the crew was just emptying their bank account. A woman with the name tag "Kelly" held her ground, but inside she was trembling. Her boss sat in his office and waited for the deed to be done. He had warned them what would happen, and to not hit the alarm. She tried to steady herself and called the next person in line, her voice broke as she greeted the man. He was tall, with the hood of his sweater pulled over his head. "How may I help you, sir?" she squeaked out, her hands shaking. A voice came from inside the hood, "Go ahead sweetheart, hit the alarm"

"I'm not allowed, I'll get fired, my boss said so" she was trembling now. The man reached up and pulled his hood down, the face of a prince, one of those princes from the fairytales, except he drank the poison, on purpose and now the evil behind his cold eyes shook Kelly to her core. A prince, a prince of darkness. Nicholas De Luca.

Act II

"Last time I checked, I was the boss around here. Now go ahead, press it"

Kelly reached under the counter and pushed the silent alarm. She held in the tears. Why was this happening to her?

"What are you doing! I said don't push the alarm" boomed a voice from around the corner. A white dress shirt, red tie and dark slacks came around the corner. Stopped in his tracks when he saw Nicholas. "I told her too, our friends will be here soon, I suggest you take your employees and leave." A cold stare mixed with zero emotion in his voice. It wasn't just a suggestion; it was a statement of fact. He knew the police were coming. The family welcomed it. The more blue shirts the better, keep the eyes off the docks. But Nicky wanted to make a statement. If he had to spell it out in blood on the sidewalk that they owned this city, then so be it.

The vault had been left open, as instructed. The three men loaded bags of cash and drug them out into the lobby. Their van, parked outside the door, was left running, no fear of anyone stealing it. The civilians had left, it was just the crew and the bags of money. A blue light flashed overhead. A helicopter in the distance, overkill at its finest. The four men all pulled out their guns from under their coats. Automatic weapons were the only way out of this. Nicky peered through the front window, SWAT vehicles, trucks, and every police car in the city surrounded the building. The intersection had been shut down and filled with law enforcement of all kinds.

Act II

Jack sat in his car, parked down the street. He had a full view of the circus, but his mind kept looking for his way out, he had to get down to the docks. Freeman's voice rang through his mind. He had to cuff Nicky. Infront of everyone. His childhood friend being taken to jail, the papers will have a field day. Angie would hang him from the bridge in his uniform just to show who runs this city. Jack flicked his cigarette to the sidewalk through his open window. He fumbled in his glove box for something, a bottle. He poured a small amount into his coffee. Liquid courage would be called upon from time to time, tonight would be one of them.

Jack stepped out and made his way toward the line of cars blocking the street. He looked toward to bank entrance, where he found all four men with automatics standing inside the door. A voice was screaming above the crowd from inside "We have hostages! Any sudden moves… they die" it was Bugsy the Butcher. He opened the front door and stood behind their van. He grabbed a large duffel bag and brought it back into the bank. Snipers on rooftops stood completely still, waiting for their signal. Every gun that had been issued from the department was drawn and pointed at the door. The bullhorn in Oscar Freeman's hand finally lit up with something to say "Nicholas, we have every exit surrounded. We don't want this to end in public warfare, but we are fully prepared if you and your team do not cooperate. Surrender your weapons and release any hostages"

"Burn it down" instructed Nicky.

Act II

Bugsy opened the bag and pulled out his trusty flamethrower and a can of gas. He doused the walls and front entrance and tipped the can over at his feet. He backed up and lit the flamethrower. The faces of the officers burned orange in the enormous glow from inside. An audible gasp whipped through the crowd. The gas went up instantly, the trail led to the van. Which was loaded with drums full of gas and explosives. It was never a getaway vehicle. It was the cover for them to escape.

The explosion shook the foundations for blocks. Police cars were sent flying, officers diving for cover, windows shattering all around. Screams and horror ripped through the street. The bank was built to withstand a blast, the glass was not, shards covered the sidewalks. The fireball lit up the night sky and could be seen for miles. This is not how everyone pictured this night going.

The ringing in Jacks ears left him temporarily deaf. No sound, just chaos all around him. He had ended up behind a truck during the blast, he got to his feet and wiped the debris off. This was perfect, he thought. A huge mess, the perfect distraction. Jack ran back to his car and jumped in. It started, unharmed from the blast thankfully. He peeled out and threw the car sideways as he turned in the street, no one would even care that he was gone now.

Firetrucks and ambulances blew past him. It was a strange feeling seeing the lights but no sound. Just a long ringing that wouldn't let up. It was a blur of lights and people running in every direction. It was a short drive to the docks, but it was made longer with the street closures and wreckage from the blast. Jack turned off his lights as he slowed into a parking spot at the very back of the lot. He sat there, waiting, no sign of anyone. He made a break for the rooftop. The entrance door was propped open, sometimes you got to have luck in this

Act II

game. That could have ruined everything. Jack opened the door to the rooftop and crawled to the parapet. An exhaust fan provided cover for him to get a good look. Through the lens of his binoculars, he located the main loading docks. What he saw shocked him. Nothing. Absolutely nothing. No boats docked. No cargo. Just a couple laborers cleaning up. Was he too late? Did Gio set him up? Was Gio smart? No, he was an idiot. This didn't make sense.

The ringing finally subsided, and he could hear the city dealing with the explosion. Sirens, screaming, no one wanted this. Jack could hear people talking from below, he couldn't tell if it was from the docks or the parking lot. Where was the shipment? It was cold out, and Jack was not dressed for the weather and a cigarette was out of the question.

Time drug on, it may have been an hour, and that hour brought the temperature down with it. The city was still bustling in the background, but all Jack could hear was waves hitting the dockyard. And his teeth chattering. Suddenly, a beeping cut through the waves. A gate was opening on the far side of the yard. Two guards pulled back the gate and let three large vans pull in. That side of the yard was dimly lit and it was difficult to see who and what was going on.

Frank Dawson emerged from the office, laughing with the two guards. A man stepped out from the van and shook hands with Frank. Are these the guns? Or are these the guys picking up the guns? Thought Jack. There was no boat. Nothing added up.

The other drivers circled up with Frank and his crew. Waiting. Mario popped out from the office; his face lit up like his cigar. They all laughed, but Jack couldn't make out anything.

Waiting sucks.

Act II

It's freezing.

Jack's head was pounding. Caffeine and nicotine withdraw.

Another car found its way around the vans. A figure stepped out in the darkness from the back seat. Everyone stopped laughing and greeted the figure. One man kissed the hand of the shadow man. There's only one person who commands this level of respect and fear. Angie had arrived.

What was he doing down here? He doesn't put himself anywhere near this stuff. Jack couldn't believe what he was seeing. He could tie everyone to the guns and take them all down. He just needed the guns. And maybe a judge who wasn't corrupt.

Jack finally let a few words slip from his mouth "Holy, Shit" was all he could muster from his deep vocabulary. It really hit the mark.

A small speed boat came flying out of the black. The guns are here. The small boat really caught Jack off guard. He was expecting a huge cargo ship, not a speed boat. How many guns could you even get on that?

The boat docked and the vans backed up into position. Three men stepped off the boat and shook hands with Angie and Frank. Jack couldn't see faces or hear anything. Very frustrating.

Three men. Small boat.

Three Huge vans. This didn't add up.

A fourth man suddenly appeared from the boat, dragging one end of a large wooden box. On the other end was a fifth man. They laid the box beside the boat. They repeated this six more times.

Act II

The sleeping quarters had been hollowed out and used to store the guns. But still appeared as sleeping quarters at first glance. Well thought out.

The men all stood around in what seemed to be a standoff. They were clearly waiting for an exchange for the guns.

Lights skipped across the water. A truck pulled through the gate and the gates slowly closed behind. Angie motioned to the truck. A hooded man jumped out and pulled a bag from the bed.

Once the exchange took place, Jack would be able to tie Angie to the guns and this would break the city wide open. And his career would be made, just try to ignore the target on his head.

The bag was laid on the ground between the groups. Hand motioning and propositioning lead to the hooded man kneeling to open up the bag. This was the show us the money part of the transaction.

In a flash, the kneeling man pulled out a submachine gun and laid all five men to waste. The shots echoed off the buildings and died off across the water. The sound of waves crashing took its place. Followed by five bodies being pushed into the water.

Angie smiled at the man cloaked in darkness. "I told you I would get you a speed boat"

"I mean it really feels Frank should get the boat" all the men laughed as the man pulled down his hood. Nicholas De Luca. Not a scratch on him.

The two men smiled and hugged. What a sweet moment between father and son.

Act II

"They knew we were moving the money to a different bank. They just didn't know we planned to blow that one up. Minor details" grinned Nicky.

"How are the boys?" asked Ang.

"Everyone's whole. Bugsy got burnt a little but that's nothing." Nicky paused for a moment.

"But the explosion took out a few blocks worth of police, so we might have an issue in the morning"

"Price of doing business my boy"

One of the guards came running from the office. Everyone turned at the commotion.

"Mr. Dawson! Mr. De Luca! Theres someone on the phone. Something about Vic."

The two men sensed the urgency and stepped inside to take the call. The guard had lost all the colour in his face. "What is it jimmy?" asked one of the men.

He caught his breath "They said, they said, Vic… Vic is dead. They cut his head off!"

The guard then threw up on his boots.

A phone smashed through the office window.

Act II

Let the Games Begin

Jack woke up three hours later. Still freezing, but at least he was in his own bed. His alarm clock triggered more ringing in his ears. That blast had done a number. Jacks third story walk up apartment on the East side was spotless. Mostly because he was never there. Jack wasn't even under the blanket, just laying on top of it. In his clothes.

The clock on the wall read five am. Too early for this, but he knew that he was going to have to sift through the rubble outside the bank with everyone else and endure the rath of Freeman and his team. Jack jumped as the phone rang.

"Hello?"

"It's Taylor, Chief is looking for ya"

"Yup, on my way. Be there in ten"

Ok. Ten minutes to get my shit together he thought. But his mind raced with images of last night. Why did they kill the guys from the boat? Who were they? Why smash the window? Question after question that he couldn't ask anyone for an answer. Time to pretend he knew nothing while knowing everything all at once.

Act II

The death of co-worker is hard. Everyone mourns differently but at the core of it is that feeling that it's all a game of chance. No one knows when it ends, or who is winning. Except most times, the death of your co-worker isn't front page news. But not the big picture with the big headline, where it should be. It's in the small picture in the bottom right. Officer killed in blast, see page 3. Instead, the big picture out front isn't the death of a public servant, someone who risked their life to keep everyone safe in their beds, no, it's the murder of a crooked slimy Real estate mogul, Victor De Luca. Angie's Cousin. A window smashing type of headline.

"This is a real mess, Oscar. A real mess," said Bill Taylor. He stood across from Oscar Freeman, a mere 15 feet from charred police vehicles, and a large team of medical staff, the press, and every onlooker in a three-mile radius.

"A mess is something you can clean up Bill. I have one dead officer and another in the ICU. And likely more who are gonna need a shrink after seeing that shit. Theres no cleaning up this mess"

"Yeah, I didn't sleep a wink. I'm gonna see that shit forever. Why is it always fire with these guys."

"I don't know. I hate them. This is going to end very badly, for all of us." Oscar lit his second consecutive cigarette. That was his breakfast, and likely lunch.

"Get Finn down here"

"Already called, boss. He's coming"

"Good, he's going in"

Act II

"Going in? are you fucking serious? He'll be dead in a week, maybe less. Death by firing squad. You might as well shoot him in the face when he shows up, save everyone the time. Jesus Oscar." Bill Taylor was not having one of his detectives try and infiltrate a deadly crime family. Friends or not, Angie and Nicholas would see right through it.

"No, it's perfect Bill. We've got one dead De Luca, we will never find out why. This city won't rat on anyone. So, we let Finn get even closer, make it look like he's trying to help them find whoever killed Victor. And then have him set off a bomb from the inside"

"Oz, you're the chief of Police, and you're talking about killing a crime family. This is lunacy"

"I don't care Bill. I don't care anymore. It's war they want; it's war they get. They want to spill our fucking blood on the street! They want to burn my officers alive! Ruin their families! He had a kid! A fucking Kid! Fuck, he was a kid. His whole fucking life ahead of him. I'm done with this mafia asshole and his fucking family. I will paint the fucking streets with their blood if it's the last fucking thing I do."

Oscar Freeman was borderline hyperventilating. Seething with rage. This was not a time to disagree with a raging bull.

"Yeah, I mean,… alright. Jackies the right man for the job," said Taylor.

"What job?" came a voice from behind them. Jack Finn had entered the fray.

Act II

Oscar turned on his heel. Took a long drag off his cigarette. Tossed it. Slowly exhaled a cloud of smoke into the air. His sunglasses reflected a young detective, a boy about to become a man in some ways. "We need to talk Jack."

The city seemed like a blur as the three men combed their way through the streets, the De Luca Mansion was their destination. Bill Taylor had the most obvious police vehicle anyone could have. A black crown Victoria. It screamed police. He rolled down his window and slapped his red light on to the roof. "I hate traffic" he said as he hit the siren. The seas parted.

"Perks of the job, boys" grinned Taylor.

The sun had fooled everyone into thinking this would be a nice day. The news of a prominent figurehead being murdered had created a shockwave in the early hours. Every newspaper, radio station and morning news show had coverage. Every one of them echoed the same sentiment. How could this happen in this city?

"If only the public really knew what happened out here," said the chief. "That family controls the media and we just smile and take it"

"It's a wonder they didn't cover this one up. Maybe last night was more of distraction than they thought it would be." Questioned Taylor, Jack had yet to interject anything into this conversation, even though he really wanted to tell his bosses about what he saw on the docks.

Screw it, he thought. This was already becoming a huge mess, might as well add to the pile.

"Probably distracted with their new gun shipment on the docks last night"

Act II

"That's what the money was really for. Nicky showed up and used it as payment for the guns. But they just killed the smugglers and kept the money."

Taylor jammed on the brakes so hard, his light when flying into the street.

"ummm. What the fuck did you just say?" asked Taylor.

"Your lights in the street Bill" said Oscar calmly. He hadn't even reacted to Jacks statement. "I know. I know" said Bill quickly to his boss. He turned his attention back to the detective. "You were at the docks last night? Instead of at the bank with us?"

"No, no, I was there, I saw the explosion, I felt it, trust me. I left after, I knew there was a meeting at the docks, so I snuck away to see if I could get some intel on what was going on" explained Jack. He was treading lightly, because he had gone rogue, even though for a good reason, was still a no-no.

Taylor shot a look at Oscar. A death stare if you may. "This is the genius you want to send into the fire? Really, Oz?" Bill Taylor's very short fuse had just gone off. He gripped the steering wheel, trying to keep it together. He kept looking back at Jack, muttering curse words under his breath.

"You" deep breath.

"Stupid" another deep breath.

"cocksucking" Jack gave a confused look.

"Oversized" Jack was tall, broad shoulders. Big hands.

"Stupid, piece of shit" end Rant.

Act II

"You went alone.. to the docks…what if they made you? Dead. You are dead." Explained Taylor

Oscar turned to Jack as well, "I think what he is trying to say, is that, you are too important to this investigation to be putting yourself in that type of situation… without us knowing"

Oscar added that last part because he was about to lay out the plan to get Jack to infiltrate the family. They didn't want him to put himself in danger, unless it was their idea. Then it was fine, typical management.

Horns blasted from behind the car. Stopping abruptly in the middle of the street will usually cause that reaction. Bill collected his light from the street, and they moved on in silence. This conversation would continue, but for now they had a small issue of a man seemingly missing his head.

The gated community. The trees hadn't grown up enough to overhang the roads. It didn't have the daunting presence that it would grow into. A much smaller version existed, more of a new subdivision. One with mid-90s super mansions. Tall Pillars. Brick on brick, with more brick. Victors' mansion was no different. Two brick pillars held up a black iron gate. His driveway went downhill rather quickly, creating a valley for his house to sit in. An impressive architectural sight. Three stories high, wealth personified. Family ties and real estate paid very well.

Flowers had been set at the gate. A small crowd had gathered on the sidewalk. Victor was a public figure, loved and hated. The crown vic pulled down the drive, the weather was cold and dense, an eerie fog sat all around the house. A three-car garage sat beside the house with a connected walkway above. This created a tunnel to the courtyard behind the house.

Act II

Another garage sat to the left at the end of the house, an absolute monster of a house.

Jack stared out the window from the back seat. "is it just us?" No sign of anyone else. No police cars anywhere. Not exactly what he had expected. "Just us, Jackie. The family has been removed as well. His wife found him; she's on watch. I hope you have an iron stomach" said Oscar has he stepped out into the cold. "Twenty bucks says he pukes" Taylor chimed in from the other side. Both men gave a laugh and looked at Jack, Am I going to end up this way? He thought to himself.

Yes. Yes, he was. That's just how it goes in this line of work.

The back door into the kitchen was left unlocked. They made their way through the maze of rooms and hallways, archways, staircases, darkened hallways that seemed to be endless. The house was silent and still. The floorboards made the only audible sound under the weight of the three men. A back stairwell led them into Victors room, no signs of struggle yet. Legs came into view as the men entered the room slowly, they disappeared beside the bed. The body came into view as they crept across the room. Silk pants, stained with blood. A silk night shirt, soaked in blood, a body sprawled out on the floor. A gold Rolex sat wrapped around a wrist that sat in a pool of dark blood. A gold chain necklace lay almost sunken into that same pool. It's hard to keep your necklace on when you're missing such a key part of the equation.

What gets seen in the run of a career for a detective or a police officer can be described as horrific to someone who has never been. The three men who stood in that room, quietly embracing the loudest silence they had ever experienced, felt an overwhelming sense of shock that none of them had felt before. The sheer amount of blood that had poured from this human body was disturbing beyond belief.

Act II

A sword gleamed in the corner, a small ounce of sunlight trickled in and just happened to catch the blade. Sat beside the sword, soaked in sunlight, the severed head of Victor De Luca.

Bill Taylor stood at the foot of the bed; Oscar stood to his left. Jack had made his way to the far side of the room, beside the body. All three men took turns giving each other the side eye, who would break the silence first.

Jack pulled the curtain back from the window to let in more light. The trees in the front entrance were bare from the cold. A crow landed on the branch that overhangs the door. An omen, maybe. Or it's just a crow.

"Jesus Christ" Oscar finally broke.

"Alright, fuck, lets look at this. Theres no clear signs of a break in. No signs of a struggle. So either the door was open or he knew the attacker."

Taylor finally chimed in "I don't think I've seen this much blood in one place, ever"

"Who would want Vic dead?" asked Jack. He knew that there had to be a long list attached to that question, but he had to seem like he knew less, let his superiors feel like they had all the answers. Oscar chuckled slightly, almost a scoff at the question " Everyone… You don't become this rich without pissing a few people off"

"Angelo is going to lose his shit. Has anyone called the coroner? They might want a heads up. Maybe get a jump on an expansion" said Taylor as he stood over Vic's body.

"Dead officers. Dead Rich assholes. It's been a nice twenty-four hours for us."

Act II

"Let's take this downstairs. We can discuss your new role Mr. Finn" said Oscar as he made his way to the door." Let the team know. They can come clean this one up" he said to Taylor. Bill made his way downstairs to make the call.

Oscar pulled a chair out from the long table in the dining room. It may have had enough chairs to seat twenty people. Jack sat across the table. This was a different Oscar Freeman than what he was used to. He seemed almost human,

Oscar took a deep breath and settled himself down.

"Look, Jackie, what I am about to ask of you is something that is going to push the boundaries of what a detective is allowed to do. This isn't undercover, this is still Detective Finn, doing his day to day. But now you're going to play on your relationship with the De Luca's. We can only assume they're angry. As they should be. Angie will be on a warpath to find Victors Killer. This, if I have thought this through enough, this should create a blind spot."

"What do you mean by blind spot, chief?" asked Jack.

"A distraction, from you, getting too close. You get yourself as deep as you can without getting made and feed us everything you can. Now, this won't come easily, and you're going to need a lot of bait and firepower to make them believe that you're on their side. We are prepared to feed you the information and back up you need to show them that you're dirty and willing to go the extra mile."

Jack sat there, in disbelief, he let everything sink in for a moment. "This is incredibly dangerous, chief, with all due respect."

"I know, but with the explosion last night and now Vic's murder, the family is going to be tied up in knots for the next little while. This is the best opportunity we have. Get them to

Act II

look this way, while we go the other. Well... you go the other. We all have to be out front fighting Angie, while you sneak in the backdoor."

"Alright, I think I get it. But how far can I go?" asked Jack.

"Full green light kid, and I don't give that to anyone. But we need this to work, so welcome to the other side"

Jack took it in some more. This was huge for him if he could pull it off. "If they catch me, or get a sniff that I'm not on the level..."

"Oh, you'll be dead in a week kid" the voice came from the other room, Bill Taylor had returned.

"Seriously, I think this is nuts and you'll be in a body bag at the bottom of the river. Or hung from the 9th street bridge. Actually, you know, they love burning people, alive. Have you ever smelled burnt hair and skin? It's fucking disgusting. Ya wanna know what is even worse? When it's your own, kid. So, don't fuck this up." Bill was such a sweetheart. He never changed.

Oscar shook his head at Bill. He turned back to Jack "Look, this conversation, never happened. And, also, it has to look like we are on the outs. So, you're suspended for your disappearing act last night. (Air quotes around "Suspended") You keep to yourself and check in with me once a week. This is gonna be a slow play at the start, but once I get the feeling that you're safe, then we go full blast. Alright?"

Jack stared at Oscar. This was a holy shit moment.

"I'm in. Let's fucking do this" the two men shook hands. Jack nodded at Bill as well, no hand shake needed there.

Act II

The three men stood up and made their way to the hall "oh, hey, kid, what kind of flowers does your mother like?" asked Taylor. Jack gave him the look of confusion "why?"

"Just getting the jump on your funeral arrangements. White lilies? Is it roses? She a carnation lady?"

"Fuck you, Bill. Fuck you." Glared Jack.

Bill stopped and they stared each other down. "You get one pass kid. And this is it. The next time you say that to me. I will take off my belt and beat you unconscious."

Jack didn't back down "Keep your head up on the other side, wouldn't want you to catch a stray"

"Enough. Get in the fucking car, the team will be here soon" Chief had gone through enough today.

  Their car pulled out onto the street as the team came down the road, Freeman turned the opposite direction and floored it. No one needed to see them together at Victors house. The less questions, the better.

  "What now?" asked Bill. He pulled out his cigarettes and offered one to Oscar. He obliged. No offer to Jack. The move was noted. "Honestly, I'm going to go sit at my desk with the door shut until someone comes and drags me out." Replied Oscar. "Because the press and I are going to be very much entangled for the next little while, and I fucking hate them, so I'll need some time to process all of this before answering any questions"

"Breaking news: Crimson Bay Real Estate King Pin Victor De Luca has been found murdered in his family home early this morning. This coming on the heels of the massive explosion that killed two local police officers, last night and injured many more, causing a large amount of damage in the city core. No

Act II

word on whether the events are linked, we will continue to update the situation as more information comes available, stayed tuned to Q97 news for more updates"

The radio told the whole story, but only one part even registered to the three men. "Did she say two dead!?"

Two dead cops. When they left the scene, it was one dead with one in the ICU. Now they've lost two men. This had become an even larger tragedy in a mere morning. Lives changed in an instant, and the only ones to blame wouldn't lose a second of sleep over it. The drive back into the city was somber. No one spoke. Their master plan to take down the De Lucas seemed miles away, left at that table.

Snow slowly fell on the streets of Crimson Bay. The cold January weather could chill anyone to the bone, but the city with a blanket of snow belonged on a postcard, it made for a consolation prize of sorts. The park, the bridge, the streetlights lit up at night. The addition of falling snow could captivate even the most cynical. The beauty that surrounded them would be lost though, when that same snow landed on a wooden casket as it was lowered into the ground.

Two young lives lost at the hands of a ruthless crime family.

As the ceremony ended, Chief Freeman sought out his detective. He walked to Jacks left side, leaned in and whispered, "As soon as the dirt hits that casket, it begins" and he moved on.

Jack didn't blink. Didn't break his gaze. Still.

It was time.

Act II

Hello Darkness, My Old Friend.

Alcohol. Alcohol will fix this. Right? Thought Jack. He wasn't debating the answer in his head, but if he didn't ask then maybe he had a problem. "Another one?" asked the bartender. The post funeral crowd had made its way down to the Duck. The Drunken Duck to be exact. A watering hole for most cops and detectives, typically jack wouldn't join but this time he was quietly preparing to get lost in the city's underworld.

"Yeah, a double please" Jack replied with a nod. The clock on the wall read Eleven Thirty-Four. AM. But no one would dare mention it to anyone in that bar. Jack sat there folding the napkin his last drink had been placed on, hiding in the far corner of the bar, dimly lit and clouded with smoke. Just the way he liked it.

The bar was packed with blue, beers, smoke, moustaches and had no signs of slowing down. A celebration of life for the two young officers they had just buried. A sad reminder of what this city could do in the blink of an eye. "I'll have one too!" came a voice through the crowd. Lou Macleod appeared through the smoke and sat next to Jack. His desk mate at the office. Lou was tall like jack but slender. More of a beanpole. Sarcastic but very smart and he knew it, he liked to fuck with people, mentally.

Act II

"Word on the street is your getting sat down for a few weeks" Lou faced the bar, they didn't need to make eye contact, Lou was a close to a friend that Jack had in there.

Jack mouthed" Thanks" to the bartender as he landed a double in front of him.

"If I had to guess, I would say Freeman sells me down the river, and when I get back, I'm taken out by the Family."

"Jesus Jackie, It's just a suspension, with pay, I doubt Freeman wants to sell his soul to have you whacked." Lou was half laughing at this point.

Jack grinned slightly "I dunno Lou, he was pretty mad this morning when I showed up"

"Yeah, I meant to ask. Where did he take you that day?" ask Lou, innocently enough. He had no reason to believe anything was up.

"Home. Made me drive down and then yelled at me the whole drive about insubordination and then kicked me out at home. My fucking car was still at the bank site. He's a dick"

"Well, at least he waited until after the funeral"

"What a sweetheart, he walked over to me and said I could go for a drink but then I was officially suspended"

Lou downed his drink and patted Jack on the shoulder, "I'll miss ya, you cranky fuck"

He disappeared into the crowd. Jack followed suit. Down went the drink and he headed into the sea of law enforcement. Once he got through the maze, Jack headed down the block toward a pay phone. He fumbled in his pocket to find change, dialed a number, "Park Bench, twenty minutes" was all he said. And he hung up.

Act II

"Is that crispy bacon I smell? Maybe a little burnt, burnt around the edges, maybe completely burnt" Jack looked up from his usual seat on the bench at City Park to see if the voice matched the ugly face he was expecting.

Gio stood five feet away leaning on his car. Smiling at himself as he lit up a cigarette. "Heard you bailed on the cookout Jackie B. Now you're drowning in hot water"

Jack tried to ignore the first comment, even though he wanted to shove Gio's face through his passenger side window.

"Just left the funeral. I am officially suspended until further notice."

"Why are you even here?" asked Gio. "I'd be home on the couch asleep or drinking or anything else but here."

"Well, if I just went home for a couple weeks, I'd fall out of the loop, get left behind. No suspension is going to keep me from having my finger on the pulse of the city" replied Jack, confidently. He had to keep everything as normal as possible, no hints at what he was really up to.

"You think you have your finger on the pulse of the city?" laughed Gio. His face turned quizzical. "Really? I mean you seriously think you have it all figured out?"

"You're damn right. Plus, our arrangement is still valid. If I disappeared, you'd come looking for me anyway"

"Very true, very true" agreed Gio as he flicked half a cigarette at stone wall behind the bench.

"Good thing there's no cops here to bust me for littering" said Gio, he sat down beside Jack and pulled out another smoke.

Act II

"So, whatcha want? I pulled myself away from my lunch time stories to rush down here. This better be good. Or else Abel is getting a phone call"

"Freeman is livid. They've got a tank now. Just one. And they're working with the special operations unit to bring in more ammo and boots on the ground. Welcome to the warzone"

"Yeah, we kinda expected that. We got our new gun shipment, so there's not much for us to worry about. These weren't just automatics; these fuckers can take down a helicopter. "

"How did they fit those big guns in that small ass boat?" asked jack. Testing to see what Gio really knew.

Gio drew back on his cigarette and waited for his response. "You asshole. You said you weren't gonna go down there. What all did you see? Did you tell anyone? I bet you did you slimy fuck."

"Shut up Gio, Jesus. I didn't tell anyone. I couldn't, they suspended me immediately. I wasn't going to give them good info just to have them yell at me even more. I was going to use it to leverage information out of you, but now I'm off duty so none of it matters."

"So, I ask again, what…the…fuck..do.. you want..Jackieeee?" asked Gio. Slowing his sentence down to emphasize how much he wanted them to get to the point. He also realized what Jack had said at the end of his sentence. "The fuck do you mean leverage? Over me?" Jack looked up at him with a slight grin.

"Wipe that smirk off your stupid fucking face. You aint even a detective right now. You're nothing. Say Nothing, do nothing, worthless."

Act II

"Well, that's kind of my point" said Jack "Freeman cut my legs out with this suspension and took me off detail on Mario. So, I'm wide open. Basically, a free agent. So… I'm open to suggestions"

The silence between them hung like a dense fog. Finally, Gio leaned a bit closer, he motioned with his finger to Jack to do the same. Gio lowered his voice, mainly for intimidation, and said, "If you think, for one second, that I am stupid enough to fall for this fake, infiltrate the family, bullshit, you got another thing coming, chico" and patted Jack on the knee. Jack stayed calm and didn't miss a beat, even though he was reeling inside. "That couldn't be farther from it, G. I told you, I just got sat down. Back to square one. No gun, no badge, nothing. I didn't work this hard to get where I'm at, just to get pushed all the way down the ladder, for some bullshit call my boss makes. They don't have it together in there and I'm tired of it. It's time to make a change, and I'm offering you my services, so you can take that however you want"

Small snowflakes began to fall from the trees and clouds above. Almost like a postcard scene. One that you would send your family and tell them how your year went at school. With the local neighborhood detective and his low life crime family friend sitting on a bench in a picturesque snow globe.

"I hate you, Jackie. I really do" said Gio. "Why would you do this to me?"

"What do you mean?" asked Jack

"Well, if your legit then I gotta take this to the boss, and it could be great. But if you're lying. Then, well, you're dead." Gio replied as he flicked another cigarette to the ground.

Act II

"How will you know?" said Jack. He knew he had him, this was his in.

"I won't Jackie, until it's too late. If they agree to bring you in, and they smell a rat. It's a nighty night for Mr. Finneas. Deceased. Loving son and friend. Gone too soon. He will be missed. Nice little obituary in the paper. 10 bell salute by the department. Your picture on the wall. Oh, what could have been, he had such potential. Definitely won't be an open casket" laughed Gio.

He stood up and shook off some of the snow. "Well, this could be the start of a beautiful partnership. Or I dump gasoline on you in a warehouse and watch your skin melt off."

Jack didn't show any emotion. "Hey, Gio"

"Yeah?" Gio turned slightly as he started to walk away.

"I still need a gun"

Gio laughed as he pulled out another cigarette. "I know. Sit tight. I'll be in touch"

Jack stayed on the bench as Gio pulled away. That almost went horribly wrong. But now he had to wait.

The police radio in Jacks car still worked. So, he could stay in touch with some of what was happening in the city. It was a time like this that he wished he had a partner. But just this time. A couple of days had passed, and Jack was starting to think that maybe the answer had been no, and everyone was warned to avoid him. He was still tailing Marios Crew, but he really had the green light to watch everyone now. A green light he wanted to take full advantage of.

There was to be no contact with anyone from the department for the first few weeks, they couldn't jeopardize anything at this point. A meeting would be set up with

Act II

Freeman but it would be through a messenger. That's all Jack knew. Keeping him in the dark in the early stages made the most sense. Cue the montage of Jack reading the paper, drinking coffee, roaming the street aimlessly. He could only tail the family if he could find them, which at times was a needle in a haystack. It was a long forty-eight hours before he finally got a call.

Jack was startled by the ringing phone. He was just resting his eyes on the couch. A slow day in the life. "Yeah, Yeah, it's Jack" he fumbled as he tried to get the receiver to his ear. A voice came through the phone, it was low and gruff "Warehouse at the end of Delmore. Twenty Minutes." The voice hung up. Jack didn't even get a chance to ask any questions or explain that he lived on the other side of town, so getting to Delmore in twenty minutes could be difficult. Not that they would have cared anyway.

Jack jumped in the car and sped off. He left his little townhouse behind; he was glad to be out of there. The mind can do some interesting things when you're running on adrenaline and fear. Jack's was racing with scenarios.

They let him in, nothing happens.

They let him in and shoot him in the head.

They hold him captive and torture him.

Torture.

Murder.

Burned alive. Which they were known for.

Maybe they just want to sit down and have a chat, drink a beer. Yeah, that was the most likely.

Act II

Jack gave his head a shake. He was going into this blind, with no weapon. Not the smartest move. The grip on his steering wheel got tighter as he pulled on to Delmore. As he approaches, the vehicles all seemed to be large SUVs and big trucks. A good sign that he was in the right place. The street narrowed to a fence and an old gate that surrounded the warehouse. Jack pulled off the road. This was the middle of the day, what would they really do?

Kill him, they didn't care what time it was.

Jack slowly made his way out of the car. No sign of anyone yet.

He walked through the open gate and turned toward the warehouse. It had three overhead doors and one man door with glass in it. The glass was all smashed. Still no sign of anyone. Did he just knock and walk in?

"You're late, Jackie" a deep voice made of gravel came from behind. Jack turned to see Mario Bruno. A full black suit, one you would wear to a funeral. The omen was not lost on Jack.

"Best I could do. I'm on the other side of town"

"Don't care. Get the fuck inside" A friendly greeting from his old pal.

Jacks insides were turning. He was sweating. This could take a bad turn at any second. He walked into the warehouse, he took notice of everything he could see. A small office in the corner, crates stacked on crates near the back and two vehicles in the bays. Nothing to write home about.

"Wait. Don't move. Arms out" Mario patted Jack down. No weapons.

"Good, now walk your ass through that door" Mario pointed at a single door near the back. "Any chance you could give me

Act II

a heads up on what this is about?" asked Jack. It was a long shot, but he was running out of nerves and options.

Mario chuckled "you got a lot of balls even coming down here, kid. I'll give ya that." He pushed Jack towards the door. "Go".

A normal heart rate ranges from 60-100 beats per minute. If they had hooked Jack up to a monitor, they may have had to shock him back into rhythm, because he was in the 180's easily.

The door slowly swung open, a room with one light and one table. It resembled a police interrogation room. This was not a good sign. "Sit down. Wait here"

Who would come through that door? Angie? Gio? Maybe a super boss that no one even knew about. Jacks thoughts spun in his head. A panic attack was coming from deep inside him. His arms froze, his chest was pounding. He tried to slow his breathing and keep his mind focused on the reality of the situation. He was just sitting in a room. Everything was fine.

The room was cold. The lightbulb above him was hanging on by a thread, it could fall at any moment. A damp basement would be the best comparison. The door finally creaked open.

Jack readied himself. Flip the table and throw the chair if he saw a weapon, or a gas can.

A hooded figure walked in. Closed the door and turned back to Jack. Jack stood up with a slight look of shock on his face.

"Nicky?"

"Jackie Boy. How have you been?"

Jack didn't even know how to reply. He stumbled over his words "I'm..I'm good Nick. I didn't really expect to meet you

Act II

down here. Honestly, I wanted to ask Gio when I could get a meeting with you"

"When your free agency, as you so eloquently put it, was brought to the table. I stepped in and asked to take the meeting. Everyone felt that I knew you the best and could make the right decision."

This was the Nicky that Jack had grown up with. Well spoken, engaging, easy to talk to. He made you feel like you had been friends for years. A natural charmer. Except there was a wolf underneath. A terrifying, murderous, blood thirsty wolf.

Nicky sat down across from Jack and motioned him to do the same. Both men sat in silence, staring at each other.

"Been awhile Jack."

Both men nodded.

"You want a coffee or anything?"

"Ah, no, I'm good."

"Jackie, why the fuck are you here?" Nicky stared at him. His glare was cold and menacing.

A moment passed that felt like an hour. "Like I told Gio, I'm open for business. Freeman kicked me to the curb and I'm sick of it. If I can be of service, then let's talk. If not, I understand, I'll be on my way."

Nicky De Luca was a very dangerous human, but he had a soft spot for his old friend. A weakness that Jack needed to exploit.

"Oh, on your way?" Said Nicky. "Just like that? If I think you're full of shit, then you just get to walk out? That's a new one."

Act II

Nicky made an amused face. "Lift up your shirt."

Jack figured they would search for a wire. He lifted his shirt. No Wire.

"This is legit, Nicky. Freeman is coming full force. He took me off every detail I was working on for the past two years. I'm back on day one. Time to get a little dirt on my hands"

That line was the first cast into the water. A dirty detective could be a huge advantage for the family. But would they bite.

Nicky tapped his fingers on the desk. He seemed to be pondering his words. He shook his head up and down "Yeah, alright, you come in here, no weapon, no wire. Huge balls for that. But you're forgetting one thing Jackie boy…"

Jack seemed a bit confused; he was trying to piece together where Nicky was taking this.

All Jack heard was a yell and he felt a forearm drive into his throat and the full weight of his old friend land on top of him. Both men spilled to the floor, with Nicky landing on top. Jack hit the concrete floor hard, it knocked the wind out of him and left him stunned.

The feeling and taste of a gun being placed in your mouth is a sensation that will live with you forever. And "placed" is a nice way to put it. "Shoved" was more like it.

"You're forgetting that we both went our separate ways. I don't owe you shit. What makes you think you can walk in here and I'll just open the doors and welcome you with both arms? Fuck You Jack Finn. You're a fucking detective that is not on my payroll."

Tears welled up in Jack's eyes. He was starting to shake. The look in Nicky's eyes was something from a horror movie. Just pure psychotic.

Act II

But then, A smile crept across Nicky's face. "Until now" Those words hit Jacks ears, and he nearly threw up on the gun from relief. Nicky pulled the gun out and Jack began coughing. The sound of the door being kicked open broke the tension in the room. Bugsy slid into the room "Boss. We have an issue. You need to see this. Oh, Hey Jacko!" Nicky turned to Bugsy and nodded. He turned back to Jack, stood up and wiped the gun off with his sleeve. Jack attempted a wave to Bugsy.

"Gio said you needed a gun. Don't try anything, it's not loaded." Nicky smiled even bigger. "Welcome to the team Jackie. I'll reach out tomorrow and get you up to speed." He dropped the gun on the floor and left the room. Jack lay on the floor for a few more minutes, gathering himself. What had just happened? Were they messing with him the whole time? Was this even real? He thought. He finally made his way outside. No one to be found. Just the lingering taste of firearm in his mouth.

Jack sat in his car for a few minutes before he started the engine. This was going to be a lot to process. He didn't have time for that.

The car fired up and the radio kicked on. "Breaking News: Labor Union President Frank Dawson was found Murdered in the street outside his home this morning. This news is currently coming to us live, we will keep everyone updated on the status as it comes available. Again, Union President Frank Dawson, A pillar in the city, has been found dead outside his home. This is the second high profile killing in recent weeks, there is no connection at this time, but we will be updating the story as it unfolds"

Jack laid his head on the steering wheel. "Oh, sweet fucking Christ"

Act II

A Blanket of Snow

The call hadn't come for Jack. Understandable, considering the circumstances. Angie really didn't deal well with his men being murdered. He had started a war with the police to create a distraction, and now it was starting to feel like someone was targeting him. These two deaths couldn't be random, and Angie knew it.

"Are you serious? We have nothing? On Either of them?" yelled Angie from behind his desk. His whisky glass smashed on the wall above Martin Wolfes head. He didn't flinch, nerves of steel. Plus, he was used to dealing with the boss. "We have a few leads, but our guys on the inside are struggling to get any information" replied Wolfe.

"What do I even pay them for? What is the good of having police officers on your payroll, if they can't do the one fucking thing, I pay them, to do!" Angie was hot, he poured another glass of whiskey. He was going to drink this one. Maritn explained the situation: "It seems as though the investigation into Victor's murder has stalled with the lack of evidence. No fingerprints, no forced entry, no surveillance. They have no witnesses to even interrogate."

"And for Frank? Anything yet?"

"Nothing, just that he was stabbed multiple times (that's an understatement) and left to die in the street in front of his

Act II

house. Same story, no witnesses, no fingerprints, not even the murder weapon this time.

Frank Dawson's Murder, coming on the heels of Victor De Luca, had shaken up the inner circle of the family. They hadn't dealt with this type of trauma. They were usually the ones causing it. They liked to dish it out, but when it was their time to receive it, they didn't take too kindly to that part of the equation. Frank was coming off the successful acquisition of their new gun shipment, as well as a few other deals that fell into Mario's lap. The union was in disarray once the news broke. It would take a few weeks to calm everyone down and get things back on track.

This business doesn't take a day off for funerals or anything really. The rest just pick up the pieces and keep moving forward. Angie had called an emergency meeting to discuss their next steps, he had his eyes trained on Konstantine. His counterpart in Blackburgh, the filthy neighboring city to Crimson Bay. There had been peace for many years between the families. A peace that was brought upon by vengeance and violence. Swiftly bringing Konstantine to his knees, leaving him with just enough to rebuild. Angie always knew that he would eventually reach the point of wanting his revenge, and now they faced that possibility.

Bringing everyone to the table was a big deal. It was a rare occurrence saved for dire straits or moments of celebration. This meeting would be a discussion of the next few weeks and how they approach this enemy at their gates.

As darkness fell on a cold wintery night, headlights illuminated the thick trees beyond Angie's estate. His mansion had a separate entrance and garage for business. The driveway lined with SUV's and Trucks. All in black, a stark contrast from the surrounding snow.

Act II

The great room, with vaulted ceilings, exposed wood beams, a stuffed Bear in the corner, and glass cases filled with war memorabilia. A step back in time as some may say. The long wooden table at the center of the room had a glossy sheen, as it rarely saw a utensil or a fingerprint for that matter. At the head of the table sat a solid wooden throne. That was the only way to describe this chair, which only one person had ever sat in.

Angie took his rightful place at the head of the table. Martin Wolfe, advisor, sat to his right. The crown prince of Crimson Bay, and heir to the throne, Nicholas sat to his left. Thomas Roth, the family lawyer followed by Mario Bruno and the rest of the crew. Gio Ricci, Big Kev, Joey Barras and Abel Mazzoni. Frank's guys sat on the opposite side, Sonny Boy, a lovely man they called "Pinky" and a very large human they referred to as "Cesar". The table finished off with Bugsy, Sid Carpino and the most entertaining Tommy brains. A group of long-standing members of the family, who had been through everything together. They were reeling from the loss of two of their own. The chair placed at the opposite end of the table, a similar throne style, only smaller, was usually reserved for Victor. This night it had a new occupant, one that became the immediate talk of the table as a tall slender man with salt and pepper hair, an expensive suit and a face for tv, or politics, walked in and took a seat.

"Arthur" announced Angie. "Glad you could join us on short notice" The man known as Arthur nodded his head, held up his glass and replied "It has been far too long for this meeting to finally happen, my condolences for the circumstances.

Gio leaned into Mario "Is that the fucking mayor?"

It was the fucking mayor. Arthur Frost sat at the end of the De Luca Crime Family table. Breaking bread with the organization

Act II

he campaigned against. On the surface. In the shadows, behind the door marked "keep out", The cities squeaky clean Mayor, was in the back pocket of the actual person running the show, Angelo De Luca.

The glasses around the table didn't stay full for long. They also didn't stay empty for long either. Cigar smoke filled the room as their food was brought to the table.

"A toast" announced Angie. He stood up from his throne. "Frank, you were one of us. Family without the name. But family, nonetheless. You will be missed my friend." Angie raised his glass along with the table.

"Now, for my namesake, my father's brother's son. Victor. Doing two of these in one night was never the plan. Both men taken in their prime." Angie paused. "Both men, who ate and drank with us. Our family. Someone has attacked our family. Every man in this room feels that, down to their core. Being at this table puts you in a different stratosphere than the rest. No one, and I absolutely mean, no one. Fucks with this family, and lives to see the light of day." Angie kept his composure, but he was boiling on the inside. Holding in the urge to yell "we are going to kill these motherfuckers" even though that's what everyone wanted to hear.

"Now, for our esteemed guest of honor. Mr. Arthur Frost, our sitting mayor. We welcome you into our inner circle" Nodded Angie.

"I have wished to grace these halls for many years. I feel the weight of the situation that you have found yourselves in and I wish to be of some help, or guidance through to the other side. Whatever that may be." He smirked at his last words. As if he hadn't already agreed to help Angie do whatever it took to find the killer or killers at large. Mayor

Act II

Frost was on the payroll, and had been for some time, but only now, with the heat from the bank explosion, and the murders, was he called to the table. It was time for Arthur to pay the piper and provide full access of the mayors many amenities, to Angie.

As the night poured on, the parties grouped off as they usually did to sections of the room and loudly discussed their plans, telling old stories that everyone had already heard, and just getting blind drunk. Angie walked across the room to where his son Nicholas was leaning on the bar in a conversation with Frank's right hand, sonny boy. A man of many talents, theft, stealing, taking things that didn't belong to him and making other people's possessions disappear. He was a master thief. Angie leaned in and whispered something to his son, they excused themselves to Angie's office.

"How did it go with your little cop friend" asked Angie. He thought the idea was a waste of time, but Nicky had stuck his neck out. "He's harmless, he just looks intimidating, I flattened him, gave him a stick and said we would let him know. If he's legit, then we milk him for info and feed him bullshit."

Angie stared at his only son. "You'll kill him, Nicholas. That's an order"

Nicky stopped in his tracks and stared back at his father. "I don't think you understand, we can use him for info, he wants to be one of us. We can use that"

"He doesn't have enough career behind him to warrant us taking that type of risk. What type of information do you think we will get from him? When there will be a check point? He's just a kid." Replied Angie "If he can provide some use, then fine, we will string him along. But you will kill him. He is now

Act II

our pawn in this chess match with Freeman. He will be displayed to send a message, and when I give the order, it will be done. No questions."

Nicky stood there, unable to make a sound, his childhood friend had done nothing wrong except become a detective. And for that choice, he would be made an example.

"Yes, Sir" squeaked Nicky. This one hurt a little. Even for a cold blooded psychopath.

"Good boy" assured Angie as he placed his hand on Nicky's shoulder. "We will do great things. And when we have removed our adversaries, we are free to roam"

The sentiment of that statement pulled back the curtain on Angie's inner monologue. Remove the Police? A city with no law enforcement, completely run by organized crime. It was a dream, and a nightmare all wrapped into one.

A voice came from the door, "Well, Angie, should we discuss our business at hand?"

Both men turned to see the mayor standing inside the doorway, drink in one hand, cigar in the other.

"Yes" smiled Angie," Absolutely Arthur, please come in, sit down" motioning to the table and chairs. "Just let me get the others, they need to be present for this" Angie leaned out the door, Mario and Martin Wolfe appeared without notice.

The group surrounded the old wood table. It had seen many of these meetings in the past. Decisions that would affect the city had been made here. "Now, gentlemen, everyone knows why we are here. Our family has clearly been targeted. This is a response to these actions that is very necessary, with appropriate force and swift punishment for those involved. With our current positioning in the ranks of the city, I find it

Act II

hard to believe that this could be orchestrated by anyone other than a member of our world." Every nodded along in agreement. "My first instinct, as I am sure much of you feel the same, is Konstantine. It lines up with his style of work, it only makes sense that it was him." Everyone agreed with Angie. This had to have been their neighbor to the south.

"Angie, how can I be of service to see this to fruition," said the Mayor. Arthur knew he had to offer and not be asked; it would seem disrespectful.

"Of Course, yes Arthur, that is much appreciated. We will discuss that arrangement outside this meeting. But everyone be sure, the Mayor is on our side through these trying times" replied Angie, toasting his guest. Arthur returned the gesture; he did not want a man of Angie's stature and temperament to feel slighted.

The night ended much later than Arthur was used to. His driver appeared to pick him up outside in the courtyard. A large full moon, a snow moon, illuminated the grounds. Pristine

Snow created a perfect coating to reflect the shining moon.

"Quite a night, Angie" said Arthur has he buttoned up his coat. He was intoxicated more than he was accustomed to, but that was just part of the life on this side.

"Indeed Arthur" assured Angie as the two men shook hands. "I look forward to our partnership. Now get home safe. Your lovely wife is likely worried."

"Tomorrow might be a rough one for me" grinned Arthur, he stepped into the back seat of his town car and disappeared into the night.

Act II

Jack stumbled into his kitchen. His fluffy robe and fuzzy slippers had seen better days. The clock on the wall read five thirty. He thought… it was very blurry, and there may have been multiple clocks. He really hoped it wasn't five thirty, PM. He smelled awful and his head was pounding. He had been frequenting the bar down the street, "Aces" was a local watering hole. It was a dive bar, let's just call it what it is. At this point he figured he had failed. The Frank Dawson murder seemed to derail everything. No one had reached out from either side, so Jack did the only thing he enjoyed the most, he drank.

One cup of coffee sat beside his plate of eggs, he really didn't remember even making the plate. He knew he had to eat but his stomach really wasn't having it. He stood up and walked into his living room. For a weeklong bender, his townhouse looked immaculate. Likely because he was never there, he lived in the bar. Jack turned on his tv, he had been disconnected for days, he figured it was time to see where the world was at.

"Channel Seven news, I'm Bruce Dickenson, we come to you live with breaking news: Mayor Arthur Frost has been found dead at his estate. The third high profile murder in the past weeks, we are waiting on words from our sources for more details, as this story breaks, we will be talking with Police Chief Freeman, he will be addressing the situation in a press conference later this morning. They have issued a brief statement asking the residents of Crimson Bay to stay inside and please report any suspicious activity as the investigation continues."

"They killed the mayor?" came a female's voice from the kitchen.

Act II

Jack jumped out of his chair, he turned to see a very attractive blond woman with her hair tied up, only wearing a white t-shirt, standing in his kitchen. "Who the fuck are you!"

"Ummm.. Kelly. Do you not remember last night, Dave?"

"Who the fuck is Dave?" The pounding in his head intensified.

The woman looked very confused. "You told me your name is Dave; you're a fire fighter"

They stood and stared at each other. Kelly broke the awkward silence "You do know that we had sex last night?" Jack still couldn't find the right words. His memory was blank.

"I'm assuming none of that is true. What is your real name?" she asked. Jack stumbled over his words as his head spun," No, my name's Jack, I'm a detective, or at least I was a detective, I Think."

Kelly started laughing, "I'm fucking with you. Can I have some coffee, Jack Finn?"

"What is happening right now?" mumbled Jack.

"How drunk can someone be to forget that there's been a hot blonde sleeping in their bed for the past two days."

"Two days?" Jack was beside himself. Confusion had fully set in. Kelly smirked again.

"You're fucking with me aren't you."

She nodded as she poured her coffee. "You're awfully gullible for someone who claims to be a detective" "Yeah, it's been a rough week" replied Jack as he ran his hand through his greasy hair. He realized his robe wasn't tied, he attempted to tie it up, this amused Kelly. "Now you're modest? That's cute"

Act II

Jack turned away from his new house guest to look back at the news. The mayor is gone too? This was snowballing fast, and he had no answers. Maybe it was time to check back in with the boss. The radio silence was driving him crazy.

"This is bad" said Jack as he stared at his television. "Very, very, bad" as he tried to collect himself. He poured a glass of water, chugged it and poured another.

Kelly sat at the table, watching Jack try to pull it together. "Coffee? The one in the other room is likely cold now." she asked. "Yeah, that's next. I need to get sober, quick," obviously time was the only fix, or more alcohol, two things Jack didn't have much of at this point.

"So...you are?" questioned Jack as he sat across from the pantless wonder.

Kelly smirked again, "You really can't remember? Aces. Last night? You sweet talked me with your 'I'm working the big Victor De Luca Case'."

Jack sat in an uncomfortable sweat. "I said…. what?"

"You said, and I quote 'I am the lead on the De Luca Case and I am going undercover to solve it'"

Jack had a quick thought to the shovel in his small backyard. How fast he could dig a hole and where his gun was. It's winter, the ground is frozen, digging a hole would be nearly impossible.

"You can chalk that up to the whiskey. I'm only new at this, they wouldn't assign something that important to a young guy like me." Would she buy it?

Kelly made a face over her coffee cup that screamed "oh, really?"

Act II

"So that's just a line you use in bars to get girls?" she asked.

Sheepishly, Jack responded with "Well, I mean, it worked, didn't it?" Jack was leaning into the sleazeball web that Kelly was spinning, it was better than the truth.

"Yeah... it clearly worked. It's only slightly upsetting that I fell for it. I read people for a living."

"How so?"

Kelly finished her drink, set the cup on the table. "Lawyer"

A lawyer, this could be good, or bad, Jack couldn't place it. "So, A detective working on a case like this would definitely pique your interest"

"I mean, you had me at detective, the rest was extra. Plus, most of the detectives I meet are small skinny nerd looking type. You're a redwood compared to them."

"A redwood, that's a new one, I'll take it." Jack enjoyed the compliment. "What type of law?"

"I work in the DA's office."

"I would have figured Defense lawyer, But you don't look old enough for that, how old are you?"

Kelly's face, or more so her eyebrow raised at the blunt exchange. "Excuse me?"

Jack didn't care. "Thirty? Thirty-Five? Fifty?...Twenty one?" She recoiled at the verbal attack. She was playing along. "Thirty-two, actually."

"hmmm.. an older women, that's a first"

"If that's how you see it, sure" she replied. They both secretly enjoyed the back-and-forth banter. Someone to match Jacks wit could serve him well, although Kelly might be one level

Act II

above him on the mid-season rankings. They both finished their coffees, Jack attempted to refocus on the news that had undoubtedly shook the entire city. The hangover was not helping.

5:30 AM

Arthur Frost Announcement

6:30 AM

Every Morning News Program and Radio show are full press on the case

6:35 AM

Jack and Kelly watched the news coverage in disbelief. Neither of them had attempted to get dressed or clean up in the slightest.

6:36 AM

Jack's kitchen starts making a strange noise. A ringing sound is coming from the wall. Jack jumps up to answer his phone, He hasn't spoken to anyone from either side and his adrenaline had just spiked.

"Hello?.. Yes..Ok..When? Yes…OK..Will Do. Perfect. Ok. Bye"

Kelly gave an interesting look to say who was that?

"Oh, that was just my mother, she's making Lasagna, wanted to know if you were coming for Dinner" replied Jack quickly. This caught Kelly completely by surprise, score one for Jackie.

"Wait.. What?" is all she could muster.

Jack couldn't keep a straight face. "I have a meeting in Fifteen minutes."

"Oh, a Meeting for the case that you're not a part of?"

Act II

Jack laughed "Yeah…something like that"

He took off for the stairs and stopped at the bottom step. "This is the part where you get the fuck out, I've got stuff to do" This was a make-or-break moment, if Kelly took offense, there likely wouldn't be a second, or first real date. But she saw right through it." Very funny Mr. Finn. I'll run along and wait by my phone for your call. Oh, dear how will I survive without you."

They both smirked. Kelly was well versed in sarcasm. If anything, Jack would need her much more than she would ever need him.

Jack made it back to the kitchen in record time, but only his shirt remained. Laid on the table, with a phone number written in lipstick on the sleeve. 'til next time.

Freeman's office hadn't changed. Smokey, a smell of stale alcohol, aftershave and a touch of stress. It had only been a few weeks since their last meeting there, but it felt much longer. Oscar hadn't lifted his head, which was typical. Jack sat quietly in the leather chair, opposite the large oak desk, covered in stacks of papers and case files. Furiously writing in a case file, Oscar finally acknowledged Jack's presence, "You smell like a brewery kid, coffees in the corner"

The Door swung open, the asshole Bill Taylor, strolled in with the paper under his arm. "Gentleman, how is everyone on this fine morning.?" He smiled at Jack and Oscar. This was alarming on many levels to both men. Bill sat next to Jack, looked over at him and nodded "Jackie my boy, I am very glad to see you're still alive" Unsettling to say the least. Bill placed his coffee cup on the table and pulled the paper from under his arm. Oscar leaned back in his chair, flipping a pen through his fingers. "What is it, Bill?" Oscar knew this act now.

Act II

Bill slammed the paper down on the desk. Arthur Frost, Dead at 47. The large black letters may as well spilled off the page. Bill's coffee bounced with the commotion. He caught it just in time.

"Our first meeting of this little taskforce, where we are basically dangling our own detective over a shark tank, and it just got turned up to eleven. Which is great! Just great! Frank Dawson, murdered!... Victor...Murdered! That was enough. Now, not only to add fuel to the fire, and it's a damn big fire now Oscar, we are now dealing with a full-blown serial killer."

"For Christ sakes Bill, calm down. It's too fucking early for this shit. The Mayor is fucking dead. The shitstorm we are about to walk into is basically insurmountable and I am fully aware of the enormous ask we are placing on Jack's shoulders. The last thing I need, and that any of us need, is your incessant whining at every turn."

Tensions were clearly very high. Dealing with big name players being murdered in a shortl time frame would cause any city to delve into mass hysteria. Crimson Bay was no exception. News outlets were flooded with calls from citizens, begging for more information, The rumors of a crazed serial killer haunting the streets were now running rampant in a very short time. The situation these men found themselves in was palpable beyond belief. A city living and breathing together, all waiting for the next news update, or worse, the next victim update.

Jack was fixated on the window of Oscars office, old and stained, but just clear enough to see the snow falling. Small snowflakes had been steadily falling since the early hours. A postcard scene to say the least when these snowfalls happen, except this time the snow that covered the city now had footprints, bloody ones.

Act II

Love Thy Neighbor

Oscar turned his attention to the young detective. "I know we said there really shouldn't be contact in public or even here, but under the circumstances, I can only imagine that you were completely shut out from the family, so please enlighten us with your early findings, if any"

A feeling of almost relief came over Jack, he had nothing at all, no inside information, no interesting stories, nothing. To hear Freeman say that they had assumed he had been shut out in the wake of Franks Murder, made his shoulders loosen up just a little bit.

"Like you said, they were about to bring me in, gave me a gun, told me to wait by the phone, and then Frank went down, and so did any communication"

"So, you did get a meeting after all?" asked Bill. His breathing still slightly labored from his rant. Cigarettes and stress will do that to a person.

"I did. I sold a sob story to Gio about how I was kicked to the curb and I'm back to square one and all of this bullshit. He was hesitant at first, don't get me wrong, I thought I had failed right out of the gate. But I got the meeting, and Nicky De Luca shoved a gun in my mouth, and I had a small brush with death, and almost pissing myself." Jack was honest with his depiction, no sugar coating in these meetings, these two would rip him

Act II

apart if they felt he was hiding anything. "Yeah..." Laughed Oscar. "Nicky De Luca shoving a gun in your mouth is usually grounds for pissing your pants. But I'm glad you came out unscathed otherwise."

"It was the day Frank was murdered, so I haven't seen or heard from anyone. I'm just assuming they went into lockdown mode, not a great time to introduce a dirty cop to the mix" added Jack. He felt a shot of energy once the realization that he was still on this case became clear.

Oscar took out a folder from his desk drawer and placed it in front of Jack. It was dark green with a white label "De Luca" written in black ink.

It was also spilling with loose papers and news clippings. "Let's start this over kid. Here's all the information we have on the family. At least, all of the information that hasn't been conveniently stolen by the degenerates on his payroll. So, use it wisely, and for Christ sakes, do not let them find this."

Jack grinned at the notion that his superiors might actually care what happens to him. He knew they didn't, but it was something to keep him going.

"I won't sir. I have a good place for it."

"Now, this is the last time we will see each other for a while. I hope. The phone bank on Jefferson and 27th, you know it? Beside the deli? Yeah? Use those phones to call with updates. That's our bank, it's all tapped. If you do get in close, make sure you use those phones to make any meetings or deals with the family. We need records and locations. Now get the fuck out of here junior" Jack got to the door before Bill Taylor left him with parting words "Hey kid, don't show your face at the fucking funeral neither"

Act II

A dark day in this city's history. Declared a holiday, temporarily, for everyone to mourn their beloved mayor. Their father figure, protector of the city. The one man that everyone looked to for leadership and guidance. He had the ability to bring everyone together and spin the web of lies through the papers and evening news to keep the citizens feeling safe. The same mayor that shook hands with the devil and watched his bank account grow without lifting a finger. The political mastermind, shake hands, kiss babies, wave at the people, make backdoor deals with crime families. Typical mayor things.

The streets lined with crowds behind a barrier for miles. Everyone had shown up for the mayor, despite the cold and snow. This city was tough, cold weather didn't bother anyone. Hand warmers, gritted teeth, red cheeks, clouds of cold breath floating above the sea of people, it was quite a scene. Every department in the city was in full dress. Police, fire, military, everyone. A somber mood fell from end to end. The full police force filled in the precession, well, almost the full force. Jack heeded the warning about not showing his face. But that didn't stop him from watching from above. Whoever was behind these killings was likely in that crowd, enjoying the fruits of their labor. Enveloping themselves in the chaos they created. Lurking, waiting for the next victim.

Jack watched from an apartment building across the street. It was a vacant drop house for rats and all sorts of other business. Lucky for him, it was vacant on the day. He couldn't risk a rooftop; they were spoken for by every sniper on the force.

A long graveside service. A white backdrop and a cold wind; a chilling addition to the proceedings. A sea of black coats and suits, painted with pops of color from the flowers around the service. Black veils, tears, tissues, grief worn by

Act II

everyone in attendance. What was this city becoming? A steady diet of minor level crime and a very low murder rate gave the city a false sense of security that only one side of the bridge really felt. The industrial side, the working side, they knew the real face. It was ugly and under reported. If they included the real stats, Crimson Bay wouldn't have a tourist for the next ten years.

Three large black SUVs sat upon the hill at the back of the cemetery. The family overlooking the service, in attendance from afar. Mingling with the politicians and law enforcement didn't land on Angie's list of things to do that day. He would save that for later, out of the public eye. The puppet strings attached to Angie's ring adorned hands connected to every office in attendance. He would call his meetings at the appropriate time; it would take a minute to find the mayors replacement. Most people thought they voted someone in, someone of Angie's choosing.

"Where are we with our preparations?" asked Angie, staring through the window, cigar smoke filling the vehicle.

Martin Wolfe, without looking up "Three vans, loaded and ready. They leave at sundown"

"Perfect. Tell them to keep Konstantine alive for me, but bring him back in a bag, leave a small hole for him to breathe."

"Yes, understood, sir" Martin scribbled into his notebook. The family had concluded that the House of Wolves, Blackburg's own crime family, and long-time rival to the De Lucas, were behind these murders. Peace between the families had been arranged many years earlier, but as De Luca's wealth and power rose to prominence, Konstantine grew ever jealous. This was according to Angie, and no way fact checked by anyone in his office.

Act II

"All of our intel points to Konstantine. His jealousy has finally gotten the best of him. Victor's refusal to work with him, Frank's deal at the port always rubbed him the wrong way. He wanted that type of access of his own and could never achieve it." Angie tapped his cigar into the ashtray and turned from the funeral toward Martin. "And now he has taken the mayor from me. I had laid the groundwork for a lifelong partnership. The last piece of the puzzle, as they say"

Martin continued writing in his notebook. He didn't dare chime in with any fact that may counter Angie's stream of consciousness. Even though he knew that most of what Angie had said was woven neatly to suit is own narrative. "I've seen enough, Dominic" Angie's driver nodded, and they pulled away. The other vehicles followed; this caught the attention of the grieving crowd. One could only assume who occupied the large black SUV's. that person would be correct. The real mayor of the city, Angie De Luca.

Jack approached his front door, light snow collecting on his front stairs, he could see something jammed into his door handle, an envelope. "Finn" in black marker written on one side.

A pocketknife did the trick to open the anonymous package. Jack laid the contents out on his kitchen table. Before him in three stacks of paper held together loosely by paper clips, were the coroners reports and crime scene photos for Victor De Luca, Frank Dawson and Arthur Frost. A similar trend appearing in each report. A full face of blood, stained, from a deliberate slice at the hair line, spilling a crimson mask on the victims. In orange highlighter, below the pictures, the words "Crimson Mask Killer" spelled out. A serial killer.

Jack felt the pressure of his new role in every part of his body. The road ahead of him would either harden him into

Act II

an unrecognizable, stone cold, ruthless detective. Or kill him. He really felt those were his only options. Transform into this or screw it all up and end up in the river. It really made him spring out of bed in the morning.

With the city on high alert, the family disappeared from view in the midst of the funeral and constant news coverage for the city's newest sensation. An unknown figure, slaughtering high-profile citizens for no reason. A short trip under the cover of darkness would solve all of Angie's problems, so he thought. The conclusion that this was clearly Konstantine Borino and his so-called House of Wolves, taking the first steps into a full-blown war, were never fully proven with any real evidence. A rare misstep from the ever so meticulous Martin Wolfe and Mario Bruno. They planned the lion share of the more violent activities that the family would participate in. This time they were pushed by blind rage from their overlord. Mistakes happen when emotion overtakes the portion of the brain that logic is developed in.

This time felt different, a calculated move it was, but the calculations had been skewed by a bloodlust. Burying their own was something the family was not used to; it was one of the few things they couldn't control and that infuriated Angie. Even the public grieving process concluding with a funeral was something that Angie despised. Frank was buried on the property with the rest of the family. Victor was too. His funeral was small and very short and a very tightly sealed casket, no one needed to see that again. No public fanfare. Just a swift goodbye.

Three vans, loaded with ammunition and hatred, shot through the tightly wound forest, along the outskirts of the city, aimed directly at ending this underground war before it had the chance to even take shape. Konstantine had fired the first

Act II

shots over the bow. So his fleet of ships would suffer the inevitable fate, in the words of the king "Burn them all"

A concrete fortress sat atop a small mountain range. The winding roads, that could make anyone nauseous, finally straightened out and met the first black gate. Konstantine lived on the outskirts of Blackburg, which made him a ripe target for an attack of this nature, but with the peace of the previous decade, he had overlooked this fact in lieu of sheer oblivious bliss. A castle with massive torches along the top of the wall and what seemed to be a draw bridge, even though there was no moat. The amount of money sunk into this architectural marvel was mind numbing.

Angie's calling card was fire. Burn them alive. Bathe in the horrific screams. Small problem, concrete didn't exactly burn well but try telling that to Mario and Nicky's guys. Once a flamethrower came out, the party started.

The last van to arrive was full of barrels. Filled with gasoline. Maybe the walls wouldn't burn, but everything and everyone inside would.

"I've never met Konstantine… is he really as scary as they say?" asked Gio from the back seat. Mario turned from the driver seat (he always drove) "why don't you run inside and have a look. Maybe go knock on his door, sell him a time share, give him a little kiss" a lot of words when a simple shut up would have sufficed.

"Yeah, he's a fucking psycho. He's a Boss. What do you expect" added Mario as he lit up another cigarette. "Just figured if this guy pissed of the old man enough to send us out here, he must be something else"

Mario laughed as he hauled in his cigarette, "Oh, he's something else, fucking guy would open fire in broad daylight,

Act II

I don't know how many people he dropped on the sidewalk and the cops said nothing. Just swept up the mess behind him. Let's just say, back in the day he and Angie had it out and it got messy."

"I heard it was a bloodbath for weeks." Added Abel from the back of the van. "You guys have no idea, I've never seen anything like it. The old man is an animal. When he walked the streets, people shit themselves. They were fucking terrified of ol' Ang. And Konstantine hated that everyone feared someone else. So, Konstantine comes over the line and walks into the casino and opens fire. At that time, the family always met in the lounge of the Casino. Konstantine took out five of our guys and a handful of others. Angie went into a blind rage. He saw red, and every other color. Once he evened the score and dropped half of Blackburg, they called a sit down and Konstantine was allowed to live, for some unknown reason, and there has been ten years of peace ever since. But if you could catch Angie off guard and ask the right question, he would tell you that he always knew Konstantine would be back"

    The three vans sat on the old access road just outside the gate. A perimeter guard would typically swing by this gate around ten o'clock. Thanks to Gio for the preliminary work, the plan was to kill the guard and then come flying through the front door. A very subtle approach, with the caveat that Konstantine be brought back in one piece. "How do we know Konstantine isn't waiting for us?" asked Abel, he was pushing the limit on his conversation skills.

"We don't. This really isn't our style. But Martin and Thomas have got Angie all wound up about this"

Mario usually took Angie's side in everything out of respect for the boss, but this time, no one liked this little adventure. There

Act II

was no real proof that Konstantine was behind anything, just a knee jerk reaction to a previous vendetta from a decade ago.

"So basically, we're fucked."

"No Able, we aren't fucked. We have a van full of gas and explosives and another van with most of Frank's guns. We will be fine." Mario was done talking.

The other vans had Nicky and his guys, and the remainder of Franks crew in the third van loaded with gas. They were the lunatics who wanted to drive the ticking time bomb into a firefight.

The aforementioned security guard hit his mark flawlessly. His truck pulled up on time. He got out and walked the perimeter, checked the guard booth, made an all-clear call on his radio, and then noticed the rear tire of a van stowed away on the access road through the trees. He didn't have time to lift his radio. His head snapped back, and he crashed to the ground.

"What a shot Bugsy." Exclaimed Nicky's in house garbage man Sid Carpino. Bugsy drew his sniper rifle back into the van. "All in a day's work boys, now let's crash the gates and light this place up"

The guard's body lay just beyond the gate, an easy grab for his keys and the gate swung open slowly. Once the body was moved of course. The moon hung over Konstantine's mansion like a painting. The reflection cast shadows through the trees, an eerie breeze picked up as the vans drew closer to the house. A pit of anxiety sat in their stomachs. Their tried and tested methods of being prepared for any situation had been thrown out the window with the short timeline given to them by the boss. This job would have taken weeks of planning, this time they had days at best. A calculated approach, mixed with endless firepower made for an unstoppable monster. This

Act II

mission had the firepower, but the planning for every outcome had been overlooked. The anxiety grew.

Gio gripped his rifle. Held it close. "Konstantine knows we are coming. I can feel it"

"Get that shit out of your head, now. That's the type of shit that makes you hesitate and end up dead" apparently Mario wasn't done talking. The vans charged down the driveway and into the large parking lot. A garage to the left connected to the house by a walkway above made the perfect entry point to the courtyard. Other than the torches above, there were no lights on anywhere in the house. There wasn't much complexity to this plan… just start shooting and don't stop until Konstantine was in the van.

Glass shattering and bullets ricocheting of the concrete made for a slow-motion symphony that only the De Lucas could enjoy. After what felt like an hour of shooting and setting anything they could find ablaze, they all finally stopped. A silence encapsulated the moment, no screaming, no one running for their life. Nothing. Half of the crew had made it into the main house. No signs of life. Maybe Konstantine had been tipped off. Maybe someone was a rat. All of these thoughts and more crossed Mario's mind as he stood in a half-demolished hallway outside the kitchen. One of four kitchens in this monstrosity. A concrete, stone, steel mansion that breathed unattainable wealth. Konstantine was in a tax bracket that most only dreamt of. Those dreamers being the top end of the proverbial food chain in Blackburg. Konstantine owned them all. The kitchen led into a great room, ladened with paintings from centuries before. A stone fireplace, still lit, burned down, illuminating the wooden table surrounded by furniture that a king or queen likely sat upon. The floor,

Act II

covered in animal fur. A lion, a tiger and even a bear. "Oh my" thought Mario has he returned to the kitchen.

 A lone door stood closed to his left, he could see a stain outside the door, like water had been spilled inside. He pulled the door open with one hand, his gun loaded in the other. The other guard crumpled in a ball on the floor of the closet posed no threat, and would need new pants, and underwear.

"Where are they?"

The guard, a younger fellow, clearly new to the team, pointed down the hall. He mumbled "last room on the right, push the fireplace poker, that's the secret room"

"Thanks, young man, I really appreciate your co-op (bang, two shots in the head)-eration. Yeah, anyway"

Mario closed the door. Blood poured from underneath into the hallway. The crew gathered in the room at the end of the hall. Guns, flamethrowers, grenades, why was there a grenade? It's tight quarters, it was a terrible idea.

Mario pushed the handle, the wall gave away beside the fireplace, a stairway below.

"Oh Konstantine… come out and play!" bellowed Mario down the concrete stairwell.

The stairs wound down to another door. A large steel trap. Mario kicked the door, surprisingly it came loose. "Last chance Konstantine, come for a little drive down the road and no one else needs to die"

Act II

They had very much caught the House of Wolves napping. They expected a firefight and all they got was a free trip to the gun range. A dim hallway lit by more small torches on the wall, revealed itself. Mario, flanked by Abel, lead the crew down into the bowels of the compound.

"Don't fuck around you dumb prick! Take the easy way out. Ang just wants to chat. No one needs to get shot.. or stabbed.. or lit on fire. Look, we may have burned all of your furniture and a couple of your kitchens. Hindsight, we probably could have let up a little, but the boys get excited, that's on me. I'll try to be better next time. I'm working on myself."

Mario's guys tried to keep their faces hid to keep from laughing at their boss. Even in stressful situations, he was an asshole.

A woman's scream broke up the comedy show. "Help me! Please" she shrieked.

More muffled screaming followed.

"I'll kill her if you come any closer" came a heavy booming voice from the darkened room. Konstantine, a scary, scary looking motherfucker in all accounts, standing six foot six, heavy on the tattoos, a gold tooth, because why not. Fueled by alcohol, steroids and cocaine. He looked like a professional bodybuilder who also ran a massive, organized crime family.

    Konstantine had been enjoying a quiet night with a lady friend when the shooting had started, as depicted by his lack of shirt, wearing a robe and silk pants. And his lady friends complete lack of clothing other than her underwear.

Act II

"You really had no idea we were coming, did you?' asked Mario. Guns pointed, locked and loaded.

"What is the purpose of this bullshit, we have peace with Angelo. You have destroyed my house for what reason" asked Konstantine, his large arm wrapped around his companion's head to keep her quiet. A lot of side eyes shifted amongst the group. This was just Konstantine acting dumb to save face. "You know why we are here. Let her go and get in the van, Ang wants to talk"

"Angelo wishes to speak? He does not own a telephone? A much simpler, cost effective way to communicate?.. Fuck you! This was an ambush!"

Konstantine spat on the floor at Mario's feet, a very disrespectful move in their culture.

"I'm gonna let that slide, this one-time, big guy. This is easy, we leave, we chat, we come to a nice resolution, Abel takes your lady friend out for a nice dinner, he's a real sweetheart, very tender lover, soft hands." Mario was on a roll.

Konstantine grew more agitated, "I will fucking kill her and all of you!"

Shooting an innocent (I mean, was she really innocent?) bystander wasn't something Mario enjoyed, but this moment really called for some drastic action.

The shot clipped Konstantine's forearm as it pierced through her neck, he dropped her to the floor and fell into his chair to grab his arm.

"You motherfucking! Arggh, my fucking arm! Son of a bitch!"

Act II

A voice from down the hall rang fear into the crew, Nicky and his guys had stayed back "We've got company" yelled Nicky as he watched out the window as five trucks stormed down the driveway. Konstantine's pain turned to amusement, "you're dead now"

Mario stayed with Konstantine, while the others went back to help Nicky. The Trucks were full of Konstantine's men, all armed and ready to kill. Suddenly, a massive explosion sent the vehicles flying, flipping through the air. Broken glass, twisting metal and screams of unimaginable pain filled the air. More flames engulfed the trucks, one exploding after another.

Nicky turned to Sid. Who held an amused grin across his face.

"You threw that grenade didn't you, you crazy bastard."

Sid stood next to one of the smashed-out windows. "I was out of ammo Boss. Plus, I've never actually used one before. Got a little excited." Explained Sid. He easily could have killed them all. The fact that he got the pin out and threw it in the right direction was a miracle. Distant yelling drew everyone's attention as Mario had finally coerced Konstantine into the hallway.

Konstantine had heard the explosion but was unaware of the severity. When they made it downstairs to the main set of doors, which no longer existed, he observed his soldiers, trucks and everything he owned, either burned or still burning. A visible rage filled the already angry, very large man. He snapped, a mere second of inattention allowed Konstantine to grab the barrel of Mario's gun and shove him into the wall. Mario's gun went off into the ceiling above, gypsum clouds filling the room. Shouting and swearing through the clouds of dust as Konstantine hit anything that moved. Bodies strewn about the room as the steroid filled mad man came at them like

Act II

an injured animal that had been cornered. Screams of "Don't shoot" and "We need him alive" kept everyone from firing into the dust clouds and chaos.

The sound of a wooden baseball breaking someone's shin bone is as disgusting as anyone could think. The noise doesn't have a word associated with it. The only sound you could describe would be the contents of anyone nearby' s stomach emptying on to the floor.

Konstantine finally dropped in the doorway. In obvious pain. "You broke my leg! I'll fucking kill you and your whole fucking worthless family!"

Nicky stood over the downed giant, "I'm starting to think that's why we're hear Connie"

"You see, we've had a few close members of our family meet very tragic ends recently and all the signs point your way, Con."

"I've not crossed the border, outside of business, in ten years. I have honored the agreement with your father."

Konstantine stared into Nicky's eyes "But now, you will meet the same fate as your family"

The wooden bat found its way to Konstantine's chin, pushing his head back. A crouched Nicky had turned his opponent into a tee. "Connie, your shin bone is currently sticking out through the skin. You're in no shape to threaten anyone" Nicky stood up and kicked the wound. Konstantine howled in pain.

"Get him in the van"

Act II

Ten Years Gone

A Crimson Bay winter, arduous as they come. The deep cold to the unpredictable winds and rain. The city was a living breathing entity. It had ebbs and flows, like the tide. Some say the brighter the moon, the higher the crime rate.

The city was hurting. The energy had been sucked out. The news fed a constant loop of fear and anguish. Stay inside, only go out during the day. Don't go out alone etc… The newspapers on every street corner painted a crude and vile picture. The gruesome details of the murders had been leaked, which was to be expected. The key detail, the connecting piece of evidence, the calling card so to say, the carved line across the forehead, leaving the victim with a disturbing amount of blood pouring down their face. A subtle nod to the city name, the Crimson Mask.

A field day, to most, is a fun trip, the media was having their own version of it. Breakfast Lunch and dinner. Force feeding the fear until everyone was sick. They had started to finger point at the police for letting this go unsolved, even if it had only been a few weeks. Families were glued to the nightly news for any update, while radio stations handled an overload of calls from every corner of the city.

"Earlier today we spoke to Detective Graham Morgan of CBPD, the newly appointed lead on the now infamously dubbed Crimson Mask Killer case." Announced the generic television news anchor they referred to as Gary Dukes.

Act II

Gary: "Now, Graham, since taking over this case, can you, in your infinite wisdom and experience, please explain to the good people of Crimson Bay, why they should still feel safe on the streets."

Graham was a long tenured Detective on the force, but he was lacking one thing, a personality.

"Oh, they shouldn't feel safe. This is one of the worst cases we have ever investigated. From the gruesome murders to the lack of witnesses and the seemingly calculated targeting of high-profile individuals. It's enough to render anyone hopeless."

Gary paused, looked at his camera man, made a face mixed of concern and sheer terror. Gary was a local celebrity, sort of, at least he thought he was. He really thought everyone lived and died from his nightly newscast. His nineties slicked back mullet and moustache, mixed with his large gold rimmed glasses made him the perfect double for almost every stereotypical pornstar, or anyone with the last name Dahmer. Get the picture?

"Ummm.. That's Great Detective Morgan, really putting our viewers at ease. Now, can you shed some light on why this investigation has seemingly stalled? What happened to the original team?"

Graham took no time to jump on that loaded question, he didn't like Jack, and this was a way to bury him on television.

"I would fully place that blame on our previous lead, Detective Jack Finn, his obvious failures have put the great people of this city at risk. He was an embarrassment, hence why he was removed from the force. Moving forward, our team will stop at nothing to bring this terror to a halt, we guarantee that." Said Graham with all the vim and vigor of a greasy used car salesman, only more monotone.

Act II

The television in Oscar Freemans office clicked as it turned off. That was an embarrassing display for the force, but he was almost happy with it, it really sold that Jack was gone. They were playing the long game here, it was risky but if it worked, it would go down in history.

His door swung open, as expected, Bill Taylor came flying through, "He's a fucking idiot! We can't put him in front of a camera! Jesus, Oscar, that was ludacris." Bill stood in the middle of the office, one hand on his hip and one running through his hair in a state of disarray.

"It's Fine Bill, Grahams a good detective, he's just a little weak in the PR department. We will get Annie to work with him, or we can get someone else to do the briefings."

"Annie is great but that's asking for a miracle, The guy just threw everyone under the bus on television. What was he thinking?"

Oscar leaned back in his chair and opened his newspaper. He peaked over the top and quipped "Yeah, but he buried Jack. Which is what we needed. Silver lining, right?"

Bill Stared at his boss. That idea hadn't washed over him until now. "Holy shit, you're right. The De Luca's will eat that up. I would almost say Grahams a genius, but he's a stupid pawn at this point."

"Our Pawn, which we will maneuver as a human shield until we crumble this damn family for good." Oscar went back to his paper and grinned at himself.

"Look, I don't want to hear any of this sob story bullshit. It's a fucking suspension. It's not the end of the world. You're going to drown yourself for a couple weeks and then come back like nothing happened. Sure, Graham buried you

Act II

on television, and Freeman basically said nothing. No big deal."

Jack looked up from his coffee. Lou Macleod's face was just as smug as he pictured it as he listened to the public narrative of his life.

"You're a sweetheart Lou. You really are." Jack set his cup down and fixed his gaze out the diner window. "I don't think I'm coming back Lou, I really don't. Freeman was livid. How do I even come back from that"

Jack's acting skills were on full display. Meeting Lou for lunch was a calculated move to show a colleague that he had been thrust to the bottom rung of the ladder and it was destroying him. It also gave him a vulnerability that drew people to tell him more details than they should. This ploy would get him the inside information he needed without compromising his situation with the family. No contact of any kind, but lunch with a friend, that could be explained.

"I'm surprised you even showed up to this Jackie. You're public enemy number one, you know, besides the obvious serial killer running around the city, causing a level of panic and fear not seen in decades, but other than that, number one."

They both brought themselves to laugh at Lou's ridiculous observation. "Yeah, that's stiff competition, but I think I've got this one in the bag. Even if they catch this guy, it'll be my face responsible for the death of our beloved Mayor." Added Jack.

"What about Vic and Frank?' asked Lou.

"Oh, fuck those scumbags, no one cares about them" shot Jack. It was supposed to have a joking undertone, but it came

Act II

off heavier. There was hate in his heart. It was a new feeling for him.

"Harsh, but rumors are old Frosty was on the take as well" explained Lou. It was an obvious take that everyone in the city had.

"I don't doubt it"

"No really Jackie, he was seen leaving Angies compound the night he died."

The sound of two plates landing on the table broke the tension. "here you go boys, two clubs with fries, how's your coffee? Need more? You don't have to answer, there's more coming"

That was the perk of being a detective in this city. Endless coffee and all the servers at any diner knew who you were. At this point, jack was running on caffeine and whisky. Usually together, sometimes separate.

"Eat, you skinny fuck" mouthed Lou as he shoved fries in his face.

Jack laughed, "You're the skinniest guy I know, don't tell me to eat." They stood eye to eye but if Lou turned sideways, or a slight breeze kicked up, he was gone.

"Have you even seen the news? Outside of the weekly murders? Have you read page two of the paper. Your buddies are making quite a haul. After the bank job, they increased their numbers and started pinching everyone. Every mom and pops, the diners, the small bookies, the big bookies. Christ, we can't keep up. The files are flooding in. I can't even see your desk; we turned it into a holding ground for all these complaints and new cases."

Act II

Jack nodded in appreciation. He wouldn't have it any other way.

"And another thing. Don't think I don't know what the fuck is actually going on" added Lou.

Jack's eyebrow twitched, slightly. What did Sweet Lou know?

Jack waited for the follow up. Lou waited for a change in Jacks demeanor. A standoff.

Jack tilted his head; played with the napkin.

Lou took a drink of his coffee. Now it was a stare down.

Jack finally broke a slightly off-center grin. "What do you know, Lou. What. Do. You. Know?"

"a suspension. An Indefinite suspension (air quotes), for chasing another lead. Insubordination as they say. Smells funny to me Jackie."

"Stop spinning Lou. Say it with your chest"

"Just be careful Jack. That's all I'll say"

"Theres nothing going on. I'm just enjoying my paid vacation"

Lou's grip on his cup tightened. "Do I look stupid motherfucker? Freemans on a war path. We have planning meetings every morning. He's gearing up for the be all end all of wars against Angie. This is going to be very ugly. And I know you're the one with the direct connection. So don't sit there and tell me there's nothing going on." Lou crushed his cup with his hand. It was Styrofoam.

Jack couldn't even reply. He was sworn to say nothing. Even to Lou. He just nodded. "Ok. We can leave it at that. That's all I will say"

Act II

"….Lou, I do need a favor though." A folded piece of paper, pulled from Jacks inside pocket, slides under Lou's palm. "A few names, I don't need it right away. Just have a look. Tell me what side they land on"

"How many names are on this list Jack?"

Jack knew that asking a detective to look into one of their own was a major favor"

"Seven"

"Theres seven fucking cops… on Angie's payroll"

"I'm not saying they are. I just need a bit more information. And then I'll make my decision on what we do with them"

Lou couldn't really believe what he was hearing. The rumours of dirty cops always swirled around. The jokes were a daily thing. The papers always questioned it. Reporters as well. They might as well plaster it on the front page each morning. Freeman hated the insinuation that they were all dirty. He resented it actually. It made him furious.

"I don't know if I can Jackie. This is a lot."

"I need one more Lou." asked Jack. This one was a long shot.

"You just asked for seven…might as well thrown another one on the pile"

"King"

Lou thought about spitting out his coffee but held it in. "You want Russell King…"

Russell King. The Fixxxer. With three x's. Yes, That's what his business card said.

Act II

He was the large man in the sunglasses in the background of every picture of Angie that had been pinned to every evidence board in the CBPD. Mario was Angie's longest running soldier. Martin Wolfe, his consultant. Thomas Roth, his lawyer. And King, his fixer, driver, clean up man, all of the above. He was the one who showed up after and made everything go away. Now these past few years had been relatively quiet for Russell. With a monopoly stranglehold, the family really didn't need much for a cleanup crew or had much use to muscle someone out or cover anything up. They operated in the open and rested on the fact that no one could do anything about it.

"He's the driver. What could you want with him" asked Lou.

"He's in the car Lou. He's in the meetings. He knows everything. He's the fly on the wall."

Lou looked through Jack. "And you think you can get him to talk. About his boss? One of the most feared individuals to ever walk the streets of this city, ha! I'd say the most feared on the east coast. I'm starting to think this whole suspension thing might be for the best. Cause pal, you are fucking losing it."

Frustration was Jack's new daily driver. It was building, growing, seething to escape. The uncertainty of his job, mixed with being undercover in plain sight, not to mention that everyone had an opinion on him and loved to express it. His thick skin was holding him together, but nothing lasts forever.

"Oh, I am definitely losing it Lou," laughed Jack. "But that's just the nature of the beast. This job drives you mad. It's an obsession. A very unhealthy one at that."

Act II

Lou raised his empty cup. "I'll drink to that" They both laughed at the thought of them losing their minds and likely their lives for the job. A different breed for sure.

Mario Bruno stood front and center in Angie's office. He waited for the large leather chair to turn around to give him his orders. Cigar smoke rolled over the top of the chair. Angie's voice carried through the smoke. "Where is he now?"

"The warehouse. Locked up. He's not exactly thrilled but he's cooperating."

"Cooperating? How so?"

"Well, he may need medical attention and he's willing to talk in exchange for said medical attention."

"What is the nature of his injury" questioned Angie, his tone and delivery was slow but direct.

Mario shrugged. His blue suit wrinkling over his shoulders. "Well, you see, maybe…just maybe.. his leg bone is uh.. possibly, sticking out through the ah, skin."

"He will lose that leg." Angie tapped his cigar in the ashtray. "Do him a courtesy and make it painless"

Mario nodded. " Understood, boss. What about after?" Angie finally turned around. The smoke cleared around him. He looked at his high-powered personal lawyer, Thomas Roth. Who sat in one of the leather chairs. Angie then looked at his consultant, Martin Wolfe. Neither man made a move. Angie studied their faces, searching for their responses. "Well?" he asked. Both men choked down their opinions. This was an angry boss. Not the normal, cold, calculated Angelo. He was agitated and it was affecting his decision making. This tension had not been felt amongst the group in many years. All three

Act II

men looking at Angelo had the opposite opinion of the situation, but none had the desire to stand up to their leader.

"Well...? What. Is. It?" Angie dragged out the question. He had an agenda, and this was not on it. "Now! Goddamnit!" Angie's large fist pounded the desk, his ashtray jump, his glass of whiskey almost tilted. Roth and wolfe, the dynamic duo, looked at each other. Silently pushing one and other to step up and say what everyone wanted to hear.

"I am going to reach into this top drawer." Angie opened the drawer.

"Next, I will pick up this revolver." Angie pulled out his revolver. Loaded.

" So, you've got three seconds…"

"Fine! Fuck! For Fuck sakes Angelo! Konstantine didn't do this. We all know that. You're not thinking straight. We all understand the stress that these murders have put on you. Someone is attacking our family. We will find them. But this was not Konstantine. He had no idea why we were there. You can ask him. And we killed his men and burnt his house down."

"This is asinine. We are looking in the wrong direction." Martin Wolfe was the one to finally break the tension with his tirade, albeit needed in the moment.

The revolver turned toward Mr.Wolfe. Angelo stood up from his desk. His walk was terrifying. He looked furious and utterly menacing. The tip of the gun found itself directly under Martin's chin. His brow was beaded sweat. But he was also angry. His glare matched Angelo's. "This is wrong Angie. What would Konstantine want with Frost? It doesn't add up. The only one on the list that had any issue with him was Vic.

Act II

Hell, Frank had never really met Konstantine. You've got to understand. Just talk to Konstantine. You'll see"

"We will see, Marty, we will." Angie was close enough for Martin to smell the cigars and booze on his breath. Angelo pulled the gun away. He grabbed Martin's face with an open palm and pulled him even closer. He loudly whispered, "Don't you ever, raise your voice to me again. Understood?"

"Yes, Angie. Never again"

"Good boy. Now let's go see our old friend"

The cold floor of the warehouse had been stained with blood. Konstantine was cuffed to a chair in the middle of the room. His poorly bandaged leg was in bad shape. He would routinely pass out from blood loss and pain.

He woke to many pairs of expensive shoes surrounding him. Konstantine was face down on the concrete, but his arm was still cuffed to a chair and table. The pain seemed to subside as he came to. Out of the corner of his eye he saw a man placing what he assumed was a needle into a box. He felt great now. What had happened?

"Morphine. It's a gift from our family to yours. Or what is left of yours" The voice sounded familiar. An old friend. And foe.

"Angelo, you must explain to me what this is. You destroy my life? Over what!? It's been ten years of peace. What have I done?" Konstantine's mouth was so dry he could barely get words out. His leg had become infected, and a fever was setting in. He began to sweat, and his consciousness became fleeting.

The side eyes and looks between the group silently screamed, we told you so. Angie felt it amongst his soldiers.

Act II

His once intimidating counterpart had been reduced to a puddle of blood, sweat, piss and tears. It was a pathetic site. A mountain of a man reduced to this; it was disgusting in Angie's eyes. "You're an embarrassment to our world. We did everyone a favour. You attacked my family, and I wipe you off the map"

"Attacked! I've done nothing of the sort! Fuck you, Angelo. I will haunt you from my grave. Do your worst you scumsucking motherfucker!" Konstantine was a mess. He was experiencing a slightly stressful, aggravating day.

Angie stood over his former foe. His black dress shoes now sticky with blood. "You have two choices, friend. We can remove the leg and send you one your way. You will bleed out and die by the time you get to the door. Or you could endure the De Luca special. Where we hang you from the ceiling and burn you alive." Angie spit on the floor beside Konstantine's head. Konstantine stared at Angie but said nothing.

"I'll take that as choice number two."

They grabbed the kicking and screaming body of their foe and strung him up by a rope hung from the roof. This rope seemingly got replaced a few times per year and usually had a gasoline and burnt hair tinge to it. Among other smells. The group surrounded, like a town hall watching a public execution. This was a rite of passage for new members of the group, something Jack would likely have to witness at some point down the road.

Other than the cries for mercy mixed with benevolent death threats from an immobilized Mob boss, the only sound in the warehouse was an industrial drum being pushed toward center stage. The smell of gasoline intensified. A pump handle had been creatively manufactured to allow someone to spray

Act II

gasoline from the drum, limiting the chance of someone igniting the entire group.

"One last chance my friend. Did you or did you not….. murder members of my family. And our dear beloved child brained Mayor?"

"I will take great pleasure in haunting you from my grave you spineless, (Konstantine broke into a coughing fit, he was in very bad shape), Fuck. I hate you Angelo, but I did nothing of the sort. I honored our agreement. You have not. You will pay for these sins Angelo. Pay dearly."

Angie nodded to the man wielding the gas pump. "You may" was all he spoke and Konstantine's injured leg was soaked in gasoline.

Angie turned and walked toward the door; he waved off his team. They would have to stay and witness this. Punishment for raising their voices at him. Angie unfolded his coat and placed it over his shoulders. He then exited through the side door. The room filled with the final screams of another human's last seconds of life. Disturbing is a word that comes to mind. But it's really the smell that sticks with you.

They say that when you cut a chicken's head off, it can still live for a short period of time after as the nerves are still firing through the body. This is not the case for burning an enemy alive. They pass out quite quickly from the shock and pain. Konstantine was dead before Angie could open the car door.

Act II

The Gallows Pole

Rain beat down on the windshield of Jack's Buick Grand National. It was clear when he left his house. It was clear when he left the payphone. The clouds rolled in, the skies seemed to darken, and the rain began. An omen, some would say. A precursor of things to come.

    The car sat running on the blacktop of the driveway. The towering mansion, seemly pulled from a fantasy novel, captivated his gaze through the rain drops. A slight movement from a second-floor curtain caught his attention. They were waiting for him. He had answered the call days earlier. The meeting was set for Thursday morning at seven am. Bright and early.

    The vehicles in the driveway told him that this meeting would not be one on one. Trucks, Vans, Fancy cars. All of them. A mix of fear and frustration built inside his chest. If this meeting went well, he would be on the inside for real. No turning back now. The crosshairs firmly planted on his back. Or he wasn't walking out of this meeting at all. The pitch black of a body bag would be the best he could hope for if this went south.

    He finally pushed open his door and thunder crashed in the distance. Was he controlling the weather? Jack quickly shut his door. He sat back in his seat, hand still on the handle.

Act II

He opened the door again, no thunder this time. It's all in his head.

The rain began to soak through his overcoat, the downpour was heavy. He made it to the overhang by a side door, a large man in a suit greeted him. King nodded, "Jack, Welcome" Russell King pushed open the door for Jack and showed him inside. The entrance was more of a mudroom than anything, definitely not the main entrance of the house. This felt like a side entrance that only certain people used. Jack was one hundred percent correct. It was the Entrance to Angie's office wing of the house. The mudroom led to a darkened hallway with a door at the end. Jacks coat suddenly flipped up and large hands were patting him down. Typical... he expected that. "Down there, they're waiting" King motioned to the door.

The noise grew as Jack got closer. With the number of vehicles outside, was this a party? Or was there a party and it's still on going? Jack put his hand around the doorknob and took a deep breath. His heart raced as he took steps into the great unknown. The door opened into what seemed like a banquet hall. He scanned the room, and then he heard a pin drop. The silence he felt in his chest. The whole family…eating breakfast together.

"Jackie boy! There he is. I figured you got spooked and threw yourself off the bridge" came the voice of Gio. The room cracked up with laughter. The tension broke and everyone went back to their conversations and coffee. A sigh of relief snuck its way out of Jacks mouth. Jack smiled at the joke and happily nodded to the group "gentleman" was all he could muster. "Oh shut the fuck up and get some food, You piggies love this shit" Nicky had chimed in on the fun.

Act II

Jack scanned the room, a large table with at least fifteen people sitting and eating. Paintings of every kind on the walls. Tall stained-glass windows around the room. Exposed beams in the ceiling with very old looking chandelier light fixtures hanging down. A room fit for a med-evil banquet. And sat at the head of the table. The King himself. Angelo De Luca.

Angie pounded the table. Everyone went still. He motioned toward Jack with an open hand. Everyone immediately rose to their feet and formed a line of sorts, a welcome line. They all shook Jacks' hand, begrudgingly. Not everyone was a huge fan of letting a detective into their ranks. A lot of very stiff handshakes and death stares. An internal competition to show who was the wolf and who was the sheep. Unbeknownst to the group and slightly to himself, Jack was no sheep. Jack was a motherfucking wolf. A crazy one. It just hadn't come to the surface just yet.

Jack sat down at the table. Gio kindly brought him another chair. He placed it between himself and Abel. Jack's new best friend. "If you look at me the wrong way, I'll cut your balls off" was Abels version of welcome to the family. Everyone finished their food, with one eye on their plate and one eye on the newest member in the room. The original tension had dissipated but there was still an uneasy undertone to the room.

Mario finally broke the mold "So, Jackie boy blue, what's say you come with us this afternoon for some on the job training. We've got a few errands to run over."

Jack lifted an eyebrow slightly, and ever so gently responded " to run..over?"

Act II

"Yeah, shithead, them detective ears still working? I've got errands to run over. They owe me money and if they don't pay up this afternoon, I'm hitting the gas and the only thing stopping me is the speed bump I make with their corpses. And I think you should tag along"

"Well, Mario, I'm here for the full experience. I'm no part-timer. Whatever you guys need, I'm there" Mario nodded in approval, it was the right answer.

The voice to Jack's left immediately overruled. " No, Jack will stay here. We have things to discuss"

Angie spoke. Mario obliged.

The rest of the breakfast was much easier. Once they finished, the conversations started to locate only between each crew. Jack felt a hand on his shoulder, it was Nicholas, he subtly nodded toward another door. Angie stood up as well. A lot could be said with body language, an old trade secret for the underworld. The less said in the open the better.

   Jack's nerves had resurfaced. He had met with Nicky. That went… well he didn't die. So all in all, it went well. A meeting with Angelo, that was new, and terrifying. The door clicked behind him. He hoped it was just the latch and not a deadbolt. The room was clearly Angie's office. The desk with the carved lion. The large leather sofas. The liquor bottles. Business was done here. It was more of a parlor than an office. And sat behind the large desk, the scariest human Jack had ever met

"Have a seat, Jack." Suggested Angie.

Nicky poured three glasses of whisky. One for each of them.

Act II

"My son has put his reputation on the line with this stunt, you know that Jack, don't you?"

How does a person even begin to answer to a mob boss with a loaded question like that.

"With all due respect Mr. De Luca." Jack started.

"Angie, please" the slight interruption showed a personal side.

"Angie, of course, I don't see this as a stunt. I am finished with the CBPD. I gave them everything and they walked me out the door over nothing. No loyalty. No respect."

Angie lit his morning cigar. He laughed to himself as he leaned back in his chair.

"The way I see it Kid, is… you're not done. You're still a detective. And you're the only detective to ever sit in this room and possibly live to tell the tale. Possibly."

Jack's insides almost became his outsides. How did Angie know?

"I say possibly because I have a proposition for you. And…really.. there's only one answer, if you catch my drift."

Jack nodded in understanding.

"You see, you're going to march back into that office and beg for that job back. Start at the bottom, be the coffee boy, shoe cleaner, dishwasher, valet, whatever the fuck you must do to get back in there. And then report back to me."

Angie pushed the newspaper to the middle of his desk and dropped his pointer finger into the front headline. It read: "Police Chief Declares war on organized crime"

Angie looked up at Jack and Nicky. The fallout from the Konstantine murder, the streets being ransacked by the De

Act II

Luca Crews, even more than usual. It was open season, and the police couldn't catch up.

"This asshole, with a serial killer on the loose, targeting my family, decides that this is the right time to go to war, with us. Fuck him." Angie's face told the whole story, more so than the words. "Jack, what do they have for leads on that case?"

The fear that had frozen Jack to the seat had let up just enough to allow him to speak again "I was the lead, Sir, and honestly. We had nothing. It's like this person is a ghost. No evidence, no clues, no trail. It's unbelievable."

"Well, you will assume your position as lead. And with your new families' help, we will find this person and justice will be served. In the meantime, you will also update us on the tactics that freeman is planning for this "war" as he calls it"

Jack didn't know how to tell Angie that the lead detective position had already been filled and that taking over the case would prove quite difficult.

Luckily Nicky came to the rescue, "He can't just assume that role. They gave it to tweedle fucking dee on the news. Real sweetheart he was."

Angie coldly ordered "We'll kill him then, simple as that"

Nicky nodded in agreement.

Jack also nodded. That was easy.

Angie fixed his eyes directly into Jack's soul. "Do not mess this up my dear boy. Your father would be disappointed to know that you'd come to the darkside. Make him proud, bring down this serial killer."

Act II

Jack stumbled "I, um.. I won't let anyone down. That's a promise"

"Good. Nicky will show you out, he has other details for you as well."

A scared little boy stood up from the sofa, he walked over to the desk and shook the devil's hand. It didn't burn, it felt good. A strong handshake. But the eyes that looked back at him. Those had seen death. They had caused death. The bringer of fear. A true psychopath in a very expensive suit.

"Thank you, Sir" Mumbled Jack. Off he went.

Jack's head was spinning. What just happened. What was the yes sir, I won't let anyone down, boy scout bullshit? Who was that? Nicky placed his hand on Jacks shoulder as the entered the dark hallway leading to the mud room. "Look, this job is easy. Just don't think about it. You'll be fine Jackie."

Jack turned and looked at his old friend. They both smiled. "You think?" asked Jack.

"Oh, fuck no Jackie, you gon die. Either we kill you or you'll get caught up in a firefight with the cops" Nicky's grip tightened on the back of Jack's neck. "So, before you cry in your car. Maybe give this whole arrangement some thought. Because if you can't get back in with the cops, Abel is going to wear your skin…now run along Jackie boy"

The drive home was a blur. The nerves had taken over. Jack could barely hold the wheel, let alone keep it between the ditches. This was going to be much more difficult than he imagined.

Most people would have went right back to the precinct, but most people aren't undercover in plain sight in a vicious power

Act II

struggle between the mob and police, while a murderous serial killer picks off the elite of the city. Just great!

"Good evening, everyone, I'm Joan Carroway for Nightwatch. In the next hour we will bring you stories of political corruption, organized Crime, unsolved Murders, and police brutality. Normally these would be multiple segments, but this time, it's just one."

We must warn you; the following hour may be disturbing to some viewers. And viewer discretion is advised. Tonight, we put the spotlight on the newly titled "Crimson Mask Killer". A name brought upon by the gruesome calling card of a knife wound across the hairline, causing blood to pour down the face of the victim. The crimson Mask. Our sources are tying this story to the De Luca family, the police, the mayor, and now a few rumors of involvement from Chief Justice Alan Daniels.

Corruption runs deep into the veins of our city, and now we have insider information stating that possible tampering, bribery, and a long list of other accusations are falling on the courts. How did the De Luca family stay out of jail for this long? We can't keep lying to ourselves, the city is falling apart, there is now a manhunt for someone who is picking off members of our society and crime rates have tripled since that news broke. Chaos can only be what follows if our police department does not step up and end this manhunt with someone in custody.

As many of us tune in every day for updates on the safety of our city, we bask in the distraction it provides. This distraction has now led to a striking uptick of crime. This journalist can see what is happening? Can you? A crime family paying off city officials. An inept police investigation that can't get out of its own way. This all screams cover up to me, but

Act II

after some deeper digging, Nightwatch has come to an early conclusion that this is a vigilante, not a serial Killer. This person is a hero. They are cleaning up our city.

"This is bullshit" echoed through the living room of Jack Finn's mostly empty house.

"What a joke. Turn this shit off" came the voice of Chief Oscar Freeman from behind the crowd in the bullpen. The officers clamored to be the ones who turned the television black. Freeman made his way down the hall to the main offices. He found Bill Taylor and another man standing over the newspaper. "Did you watch that?" asked Freeman, both men turned around, Bill pointed at the broken television in the corner. A signed baseball planted in the screen; shards of the screen scattered on the floor.

Bill realized he hadn't introduced his guest. "Oscar, this is District Attorney Vincent Carvallo, we went to school together growing up."

"I've heard the name, what happened to ah…" he snapped his fingers to try and remember the missing name in his head.

"Hall. Anthony Hall" answered Carvallo.

"Yes, Tony. I just saw him a few weeks ago?"

"Early retirement I was told" responded Carvallo. The two men briefly shook hands. "Well, welcome abord, I'm sure with all this nonsense going on, that our paths will cross many times."

"That's why he's here, Chief. I think it's time we pull everyone together and end this. Finn and Morgan obviously couldn't handle it. So we are going to have to step in. One more murder and this city is going to burn down. They are protesting outside

Act II

city hall, they are protesting outside, right now! Don't tell me you don't see that."

"Calm Down, Bill"

"Don't fucking tell me to calm down. I'm sick of this shit. I've got a family to think about. What if this creep starts targeting us and our families. I can't stand by and just let those idiots fumble fuck around while the good people of this city die in the streets."

Bill Taylor was a little hot under the collar as they say. It was all a show though, for the new DA. Only three men knew the real plan (maybe 4) and it had to be kept tight lipped, but the public perception was going in the toilet and fast. So, this new team had to assemble quickly and make an immediate impact.

"I mean...good people? That's a bit of stretch" Joked Carvallo. "Maybe the Mayor, But De Luca and Frank Dawson, they were scum"

"You're not wrong. Arthur was a good man.'

A distant sound of a phone ringing interrupted the men, Oscar leaned into the hall, "Oh that's me" he stepped out and disappeared into his office. Carvallo and Bill just continued mocking the whole system and the weak attempt for law enforcement to bring down this serial killer. Throwing everyone under the bus in the process.

Oscar took one step into Bills office and said "Sorry fellas, this one's important. I'll take it myself" and he took off down the hall towards the back stairwell.

Act II

The two men didn't even seem to care. Which worked out well. The less eyes on Freeman the better. The voice on the other end of that phone call held the key to solving this case.

Oscars classic Crown Victoria slowed to a stop just beyond the service entry to the park. It was dark and still cold out. He could barely see the car he was supposed to see. He squinted through the windshield; he crawled forward a few more feet and lined up his window opposite his friend. Oscar rolled down his window, he still couldn't see that well. His police issued revolver sitting on his thigh, ready to go if anything went sideways.

The sound of trees rustling is all he could hear. The other car slowly dropped its driver side window. A matchbox strike broke the tension, the flame lit up the informant's face as he hauled on his cigarette. "I'm back" grinned Jack Finn.

"You really think we are pulling you back into this?" asked Oscar.

"According to my new boss, Angelo De Luca. You've got no choice."

Freeman paused for a moment and let everything sink in. "Say again?"

"I'm in Chief. I sat down with Angie. He wants me to go undercover; can you believe that? I'm a double agent now." Laughed Jack. His meeting with Angie had really shaken him up. The confidence he once had about this job had been replaced with new attitude of "I'm dead either way, so I really don't care anymore, so don't fuck with me"

Act II

It was that new attitude he needed to bring down a serial killer or die trying. Most likely die trying.

Freeman shook his head. He knew that laugh. It wasn't coming from a good place.

"So, he's taken the bait…how do we know he's not going to stab you in the back as soon as he get's the information he wants. You're a sacrificial lamb Jack. You know that."

"Everyone knew the risks. You laid it out for me quite clearly." Jack adjusted his side mirror. He was fidgeting with anything in his reach.

Freeman noticed all the nuances about his detective. "You don't look great Jack. Don't take this the wrong way, or do, I don't care, but if Angie has you working us, and I find out. I will personally throw the dirt on your coffin."

Jack figured this might happen. Who can trust who? He finished his cigarette, flicked it into the night. "Do you really think I'm going to feed real information back to them? We've got to come up with an airtight bullshit plan."

Freeman had already started thinking about the next part of the plan, feed Angie false information, but they hadn't discussed how they would execute it.

Jack added "I'm going to need the names Chief. And you're going to have to pull the strings"

This was the part they left Bill Taylor in the dark on. They were going to feed false information

Down the pipe and use the officers that Freeman believed to be on the take as bait. He would set up fake stings and leave them to take the wrath of Angie. It was genius.

Act II

"You'll have them in the morning. Oh, and try not to get yourself killed. Tell them you're back in. I'll arrange it. Be back in Monday morning, there's more to catch you up on." Freeman rolled up his window and backed away into the darkness. Jack lit up another smoke. The match poured light on to his coffee cup, with not an ounce of coffee in it. A much stronger coffee had taken its place; a type of coffee aged in barrels for years and served on ice.

That meeting took place on a Thursday night. Jack now had three days to get everything lined up for his return. He needed to square up his duties with the family and let them know he talked his way back into the job. This double life was going to be complicated.

The nightlife in Crimson Bay had taken a slight hit during the coverage of the serial killer and the explosive relationship between the police and the underworld, but alcohol has a magical way of convincing people to do things they normally wouldn't. Exhibit A: The news says there's a serial killer slicing people open in the street, please be advised and stay in your homes. This lasts for maybe a few weeks, until it feels like everyone is comfortable with the new way of life and then they resume their old habits. This was the new way to consume the news updates. Each pub had a television behind the bar and the crowds would pile in, get drunk and wait to see who else got killed from the world of the rich and famous.

Some patrons would even place bets on who it would be next. The Mayor was the biggest payout and had the biggest shock value. The crowd was the usual fare. The pub "Donnellys" was on the industry side of the bridge, so people felt a little safer. All of the murders had taken place in the white-collar neighborhoods. The feeling of two cities had never been

Act II

greater, the gritty, factory-ladened side of the bridge had taken to peacocking when the scenario presented itself. No Serial Killers over here, just regular criminals and the odd murder, maybe even a double homicide. But definitely no Serial Killers.

The eleven-o'clock news brought a collective groan with its lack of murder. Just another cry from politicians and the city officials for information and a plea for safety amongst the people. Everyone look out for each other, report what you see, any tip can help. All that nonsense. This was a blue-collar neighborhood, it was going to take more than some fear mongering from the television to keep everyone from drinking in a pub.

A busy Thursday night finished with a crowd spilling into the street. Attempts at an afterparty always swirled through different groups. Eventually everyone stumbles down the sidewalk under the streetlamps. The early morning fog was floating through the streets, illuminated only by the overhead lights. The still of the night set in as the voices faded. The silence was beautiful, accompanied by a slight breeze off the water. An oddly warm March was welcomed by everyone in Crimson Bay, normally the cold and wet lasted until June.

The museum of Industry was a main attraction on this side of the bridge. It was illuminated by spotlights and carried many flags out front. An early-century vehicle and cannon sat on the concrete pier in front of the building. Two local pipefitters, still in their best work attire, turned the corner and headed toward the museum, they had apartments on the street in behind. It was only a few short steps before the men stopped in their tracks. Boots, untied, dangling a few feet above the sidewalk. They followed the obvious sight line to the cannon set on the pier above. A rope tied around the barrel hung into the darkness below, the pier created a shadow that

Act II

covered the sidewalk. The rope appeared to drop into darkness, but the outline was something hanging. The two men slowly moved toward the cannon, neither could make a sound. Was this… a person? They moved closer. The figure started to take a human shape, the boots were visible, they had legs attached. There was a pool of blood on the concrete below, it ran down the legs and into the boots. The two men, let's call them Bob and Doug, started to shake. Bob finally spoke "That's a guy, man"

"No shit, bud" replied Doug. Dougie to his friends.

"Dougie, look at his face, holy fuck" both men were now close enough to see the body of Abel Mazzoni, Mario Brunos muscle, hung from the cannon barrel with his forehead slashed into the Crimson Mask. The calling card. This was the first public display. A public execution.

Act II

The Pain of War, Cannot Exceed, the Woe of Aftermath

"I thought you said Monday, Chief?" came a moderately hungover gravel tone of the newly reinstated Detective Jack Finn. Oscar Freeman, standing in a group with his right-hand Bill Taylor, The new DA Vincent Carvallo and the case lead, Graham Morgan. The look of shock on his face gave Jack the warm and fuzzies. All four men turned to see who had the gall to interrupt the bosses, especially at a murder scene. "Fashionably late, Finn. I guess the more things change, the more they stay the same?" Freeman sarcastically floated to the group.

Jack took a sip of his coffee, it was too hot, he made a face, squinted his eyes and said "The boss man is getting philosophical in his old age" Freeman was the ripe old age of forty-one at the time.

DA Carvallo spoke up "And you are?"

Jack stepped forward and extended his hand "Oh, sorry, I'm Detective Jack Finn, it's my first day, very excited to be a part of the team"

Carvallo shook hands with a confused look on his face, he wasn't in on the joke yet.

Act II

Jack nodded at the other two, "Bill, Grant, how are you?" he started to walk passed them.

"It's Graham, Jack, you know that." Stated Det. Morgan. "Actually, it's lead Detective Morgan, asshole."

"My apologies, I'm new, like I said, first day, just learning everyone's names. So! What do we have guys? I get drug out of bed at five am to come down to the museum, I don't think it even opens until nine."

Bill Taylor finally chimed in "Are you still drunk Finn? Christ shut up."

Jack stood up straight, took another sip of lava water and pulled out his cigarettes. "Sorry, just excited to be back"

Jack's new outlook on life was bleeding into his work. His normally calm, stoic, intimidating persona had been replaced with a slightly unhinged, almost too loose demeanor. This made the overlords a little nervous. Maybe this was all part of his plan?

Jack made his way closer to the crime scene. The body had been removed, the crime scene techs had the sidewalk blocked off and all their gear spread out. The rope remained, same as the blood-stained sidewalk. Jack glanced at Freeman; the chief motioned up the stairs. Jack followed the lead. This was going to be a dance, they had to pretend not to get along, no one could know they were in on everything. They crossed paths, Jack leaned in, "It's Abel" whispered Freeman. The men both turned away from each other. Jack tried to keep his face from giving him away. They circled back around, "I should go then" mouthed Jack. "Yes, do what you have to"

Act II

Said Freeman, into his hand. Both men gave a nod and went their separate ways. The dance had begun. "Well, this looks pretty cut and dry gents, I'm off for now, lots of people to get re-acquainted with." Jack patted Bill on the shoulder as he landed on the sidewalk, two quick steps later and he was in the wind.

All three men turned to the Chief as he stood above the crime scene. "Is this a joke Oscar? He's blacklisted; everyone knows that. He's a fuck up." Blasted Bill Taylor, playing is part to perfection. "He's not fucking blacklisted Bill, Jesus, He was suspended for due cause. Everyone gets a second chance. If we cut people loose for every indiscretion, we wouldn't have a police force. Of all people, you should know that best" laughed Oscar as he planted his finger into Lieutenant Taylors chest. Bill's eyes glared at his boss, same team or not, that was a shot.

The early morning sun flooded the city. The city started to wake. The early morning traffic began to flow. The hustle and bustle of a Friday in the city took over. Along the busy streets, lined with shops, televisions hung in windows, the morning news ticker flashed across the bottom. Another murder. This time, it was in public. The news stretched through the city. The diners were all a buzz with the news. This wasn't one of the city elites. What is the link? Many assumed this one had ties to the underworld, and they would be correct.

The payphone was still cold and damp from the early morning. "Yeah, it's me. Have you seen? Yeah, I was there. I'm back on the team. Ok, when and where? Got it." Click. Quick and easy. No real information exchanged, but everyone got what they needed.

Act II

Jack pulled into his old parking lot, across the street from the precinct. A small rundown lot that had half a fence and looked more like a small forest than a parking lot. There was always a spot in there, no one wanted to park in the jungle. Coffee, check, smokes, check, whiskey, check, banana for added potassium, check. No time to hit the diner for breakfast, the big three would do the trick today, caffeine, nicotine, and fresh fruit.

  The suspension lasted over a month, which was a lifetime in cop years. He was returning as a different person on the inside, still a surly bastard on the outside. A lot changed in a month, the bullpen had been rearranged, Jack's desk was no longer a pile of papers and whatever else they could stack on it. It no longer existed.

Jack pulled open the front doors, he braced himself for a barrage of insults and comments that would get someone cancelled in thirty years.

Crickets.

Front desk. Nothing. No one even looked up. He walked by.

The offices before the back stair, everyone glued to the television, no looks.

Up the stairs, it was oddly quiet.

The bullpen doors, just as heavy as he remembered. They swung open, the anticipation for the wave of sound he was used to. Nothing.

No one even turned when the door opened. Jack walked in slowly, two televisions held everyone's attention. The old wooden floors echoed Jacks footsteps in the silence. Jack had already seen this episode, up close and personal. A new face, at least to Jack, entered his view to the right. They made eye

Act II

contact. Younger guy, dark hair, police moustache, big glasses, deer in the headlights in human form. "This is wild" is all Jack could make out from Bambi.

"Yeah" mouthed Jack. "I knew that one"

"Which one?" asked Rudolph.

Jack looked confused; he pointed to the Television "That… one?"

Bambi's mom raised his hand from the desk and held up four fingers. "There was four this morning"

"Four? How? What did you say?"

"Yeah, one by the museum and three in the parking lot at the dockyard. It looks like the three were all stuffed into the trunk of a car and then the car was set on fire."

"That doesn't line up with the others?" asked Jack.

"No, it does, they all had the marking on their face. The fire department managed to drag them out before they were burned up. Still dead though."

"Thanks for clarifying," said Jack. Deer boy smiled, obviously not well versed in sarcasm.

"What's your name hop along?" asked Jack

"Cole, detective, Um.. Cole., Andy Cole." Fumbled Andy. He had transferred two weeks earlier.

"I was on the street for four years up in Brighton. Not enough going on up there, I asked for somewhere with an open spot"

Jack grinned slightly "And one just magically opened up a few weeks ago"

"Yeah!?, how did you know?"

Act II

"You're looking at the open spot" Jack was transfixed on the news now too. He knew he had to get out of there but needed to show face to the team and see what intel he could drag back to Angie. Even though Angie was probably switching into full war mode now with the news update. Jack was trying to see if they had released names of the other three. Nothing yet.

"Any ID's?" came a voice from behind Lou McLeod. He turned with an intrigued expression. That voice sounded familiar, but it couldn't be. "Wait, am I dead? Did I die again? Cause you're a ghost. Dead and gone"

The two men locked in a stare down as the rest of the group started to take notice.

"Boo" said Jack, followed with a grin.

Both men started laughing and threw a quick hug in just because. "Welcome back you ugly fucking waste of time"

"Thanks Lou. I will always hate you and wish nothing but despair to you and yours"

"Get a room, lovebirds" Bill Taylor had returned. Everyone scrambled back to their desks and pretended to work. Even back then, Bill was feared by everyone.

"McLeod, Finn, Malone, Raines, War Room. Now" bellowed Taylor. His tone was loving and warm (it wasn't).

Jack turned to his Lieutenant " I want him too" he pointed to Andy Cole. Andy turned white.

Bill was halfway into the hall "Fuck no Finn" came his response. Sheer terror crossed Andy's face "Me?"

"Get up, you're with me, kid," said Jack. He motioned toward the door.

Detective Lou McLeod

Act II

Detective Ellis Raines

Detective Calvin Malone

The A team.

Down the hall, which was now filled with officers and the usual chaos, the team made their way to the War Room at the end of the hall. Inside they would be greeted by Bill Taylor, Chief Oscar Freeman, lead detective Graham Morgan, Captain Len Basso and the DA Carvallo. Not a female in sight.

A room that was not big enough for this crowd, or the egos. Blackboards, with names and descriptions of potential suspects, tackboards with pictures and a family tree of the De Luca Crime Family. A Red pen scratched out the deceased. Len Basso grabbed it and scratched out all of Frank's crew. Sonny Boy, Cesar, and Pinky. "Three more, plus Abel. That's four in one shot. Who the hell is this?" Len tossed the pen on the table. Newspaper clippings, charts, files and coffee cups filled the room. These walls had stories, years of them.

  Chief Freeman stepped out into the middle of the room, everyone waited for his address. "It's obvious why everyone's here. We have just added four names to the ever-growing list of victims. Six weeks, Seven murders, all with a calling card. Now, this is really a first for us, we have yet to deal with an active serial killer. As you can see, over the last month we have compiled all the evidence available to us. Thus far, we have hit every dead end. This stops, today." Freeman was fired up, as usual, but this time he had a desperation in his tone. This group of decorated law enforcement officers didn't take the sting of losing well.

"What are our leads, Chief?" asked Lou. He was new to the team, same as Jack (sort of). "You see Lou, there lies a great question, and my response to that is one that has been

Act II

reoccurring now for weeks and reiterated by the papers and nightly news, We got fucking nothing! No fingerprints, no murder weapons, nothing left at the scenes, no witnesses. The only thing that ties any of this together is they are all members of the De Luca Crime family, except the Mayor, which begs the question. Anyway, it's all here in these files. Now, I have

brought you all here to join this taskforce. This will be your only job. We have to find this guy, and we must find him now. The fucking city is about to enter into a political campaign for the new Mayor and guess who is going to be used as bait for every candidate, you guessed it, us." Chief Freeman grabbed his coffee and headed to the door "I'll be in my office"

 Graham Morgan was almost dancing in one spot; he was so agitated that a taskforce had been brought in to undermine his investigation. He didn't know whether to start screaming and just leave. Jack looked at this team, his gut immediately started churning. He trusted Lou, but Raines and Malone were grade A assholes and Bill Taylor loved them.

 Taylor, Basso and the new DA followed Freeman. The door swung shut behind them, Graham Morgan turned to the group and expressed himself "This is my investigation! Everyone here answers to me. If I say jump, you say how high? If I call you at three in the morning, you better fucking answer. I'm the lead here, not you (points at Lou), not you (points at Jack) and definitely not you two (points at Raines and Malone) Now, Ellis Raines, a fifteen-year vet on the force, had a long pedigree, he was just mean for the sake of mean, and he took shit from no one. Graham's index finger did not make it back to his balled-up fist. Ellis caught it in his hand and pulled Graham toward him. If you asked someone to describe "Badass looking detective or cop" the description would be Ellis. Tall, muscles, bald, basically an enforcer with a police

Act II

issued firearm. The three other men immediately jumped in to break up any attempt of a fight, or a murder.

The scuffle could be heard from outside, but no one made a move towards the door. They all knew to leave anything they heard in the war room, alone. "You fucking sonofa…" followed by more shouting. The noise finally settled down as they got the two combatants separated. Lou had Graham wrapped up and everyone else had Ellis. "Ok! Ok! Calm the fuck down" yelled lou, "Jesus, we're professionals" They all started to settle and pull themselves together. Jack really didn't try to restrain Ellis, he was just waiting for a left hook and a chance to pop someone himself, if it got out of hand.

Jack noticed a blur in the corner. Andy Cole had been left alone; they had forgotten about him. Taylor hadn't even noticed that they had brought him in. "C'mon guys, you're scaring the wee child," said Jack in his finest Irish accent.

The room all turned to see Andy Cole standing in the corner. His eyes couldn't hide the fear.

His expression screamed "What the fuck is this".

"And this is?" shouted Graham, still wound up with adrenaline.

Andy collected himself enough to try and answer, " I just transferred, I'm…."

"I don't care! Get the fuck out of my room!" yelled Graham

"Jesus, Morton, shut the fuck up."

"It's Morgan!, you damn well know…

"Oh, just fuck right off, Graham, we all hate your guts. You threw me under the bus on national fucking television! You can walk down those steps, out the front door, go find your

Act II

shitbox of a car, start the engine, walk around back and shove that tail pipe in your fat mouth you low life cocksucker."

The group readjusted who they were holding back. It was now everyone in the middle of Graham and Jack.

"Shit, I wouldn't be surprised if you were dirty. On the take, looking sideways for Angelo. You greasy, ass kissing, whiny bitch!" Jack was in full force now.

In that office, calling someone dirty, or even alluding to the fact that they were working both sides, was grounds for firing or a fist fight, depending on who heard it. The next few minutes could be heard all through the office. Eventually Freeman had to come back down the hall and kick the door in. All six men looked up; it was a parent walking in on siblings fighting. A couple bloody noses, lips, knuckles and a pair of broken glasses. Freeman broke the tension "did you get it out of your system?" no one answered. "Good, now find me this psycho."

The rest of the day was a montage of files being strewn about, coffee, cigarettes, the odd argument or two, and a group of detectives getting absolutely nowhere. Finally, Jack left, he told them he was grabbing food and running an errand, no one batted an eye, not even Lou. He had to get to Angie, they were likely planning something big.

The back room in the De Luca's storage warehouse was dimly lit, smoke filled but much quieter than usual. Four dead family members did not sit well with the family. This was the start of an all-out war, but there was one problem. Who are they fighting?

The side door creaked open, Nicky's ears perked up, he walked out on to the warehouse floor, the door was held by a chain across it. Nicky unhooked the lock and let it drop to

Act II

the ground. The door swung loose. Detective Jack Finn, darkening the doorway.

They both nodded, there wasn't much to say. "They're in there" mumbled Nicky, he was more rattled than ever, not a side Jack had really seen. The remaining members of the family sat around a long table, minus Angie and his associates (Roth and Wolfe). The room looked bigger, less people this time. Mario Bruno handed Jack a beer, motioned for him to sit.

"Well, what's the word in there? Let's cut the bullshit, just tell it straight," said Mario, he had chosen a sharp black suit for the occasion. Jack looked around the table, everyone had been through a lot in the last twenty-four hours. Gio sat across from him, he couldn't bring his eyes up from the floor. Abel was his best friend, this one hurt.

"We have a taskforce on the case now. I'm on it. It's the best ones we have. The fucking DA lives in our office, even Captain Basso came out of hiding. This is Freemans best shot at it, and they have nothing, it's pathetic."

Nicky chimed in from the doorway "Yeah well we've got all we need on them."

Jack looked sideways at his old friend "Say again?"

"You heard me. Those assholes in blue are behind this. Your little team…. Is all for show."

"You think Freeman… killed Victor..and..and.. Frank? The mayor? You think Freeman is behind this?"

"………did I fucking stutter, Jackie?"

The temperature in the room started to rise.

Nicky added "If you think we have been tough on them these last few months, they've got another thing coming."

Act II

"It's time they drew a chalk line around some of their own." Mario said, through his cigar smoke. Jack sat in the middle of a scorned crime family, hellbent on evening the score with an unknown enemy. The pressure and fear of the situation was finally cracking the armor. The ludicrous notion that the police are behind the most brutal serial killings this city has ever seen.

    Jack tried to speak but broke out into a coughing fit. "You wanna walk me through that? Just so I know what to look for when I go back?" asked Jack, cautiously. Nicky pulled out a chair, sat down and put his feet up on the table. "Well, it's pretty obvious, yeah, it's really obvious actually. Freeman hates us. We know that. You even said it yourself, he was out to get us."

Jack tried to interject " Yeah, but.."

Nicky put his finger in the air. Signaling Jack to wait until he was done. "Now, we have Victor, who on the surface was a decent businessman (not true). Hard working family man, sure, he bent a few rules when it came to his developments. A couple city officials go missing a few years back, Freeman can't figure it out, blames Victor but can't prove it. That's the first domino."

Mario chimed in "He always hated Frank too, he knew what went on, he probably wanted in, who knows, a lot of shit moved through that port. Freeman was likely jealous of the whole thing." Mario was slightly delusional, he drank his own Kool-Aid, as they say.

Jack played his part "Yeah, I can see that, but what about, Abel?...or, the mayor? They were friends.?"

"They were not friends" the matter-of-fact voice of reason, Martin Edgar Wolfe. No one had even noticed he entered the room. Followed by Thomas Jonathan Roth and the overlord

Act II

himself, bringing up the end of the line, Angelo Salvatore De Luca. The mood altered slightly, the temperature was still high.

Everyone sat and stared at their boss. He took his seat at the head of the table. He undid the button on his coat as he sat down. Pulled in his chair slightly. A glass of whiskey seemingly appeared from nowhere. The room waited with baited breath… this was the first address of the group after the murders.

"This time tomorrow… I want the person responsible, brought to me. If it's Oscar Freeman, then so be it. We will kill them all. One….by….fucking…one until they confess to being this crimson mask killer." Angie pulled out his knife and started to carve pieces of apple. (where did he get an apple?) Jacks mind did a full lap through everyone on the taskforce and all of his superiors. Could they be behind this? Was he a decoy? Holy fuck I'm a decoy. This rang in Jacks head.

Was he just naive? Did they pull the strings, and he just played his part? He could have been killed the first day and they wouldn't have cared. Welcome to the Mindfuck.

"Twenty-four hours. Flush them out, and if there's no bites, then you make an example of one. A big example. Understood?"

The room knew their assignment. This was going to get ugly. Everyone finished their drinks and headed for the door.

"Jackie. You stay," Angie said.

"Great" thought Jack. Just fucking great.

Act II

An Outlaw Torn

A full moon sat above the city skyline. Casting eerie shadows down to the streets below. Shadows for some, darkness for the rest. Corridors, alleyways, all cloaked in the night. Lou sat and waited in his old caprice. Parked in the pocket between two streetlights. He sat in the entertainment district, bars and clubs lined the streets. Hiding in plain sight, he had his orders to keep eyes on the remaining members of the family. Similar to the night Abel was found, it was unseasonably warm, Lou had his window cracked slightly. The music and chaos laid the soundtrack for his night.

The De Luca's had become more tactical with their operations, but they did not cease to exist. Business still had to be handled. Money wasn't going to launder itself. Bookies and shop keeps weren't going to be berated into handing over their savings all on their own. And of course, the weapons and drugs weren't going to sell themselves either. Lou was staked out with his eyes on Nicky's crew. Two black vans parked outside a local establishment known for it's cheap booze and allowing their serving staff to get on stage and dance in exchange for compensation in the form of dollar bills. Classic Crime organization hang out. The strip club.

Lou got his intel from a crew of informants he had been working with for years. They were his eyes and ears on the street. It was off the book, but Freeman knew about it.

Act II

They got paid off in cash that was pulled from the evidence room. Also Freemans idea.

He was to follow Nicky's crew, who were supposed to meet a buyer for a slew of items. Drugs, guns and stolen goods. Freeman wanted to follow each crew as much as possible. When the next murder happened, they needed to be there to catch this guy. It was clear to everyone that civilians were not the target. The news reporters had made that very clear, but it didn't ease any of the tension in the streets.

Lou flicked his cigarette out the cracked window. A steady diet of smokes and coffee were on deck for the evening. It was eleven and this establishment closed at four, but he didn't expect them to do any business here. Two birds one stone, maybe even three. The buyers, a serial killer and the De Lucas. That's a retirement lineup. All three groups locked up sounded like a raise and promotion to Lou. Instead of Lead Detective he could be super lead detective. Or Senior Lead Detective, overlord of the detectives. He wasn't picky.

Movement. Another van pulled in behind the first two.

Three men. Two taller ones and a small one. Leather coats and briefcases. Likely full of money.

Standing by.

More Movement. It's the full group now. Nicky, Sid, Tommy and Bugsy. The three amigos with briefcases and following behind them was Russell King. He took the first van, Nicky the second and the unknowns in their van. Now Lou got to have some fun.

Act II

He fired up the caprice as the three vans pulled away. He hung back in the traffic just enough to not be suspicious. These guys would have their heads on a swivel now.

They all turn at the next light. Out of the entertainment district. Straight for the bridges.

They skipped the bridges.

Now they entered the warehouse section of the city, more of a business park along the water.

Large industrial warehouses with high fences topped with barbwire. A very nice place indeed.

This wasn't their typical spot, this was a legitimate section of the city that housed a lot of important businesses. Lou clued into what was happening, they were getting away from traffic to see if they were being tailed. Shit he thought, they've made me. He pulled down a side road quickly. He parked, keeping his line of vision on their taillights. As the Vans made it to the end of the drive, they turned right. Just as Lou went to start up his Caprice, a black muscle car flew by him. This was perfect, he could use them as cover.

The three vans sped up.

The muscle car made up ground quickly. Staying with them every turn. Lou kept his distance and enjoyed the show.

"Is this the buyers? Or… holy shit is this the killer? This could be huge." Thought Lou.

Act II

    The highway was there only option at this point. It hugged the coastline with a lot of little stopping areas. Lou figured this was the meet up spot out here, but who was in this muscle car?

Lou followed the parade for a few miles. Finally, the three vans turned off down a side road, it wasn't even a marked highway exit. The muscle car didn't signal, so maybe this was all a big coincidence?

Nope, the black muscle car waited until the last possible second and cut across the lane and took the makeshift exit at an alarming speed. Dust kicked up in Lou's headlights. Rocks and debris flew. The road led through a heavily forested area on the opposite side of the highway. The road was likely a side entrance or a trucking lane for someone's business. Likely something Angie was running.

    The vans finally pulled into a small gravel parking lot beside an old tin can of a warehouse with one light pole outside. Not one of the usual drop points for these guys. Tall trees heavily covered the building, you wouldn't know there was ever a building back here. Lou killed his lights and slowed to a crawl. He could see the building through the trees, hopefully they couldn't see him. The road was twisting enough to give him some cover, he doubted they noticed him behind the speeding muscle car. Time would tell.

    Lou had called in backup when he left the highway. They were at least twenty minutes behind. He lay low in his seat with his gun on his lap. The hanging light swung in the wind; it picked up the shape of another car parked around the back of the building. Someone was already inside.

Act II

    The three vans all emptied: guns drawn. They made their way towards the building. Bugsy kicked on the door and it swung open. There was a light on inside, but that was all Lou could see.

The speeding black muscle car made the last turn and slid in behind the vans. No one even acknowledged the car. So, it was either one of the crew or a buyer. The three-briefcase gentleman followed the group into the building, it all seemed rather casual, minus the guns out. The trailer in the car jumped out, Lou couldn't see a face, he had his hood pulled up.

    Lou scanned the building, how could he get closer to see. It was a major risk but if he could see or even hear something that could blow this wide open, it was worth it.

    Inside the warehouse, Nicky and his guys started unloading lockers full of guns and ammo. They had dropped it off days earlier, they had to be more careful with the transactions these days. More lights turned on inside the building, Lou noticed the trees light up on the right side. There must be a window or a louvre, maybe a door over there. Time to find out.

The thick forest made a great cover. It was pitch black there. Easy for Lou to sneak around. The side of the building seemed to be miles away, it wasn't, but it felt that way. Critters, spiders, bugs, maybe a snake, all in the path of Lou. He hated every second of it. Not a woodsy type of guy.

    "Alright, Alright, get everything lined up. Our guests are patiently waiting. The long coats of their three guests near dragging on the floor. The Moretti's placed their briefcases on the table with the guns. Sal, Vince and Dante. Sal was the shorter of the three. He was also the grandfather of Dante, and father of Vince. They ran most of Ashford, a smaller city, an

Act II

hour west of Crimson Bay. They were about to enter a war with the Bellantti's a brutal crime syndicate that rans mostly drugs. The Moretti's were small time in the drug business but big in the weapons and extortion, this was a buy to push their move into drugs. The De Luca's were happy to oblige.

Pleasantries exchanged, merchandise reviewed, briefcases full of cash, transferred to the De Luca's. Easy business. Sal motioned to Nicky that he wanted a word in private, so Nicky showed him to the back. Russel King tagged along, as well as Vince Moretti. Dante stayed behind, he had an automatic hanging on his hip, covered by his coat, so no need to be worried.

An exhaust vent louvre made for a good place to observe the meeting from the outside. Lou peered through the holes and tried to take a mental note of who was involved in this meeting. Nicky's crew was intact, Russell was there, the three Moretti's, rounding up their weapons. And a side profile of the muscle car guy. Although he didn't have his hoodie on, maybe this was the guy from the car parked out back.

Lou was careful with every move, he couldn't make any noise, no trees snapping, not anything.

So when he saw the face of the new guy, he held his mouth shut so that he didn't scream.

Jack Finn.

With the De Lucas?

Shaking hands? Loading product with the Moretti's?

What is happening? He wasn't on undercover detail; they would have been told at the meeting.

Lou's heart was racing, what the fuck was happening. He took deep breaths to calm himself; it didn't do much.

Act II

How much time had passed? Backup must be coming soon.

Jack didn't have a muscle car though. Unless he had a double life, which at this point seemed very plausible. He also didn't have a black hoodie, and there didn't seem to be any other clothing laying around on the benches.

Click

A cold chill shot down Lou's left side. He kept one hand on the wall, bracing himself, and his other on his gun. The cold steel pressed into the back of his head.

"Get up Lou" came the voice. "Get up slowly, take you hand of the piece, and do not turn around"

Lou followed the orders. He kept his eyes ahead. He wasn't someone who would be able to wrestle someone to the ground. His captor kicked open the door to the room, it startled everyone inside and all they heard was yelling and guns be armed.

"The fuck is this!" yelled one of them

In walked Lou MacLeod, with his hands up and a gun buried in the back of his head. Another man pushing him into the room.

Everyone emerged from the private talk in the back to assess the noise. "I wondered when the boys in blue would make an appearance. Hiding in the woods and watching us seems to be your guy's M.O lately."

Even in this stressful situation, Lou couldn't help himself "I mean, that's kinda all we do anyway, I wouldn't flatter yourself"

Lou dropped to the ground as the back of Nicky's right hand connected with his jaw. Lou laid on the ground, his vision

Act II

blurry, once he came back around, he turned his head to the left, he locked eyes with a man standing a few feet away. His friend, Jack Finn.

Jack had a mixed reaction painted on his face. He was made. He couldn't explain to Lou what was actually happening, they would both be killed immediately. Jack kept moving his eyes upward, above Lou, Lou finally caught what he was doing and turned back to the man standing over him, fucking Calvin Malone. Nothing made sense now.

"Calvin?.... Jack?... What the fuck is.." Nicky kicked Lou in the chest, the air gone from his lungs, he crashed into the legs of a bench. He was in bad shape.

Jack didn't know about Calvin. He had got here first; Calvin was in the muscle car. He was the dirty one, they had turned him.

Calvin sneered at Jack; he could tell he hated him being there. "Oh no Jack, looks like your boy is gonna need a doctor." Calvin walked closer to Jack. "It looks like his nose is broken, and from that wheezing, I would say a rib or two, maybe a collapsed lung."

Calvin moved closer. "What is Freeman going to say about this? Is his little buddy dirty? He's actually in with the family. His heart will be broken." Calvin stopped about ten feet from Jack.

He pointed his gun at Lou.

Jack didn't flinch.

"How's the next meeting gonna go Jackie? Oh, big bad Calvin killed Lou, Oscar. How do you know that, Jack? Where you there? Hmmm? Yeah, I guess you could say, you're fucked.

Two shots rang out from Jacks gun. Everyone jumped.

183

Act II

Lou rolled over into the puddle of his own blood. It poured from the exit wound in his neck. He was dead.

Calvin turned back to face Jack, he couldn't believe what just took place.

The next thing that went through Calvin's mind was two shots of hot lead. He collapsed on the warehouse floor. The blood poured from his skull, half of it was missing.

The appropriate amount of yelling came from the bystanders. It was a small warehouse made of metal, so gun shots really hurt the ears.

"Fuck sakes Jackie! What was that for?" asked Bugsy, wiping the blood splatter from his coat. "I just got this coat, dammit."

"I'll buy you a new one, Jesus" replied Jack as he tucked his gun away. "They are both on the taskforce with me. Lou wasn't on this detail, Calvin was. They wanted to flush out Calvin, neither my bosses nor Angie trusted him. "

"This guy wasn't assigned to us?" asked Nicky. "He's the fucking killer!" the whole room erupted.

"He's the killer!" repeatedly. From everyone. It was almost a mix of panic and relief. No one knew how to feel.

Jack stepped back, the pit of his stomach was about to meet the warehouse floor.

Nicky's hand landed on Jacks shoulder. "You're about to be a hero my friend. Put your detective face on."

"Everyone else, move this shit out the back." The Moretti's, who enjoyed the show, needed to get out of there before the blue and red lights came down the driveway. Nicky grabbed

Act II

Sal, "Theres a back road behind the building, it's a little rough but it'll get you back to the highway"

Sal nodded, grabbed Nickys arm, "Be well my friend, until the next time" and the three men disappeared outside into the darkness.

Minutes felt like seconds as they cleaned up the warehouse. This place would be crawling with cops. Normally they would just bury the body, but Angie needed to see this and they knew that either Calvin would have had back up on standby, or someone would have heard the shots.

"Shit, hold on" said Jack, he went over to Lou's body and searched for his gun. "Oh, right," he moved over the Calvins body, Lou's gun lay beside him. Jack looked around for a glove, nothing there, he ripped Calvin's shirt and used it to pick up the gun.

"What is it Jackie?" asked Nicky.

"Everyone move away" Jack fired two rounds into Calvin's head. The mess grew. Blood was now everywhere.

"Ok, Lou broke in, killed Calvin, I killed Lou, he's the Crimson mask killer. We can all go back to our normal lives, what the fuck." He exhaled.

Everyone looked at each other, yeah that makes sense. "You heard him" said Nicky, addressing the team. Not that any of them would talk to the police anyway.

"I'll talk to the cops. You guys can get out of here. The less heat on the family for this the better."

"Well, maybe jack, we should stay, it proves this Lou guy was trying to kill us"

Act II

Jack stirred Nicky's idea. "as long as there's nothing else in here"

"There isn't, it's just a drop point for meetings. Guns are gone; money will be gone too."

"Then what do we tell the cops? Why the fuck are we out here?" asked Jack

"We figured if the killer was picking us off, then we would bait him out here. So, we told Calvin, and he told Lou at your meeting? It all lines up. He followed Calvin. We waited for him. It was all your idea, right, Jack?"

Nicky's plan made too much sense. Nothing that came together this easily usually worked. But It was all they had. The alternative was jail time.

Blue lights cut through the trees. Jack stood over the bodies of his only friend and Calvin Malone, the piece of shit. This was his fucking fault.

The Crimson Bay Chronicle finally got to print something positive: "IT'S OVER! IT'S OVER! CRIMSON MASK KILLER CAUGHT"

The article got right to the point. Detective Jack Finn painted as the hero, Lou Macleod, troubled ex-detective, working alone, targeting the underworld and the elite. Not a word of it was true. But it made everyone happy.

Jack sat at his kitchen table reading the headline. He was disgusted with the whole thing. Not an ounce of truth. They jumped on this idea that Lou was the killer with no evidence at all. How was this justice?

Act II

Suddenly Lou is this maniacal vigilante that is nearly untraceable in his work as a serial killer? The newspaper headline was haunting in its ability to ruin someone's life who has no chance of defending themselves. The man Jack knew, was not a serial killer. Which is likely a sentence heard at every trial for every serial killer, ever. But nonetheless, Lou wasn't the killer. He was the scapegoat for a city that needed a win. A city that needed a sense of normalcy again.

The fear had produced large cracks in every facet of Crimson Bay. The economy suffered, the overall wellbeing of the people that shouldered the burden and was about to break. That newspaper headline popped the proverbial anxiety balloon that the city was floating in, and now they had come crashing down to reality. Even though the reality they were being shown was false in nature. None of this added up.

10:00am. City Hall.

Jack stood against the back wall of a jam-packed room, full of city officials, officers, detectives, Journalist, anyone who had an opinion, and a few waiters. He wanted none of this. He had skipped the morning meeting at the precinct. He walked into city hall in his best suit, a flask in his inner pocket and a sick feeling in his stomach. Not alcohol related.

A half hour in the meet and greet. Handshakes, pats on the back, just a room full of elation and relief. Chief Freeman finally made his way over to Jack. They were only a few hours from their first meeting early that morning in the woods.

"You smell terrible."

"Thanks Boss."

Act II

"How drunk are you?"

"Eleven"

"Christ Jack, you fucking drove here." Freeman kept his voice low on purpose, no one needed to listen in.

"I'm experienced in such matters."

"Just stop talking. Thank fuck you don't have to speak at this thing."

Jack raised his eyebrows "wouldn't want too anyway. It's a farce. For all we know, Calvin is the real killer."

Freeman eyed up Jack. "What do you mean? That's not what everyone said this morning."

"It just can't be Lou, it makes no fucking sense Chief." Jack was starting to lose it. No sleep, the stress, booze. His eyes were getting heavy. "Boss, I gotta go. I need to lay down, or throw up"

"Just keep it together Jack. After this go sleep it off and then come see me. We need to chat"

   The interim Mayor, Riley Cortez took the stage in front of a mass of media. Flashbulbs, microphones, the whole works. He stood with such power. A real leader. The man Crimson Bay needed to lead them into the next chapter. He was the favorite to win the election as well, and now he got to deliver the news that everyone was begging to hear. Check and Mate.

   Cortez had wavy dark hair, pushed back, stylish. The strong jaw, broad shoulders and stood an astonishingly normal six foot one. A clean slate for this Mayor. But for how long.

The crowd fell hushed as Riley Cortez approached the microphone. The room was hot, poorly ventilated, even for ten

Act II

in the morning. It was the big room at city hall. The one everyone saw on the six o'clock news. The one everyone was hoping for.

"Ladies and Gentlemen, as many of you have already read, our beloved city can breathe a much-needed sigh of relief, this morning, as our diligent, determined and bravely distinguished CBPD taskforce has caught and terminated the now infamous "Crimson Mask" killer."

Mayor Cortez held for applause; he was hit with a wall of sound. It was unprofessionally loud in that room. Jack's hatred grew. Just as the crowd calmed itself, Mayor Cortez's assistant Julia Garcia, approached the platform and caught Riley off guard, she seemed upset, and cupped her hand over Riley's ear to whisper something to him. The mayor had a good poker face. He nodded along until she left. He composed himself, took a sip of his water and continued to deliver his victory address. The crowd ate it up. Until a noticeable surge of side conversations broke out. Journalist running to the phone banks, people running into the room to grab a colleague, tell them something, and run out. A simmering chaos engulphed the formerly happy press conference.

"What is going on out there?" said Bill Taylor from the side of the stage. There was a room just behind the curtain where everyone waited. It had a television mounted in the upper corner, someone ran in and turned it on. Breaking news : Two new victims found. Both Hanging from the bridge, both faces covered in blood. Both men, in suits, each with a large sign attached to their lifeless bodies.

One read: **Greed**

The other read: **Corruption.**

Act II

Crudely spray painted in red on what looked to be plywood. More televisions in the building depicting the event on the bridge turned on. The previous half hour of cheering and excitement had been replaced by a wave of horror. He was still out there. They had it wrong.

Jack saw the breaking news, the same as everyone else. The rage inside him boiled. They used his friend, to keep the economy going, to keep profits up, to make their lives easier because they couldn't figure out this riddle. Fuck them.

Chief Freeman found Jacks eyes, they locked in.

Jack walked slowly passed his boss, "Fuck you, I quit" he said in his ear.

"Jack we need to talk about this in private, lets just calm down, we are going to figure this out"

Jack looked at the horrifying images on the screen. Two men in their business suits hanging from a bridge. Why are they showing this.

Something caught Jack's eye. He knew these men.

It was Thomas Roth, and Martin Wolfe.

Jack turned back to Oscar, he had also realized who was hanging from that bridge." Oh, I am fucking done. And from the looks of it," Jack stood as close as he could to Oscar. Stared him right in the eyes, the smell of alcohol seeping out of Jack. He took a deep breath. "Angie is gonna fucking kill you."

Jack pushed his way through the crowd and the sideways glances. The doors seemed heavier this time, reaffirmation of his weakened state. The crisp air brought him back around. He fought another flow of reporters and onlookers, finally freeing himself as the bottom of the City Hall Steps. Jack undid the buttons on his shirt and pulled his

Act II

tie loose. He threw the tie into the bushes; he peeled off his police issued shirt (fancy dress for being on television). He just let it fall to the concrete. His white undershirt was good enough for now. The fog had lifted off the city, but it was still cloudy as Jack made his way around the building. A crowd had formed halfway down the block. He could hear yelling and screaming and see smoke rising above the crowd. He picked up his stride, the crowd broke slightly, just enough for him to see fire and smoke. A car was on fire with, with its wheels slashed. It sat on the rims, roasting like a marshmallow. Jack's Buick was melted.

  The crowd pulled back as the firetrucks showed up. The chatter amongst the people was pedestrian. "Who would do this?" "Whose car is that?". Jack stood off to the side and just watched, maybe he would catch a glimpse of something that would tip him off. Nothing.

  Jack just walked away from the crowd; it wasn't worth hanging around. The papers in the car were melted, no way to identify the car now. Half a block away there just happened to be a parking lot, he wasn't a cop anymore, time to steal a car. A man in his mid-forties was about to get into a jet black '88 Monte Carlo SS. "Hey! Stop! Police, I need your vehicle!" called Jack as he pulled his badge from under his shirt. He wasn't throwing that away. Fear and confusion read on the mans face. He didn't put up a fight, he just backed away and tossed the keys "Thanks, I'll get it back to you as soon as possible" lied Jack. The 454 fired up and may as well shot flames from the tailpipe. Jack threw it in reverse, peeled a strip off the tires and fishtailed it out on to the road. "Hey, wait! Don't you need my information!" yelled the nice man. He realized then that he should probably look for a new car.

Act II

Shouting Gun, On They Run…..
Through The Endless Grey

The thick fog had kept the bodies under a blanket for some time, only the coroner would be able to give a time of death. The security cameras on the bridge may give some insight, but they aren't the best at night. Everyone had been focused on the call to the warehouse, the excitement of possibly catching the serial killer. The ending of weeks and weeks of stress and fear. Everyone had let their guard down, which is what he wanted.

Jack was officially gone from the force. He was removed from records. His files were packed up and lost somewhere deep in the bowels of the precincts archive. That moment of celebrating a victory too early and letting the other team come back to win was humbling. No one could wrap their minds around the lack of evidence, all they had was motive to kill the elite and now motive to take out the family. The spray-painted plywood signs, it was clear someone was sick of corruption, and this was their only way to get back at the ones who caused it. All the remaining detectives set forth to investigate who had suffered the most from these practices, who had suffered to the point of breaking.

Housing demolished for new developments, signed off on without merit, breaking city laws in broad daylight. Officials pocketing the bribes and smiling. The proverbial foot placed on the throat of the lower class, and they were meant to suffer and say nothing. This could be anyone. Just those actions alone

Act II

affected thousands. When they add in the extortion from small businesses, the breaking of procurement law with bid rigging for projects paid for with public money. The concrete tipping fees going straight to the De Luca's. The Dockyard, The Unions, everything fed back. And every one of these took food off the table of many, many people. The pool of suspects just got deeper, and full of sharks.

The black Monte Carlo tore through the streets, running every red light, zero concern for public safety. "So now I'm a target" Jack thought. Which was bound to happen. He was on both sides of this mess. The city faded in his rearview, he finally let his foot off the gas, just a little. Jack searched for a radio station that wasn't broadcasting pure panic riddled rhetoric about how he screwed up. Even if that's not the case, it was how everyone would paint it. One more turn of the dial, "..And in other news, three bodies of the notorious Moretti family were found in a black van early this morning. The van appeared to be riddled with bullet holes. The Moretti's hail from Ashford, their business in Crimson Bay is still unknown" Jack turned off the radio. The thousand-yard stare took over. He just sat there, silent. That was who he was aligned with. Shake your hand and then stab you in the back. When was it his turn? Once the killer was found, would they just make him disappear too?

A gas station up ahead came along at the perfect time. Jack was low on gas, smokes, alcohol, coffee and firearms. A woman pumping her gas. A full-service attendant washing the window of another car.

Jack looked through the window at the cashier, just a teenager. He threw the door open, took two steps and jumped over the cash. The poor kid screamed. Jack grabbed him by the shirt "Where's the gun?"

Act II

The trembling voice came "I..I..I..dont know, I don't have one"

"Where is it? The safe?"

The poor kid was almost in tears "I really don't know"

The cashier's eyes drifted behind Jack. He turned to see the nice lady who had been pumping her gas, had ventured inside and was now pointing her handgun at his face. "Let him go, asshole" Jack obliged. "Sorry, Ma'am. I'm...I'm a detective and I'm chasing a suspect. They stole my gun." He pulled out his badge for proof. The television above the cash was plastered with the morning newscast of the shitstorm from last night. "Is that you?" she nodded toward the television.

"Unfortunately, yes" sighed Jack.

The nice lady calmly lowered her gun; Jack's bladder held its ground. "You see that car out there?" she asked.

"Yeah" said Jack.

"Glock 9mm in the glove box. Sig 9 in the trunk. Take your pick. You can't have this one, this was my mommas, it's my handbag gun." She spoke with a full deadpan delivery that was chilling and moderately adorable.

Jack gave a half smile. He reached over and grabbed a carton of cigarettes, looked at the cashier and nodded. "Coffee?" he asked. The cashier pointed behind Jack. "Ok, good. Whiskey?" The cashier pointed to the shelf beside the coffee. "Convenient" Jack pulled out some cash, hit the button on the coffee machine and grabbed a bottle of brown liquor. The coffee machine sputtered a bit before starting to slowly pour. The three of them stood and waited. The main entrance door opened, and another man walked in, an older gentleman. He surveyed the situation. He saw the teary-eyed teenager with a

Act II

ruffled shirt; he saw a late twenties detective (the badge around the neck gave it away) and the gun-wielding lady patiently waiting in line. Everyone stood still as the man shuffled in behind the nice lady and took his place in line. He calmly nodded to Jack and fixed his gaze into the ceiling. The outskirts of the city seemed to be a bit different than downtown. The coffee machine finished, and Jack loaded up and headed to the door, he turned and thanked everyone for their cooperation in this on-going investigation.

    Miles down the road there would be an old dirt path that was starting to grow over, just past a large horse ranch. It followed a tree line back to a bunch of lakes. Several fishing cabins were slowly deteriorating back there. One was Jacks. Somehow the Monte Carlo made it back unharmed, not exactly an offroad vehicle, but the trail was flat. A small cabin overlooking the lake with a small porch and a green door waited for Jack to turn off his engine. It had a bed, a kitchen, and a bathroom technically, if you could call it that. There was electricity strung down from a row of old power poles, a deal that someone made with the farm. It also contained a coffee table in the "living Room" that doubled as a trunk that doubled as an ammo case. And it was full.

Jack had picked the Glock, because he knew he had the same gun at his camp. Now he had two guns and a lot of ammunition.

    The De Luca's, as far as Jack knew, still held him in high regard. He was still their man on the inside. But once they found out that he actually quit and would no longer have inside access, then they would get rid of him in a heartbeat. He needed a good reason for quitting, maybe they would spare him (nope, they wouldn't, they're the mob). Telling a mob boss that you quit because you're secretly feeding information back

Act II

to the police, the one thing you said you wouldn't do, right to Angie's face, wouldn't go well. Maybe he would understand that you didn't want to play both sides and also keep secrets for both sides and try to keep everything straight until your best friend gets killed and everything is a total shit show. Yeah, he would understand.

Both guns sat on the passenger seat, fully loaded. The Monte Carlo burned down the road back toward the city. He turned the radio back on to tune in to the shitshow updates. "Mass chaos has erupted downtown outside city hall, where Mayor Cortez was giving his victory speech in the wake of last nights capture and killing of a major suspect in the Crimson mask killings.

As the Mayor gave his speech, he was informed, along with the rest of the city that two more bodies had been found and that they may have apprehended and killed the wrong person. This led to a car being burned and flash grenades being thrown into crowds outside of City Hall. A riot has broken out between the police and protesters who seem to be sick of the police and their lack of evidence in the case. Ambulances and first responders are on scene as many people have fallen victim to various injuries in the rioting. Please avoid the scene and surrounding areas as it seems to be spilling into neighboring streets"

Jack turned off the radio.

Lit up a cigarette.

He dropped the glove box and a tape fell out. It was black with red lettering. "Thunder Jeep" the 80's metal band. He popped it in the tape deck and turned up the volume just as the skyscrapers came into view. The screaming guitars and thunderous drums, this would be his soundtrack.

Act II

The sirens filled the air as the buildings grew larger, and the haze of smokestacks clouded the sky. Distant flares caught Jack's eye. He turned away from the mess and headed toward the De Luca's main warehouse, maybe a chat with Gio and Nicky could buy him some time. The gate was open, nothing out of the ordinary there. No vehicles other than Gio's truck. Jack pushed the side door open, both guns in his waist band, hidden under his old jacket he found at the fishing camp. "Hey, Gio it's me" Jack called out. No response. He walked down the hall and turned into the main warehouse; he stopped dead in his tracks.

The room was silent. So quiet you could hear a pin drop, except there were no pins, just blood periodically splashing on to the cold concrete. A gruesome visual hung above the puddle. Gio's lifeless body hung from the beams above. His clothes were torn; his arms and legs were bloodied. It almost looked like he had been drug behind a vehicle. He was alive at that point. The rope around his neck finished him off, or maybe the lack of blood in his body was the final nail. Jack pulled out both guns. Maybe he was still there. Who was this psycho?

He walked closer.

He paused. The blood on the concrete seemed to spell something.

ANGIE spelled out crudely.

Jack's stomach jumped into his throat. He looked up at his other friend. He did consider Gio a friend, and now he had two dead ones. He stared up at someone who really didn't deserve this end. The rage that hides deep down in your soul, the kind that pushes you over the edge, the blackout, seeing

Act II

red, wake up after and have no recollection of anything, type of rage.

The thoughts raced through Jack's mind.

If I can save Angie, I'm immortal.

If they kill Angie, then I stay on the list to be hunted.

"Fuck sakes" Jack heel turned and headed back to his car.

The city seemed like a blur. Get back to the house, call Nicky.

The Monte Carlo came to a stop outside Jack's house. On the step sat a man he did not want to see. Chief Oscar Freeman.

The car door slammed; Oscar stood up. "Look jack, we need to talk"

Jack didn't break stride. Oscar's face turned uneasy. "Jack wait!" he yelled.

No waiting, no stopping. Jack put his shoulder into Oscar's chest, wrapped his arms around him and speared him through his front door. Wood splintered all around them. A broken door slammed into the floor; the small viewing window shattered everywhere. Jack landed on top of his old boss. Adrenaline had taken over.

"Fuck you!" Jack pushed himself up, grabbed Oscar by the shirt and started to rain down punches until his knuckles were battered and bloodied. He finally stopped when he realized Oscar was unconscious.

He stood over Oscars body. "You asked me to put it all on the line. And I did. And you cowardly pieces of shit jumped on the first scapegoat that came along. You fucking lied about the assignments. You changed them. You got Lou killed. I would have been next." Jack started screaming. "And that cocksucker

Act II

Bill Taylor just sat back and watched. You both fucking knew that changing the details was dangerous! You fucking idiots!"

Jack was seething. He had just screamed at someone who heard none of it. He walked into his kitchen, poured a glass of water and walked back to Oscar. He splashed it on Oscar's face. Nothing happened.

Jack checked for a pulse.

His heart was beating. Not dead, yet.

"Get up"

Nothing.

Jack pulled the deadweight up on to his couch. He picked up the broken door and leaned it back into place.

The phone started ringing in the kitchen.

"Hello?"

"It's Nicky. They got Gio. I'm at the warehouse now. Meet me at the house. We are loading up"

Jack only got one word in before he hung up. He turned to leave in haste, but his visitor was starting to stir. Jack set a cold beer on the coffee table and observed the damage he had inflicted. His hand was swollen and bumpy. Likely a broken bone in there somewhere. Oscar's nose had clearly been broken, it was now sideways, and he had cuts and bruising on his cheeks. Freeman leaned forward and spit blood and a tooth onto the floor.

    Jack stood staring. Boiling. He couldn't keep still, shifting his weight from one foot to the other. He needed to leave, but this needed to be dealt with.

Act II

"You've got one minute," said Jack, without moving a muscle in his face.

Freeman leaned forward again and grabbed the beer, opened it and had a drink.

"I think you broke my nose, kid"

"I definitely broke your nose"

"Thirty seconds." Jack wasn't sticking around.

"Alright, Jesus. I'm sorry for Lou. We were trying to flush out the rats. We gave everyone details that night and then pulled them all aside later to give them their real ones. Lou was supposed to be on Mario, but we switched him. We figured it was Calvin who was dirty, and we needed Lou to take him down. We didn't factor in that you might be there and how that would all pan out"

"All pan out! They're both fucking dead! Lou was about to make me, and so was Calvin. I had to kill them both." Jack was at the tipping point, and he was now fully toppling over. "That's right asshole! I fucking killed them. And then I had to stand there and watch everyone drag Lou through the mud and make him the scapegoat because we couldn't do our jobs!"

Jack pulled out his gun and fixed it on Freeman's forehead. "Maybe it should have been this way. Maybe I put two in your skull, carve a line across your face and disappear. Killer got us both....huh?... How does that fucking sound Oscar!" If the neighbors were awake (they weren't) then they likely heard all of this. Jack was screaming now.

Jack turned the gun and put it under his chin. Freemans eyes lit up. "Jack, no, this is ridiculous"

Act II

"Oh, it's ridiculous!? Oscar? Maybe I just blow your head off and then I do the same. See you on the other side. End this whole fucking mess."

"Christ Jack. I'm Sorry! I fucked up. Lou shouldn't have been there. I will right that wrong. Restore his name. I'll tell everyone our plan, pull back the curtain on everything."

"Shut the fuck up Oscar. You don't get it. You can't. The damage is already done" Jack crouched down beside Oscar. Staring into his eyes. "Oscar, I'm walking out that door. I would say lock up but clearly my door is fucked. Maybe the racoons will make a home here. If you call me, come near me, contact me in anyway. I'll kill you." Jack tapped his gun on Oscar's forehead, turned and walked toward the door. "What are you gonna do, Jack? Go this alone? Vigilante justice? A renegade?" asked Oscar through his broken nose and missing teeth.

Jack stopped. Turned around. "Tell me, Oscar. Have you ever seen a wolf in the wild?"

"No, I haven't" replied Oscar.

"But you know they exist, even without seeing them?"

"I mean, Yeah, I've seen them on television, in books"

"So, you believe there is something out there, watching. Think about that long and hard, chief"

Oscar put his empty beer bottle down "You've lost your fucking mind Finn"

Jack's face almost broke into a smile. Finally, someone saw what was happening with him. There was no turning back now. Jack mumbled "Yeah" and stepped over the broken door. He disappeared around the corner. The monte Carlo fired up in the distance.

Act II

Oscar tried to collect himself when a coffee cup appeared beside him. It was connected to a hand, which was then connected to a blonde-haired woman in a robe.

Oscar did a full jump scare. "Who the f-"

"I'm Kelly, I stay here sometimes. I am Jacks... friend? Who is a girl? But not his girlfriend. Does that make sense?" she asked.

Oscar tried to stand up, he stumbled but caught himself. He steadied on the arm of the couch. "At this point, if something actually made sense, I would be terrified." Kelly agreed. Jack's life was a tornado right now. He had spiraled trying to keep up with both sides.

"Do you happen to know where he's going?" asked Oscar. "Oh. God no. I work for the DA. I want nothing to do with the shit he's tied into. I'm busy enough." She replied. "This is a very casual arrangement"

Oscar nodded in understanding. "I'll umm.. see myself out"

"You guys royally fucked this up. Just so you know" added Kelly. Salt in the wound. Oscar took two steps and dropped to one knee. He clutched his side. "Ahh fuck, I think he broke my rib. Call an ambulance, please" Oscar laid on the floor. Cursing Jack for standing up against the system.

  Armed to the teeth. Would be the best way to describe the man flying down seventh street in a black Monte Carlo, blasting Thunder Jeep songs for all to hear. Jack had grabbed his hidden go bag before he jumped into the car. Ammo, automatics, a hand grenade, because why not?

Nicky, Mario and remaining members of the family all stood in the driveway of Angies house. They were loading the vans and trucks just as Jack had. In broad daylight, nonetheless.

Act II

Weapons of all sizes. Not a care for repercussions if anyone saw them. This was a free for all now.

Jack came flying up the driveway. The screeching halt tossed everything from his front seat to the floor. He jumped out of the car and tucked two 9mm's in his side holsters and one behind him. He grabbed his bag of goodies and threw it over his shoulder. The perfect hair didn't move. His aviator sunglasses covered up his bloodshot eyes. He walked toward the group. Unhinged was here to play.

Mario met Jack in the driveway. "Nice wheels Jackie"

"Sometimes you need an upgrade" replied Jack. "What's the plan?"

Mario laid it all out, it was straightforward "We use the riots as cover and run everything down the throats of HQ."

"Angie still thinks its Oscar and Bill?"

"It has to be at this point. We've killed our enemies. The only one left is the big man in the tower. And it's his time to pay." Said Mario without batting an eye. He meant business, as always. Mario turned to the group as the worked, "Nicky's got it all mapped out. He can barely talk he's so mad. Gio and him were close and the two suits were like his uncles."

"Yeah, I get it. Would it help if I just beat the shit out of Freeman on my front step? Cause I Did" Jack was going to keep that one to himself, but clearly, they didn't care anymore about gathering information from the inside. They were planning on walking in the front door and taking out anyone who stood in their way. This was going to be a very bad day for the city.

"It's a good start. Soften him up for what's to come." Mario put some weight behind that comment. There was a lot in

Act II

store for Oscar and his group. And they had no idea it was coming.

"Jackie boy, come inside, we need to talk" the voice of the devil himself hath beckoned.

Angie stood in the front entrance of the house. Rebecca stood atop the stairwell, observing. Nicky joined them from the side entrance hallway. "We are loaded up and ready" he said to his father. "Good. This will be the day of reckoning for the city and the people of Crimson Bay. The reign of terror brought upon us, by the men and women sworn to protect us. Shall end tonight. A crusade that will end in blood, fire and brimstone. Jackie, these men, shrouded as heroes, have taken the law into their own hands in hopes to eliminate our family name. It has taken us this long to figure it all out, a clever plan when you think of it, no one would suspect the people who are investigating the murder. Greed? Corruption? All perfectly placed to distract from the real killers. I almost bought it, but now I see clearly. They will all die."

Rebecca raised her wine glass from the top of the stairs " to my boys, to taking back our city" she was also completely insane but in a nicer, easier to swallow way. IF this had of been a previous meeting, jack would be a puddle of sweat and others. But now, he just smiled at Rebecca. Basking in the insanity they were about to partake in.

Angie placed his hand on Jack's shoulder. He then placed his other hand on his first-born heir to the throne, son's shoulder. "Tonight, we take back what is ours. What we have built, and what we will continue to build." Angie's grip tightened. "No one, absolutely no one, fucks with this family. Ever" His cold eyes stared through Jack's head. Like he was looking at a painting behind him. "Now run along kids, make

Act II

me proud" he patted them on the back and pulled out another cigar.

Nicky looked confused "You don't want to be there for this?"

"I'll be there. Later, I must see a man about a horse. And then I will join you" Angie grinned. That was his favorite "Fuck off and don't ask about my business" saying.

"Save Mr. Freeman for me. Bring him back here, alive. I need to look in his eyes"

Jack's mind began to race. Angie wasn't going? This might work out well. Jack could get lost in the shuffle and duck out to follow Angie, save him, catch the killer and be set for life. Be the hero for both sides. But if anyone noticed him trying to leave. They would shoot him where he stood.

"I thought he was pissed?" asked Jack as the stepped outside. "Oh, he's going to burn the entire city down to get to Oscar Freeman and Bill Taylor. He gets like this. Almost happy. He enjoys war. It's a wonder we have had peace for so long." Explained Nicky.

"Where would he be going that's more important than this?" Jack was perplexed. "This is all business, Jackie. Murder a police Chief at seven. Meet with international arms dealers at eight. Dinner with mom at nine. You know, typical mob boss shit." Nicky smirked as he loaded a bag into his truck. It was full of guns. He laughed even more as a clip of ammo fell out. "I mean, this is just another fucking Thursday for us." He turned to measure Jack's take on the situation. "This is where we make them remember who runs this fucking city. Sometimes it's a simple reminder, and sometimes…it takes a bit more effort."

"Isn't he at least a little concerned about his own safety?" Jack was trying to dig a little deeper.

Act II

"Pfft.. He's got King with him. A registered psychopath driving his car and the will to die for him. He doesn't bat an eye."

"Didn't he snap at the mere thought of Konstantine?"

"I will say that was a little out of character. He usually doesn't get tunnel vision like that." Nicky paused." Wait, how the fuck did you know about Konstantine?" Jack caught himself. He held a pause. Smirked a little, "Gio". Nicky made the "Yeah I figured" face. "Typically. If he wasn't already dead."

Jack was trying to fit into the conversation a question about Gio's murder. A question about what was written on the floor. They walked over to the rest of the group in the driveway. It was not the right time. "Alright, load up. This one's not exactly typical, no matter what Nick says. We are walking into a pre-existing riot, that we didn't even start. It's almost disappointing, but we are gonna finish it." Laughed Mario as he handed out assignments.

"Our knight in shining armor, Little Jackie, you're going in first. That'll be our distraction to get set up."

Jack spoke up "You realize they're going to have the full tactical team, with tanks and riot gear, the whole works. Just be ready for that." Bugsy leaned over to Jack, "That's why you're going first, genius"

"Look, Theres eight of us here right now. There should be at least thirteen." Nicky had started his rally cry for the troops.

"Twelve, This Homicide Detective still don't count." Marios's pitbull Joey Barras never trusted a cop. Ever. "He hasn't proved anything yet. This could all be a setup"

"Jackie, why don't you tell Joey what you did this morning"

Act II

Jack looked a bit confused. It had been a long day. Which thing was he referring to?

"Yes, shit… I beat the living daylights out of Chief Freeman on my living room floor. Broke his nose and left him in a puddle." Jack held up his busted hand as proof.

"Proves nothing. I hope they shoot you first" said Joey "Fuck this let's go."

The day was running long; the sun was starting to drop. The riot had continued on for hours and showed no signs of stopping. The police had sectioned off parts of the city to try and keep it contained but the protest groups had them heavily outnumbered. The rumors were they had this planned for weeks and were finally unleashing their hatred for the lack of progress in the city's first serial killer case. A case that had nearly crippled the city. Kept people from their everyday lives, causing fear and unrest. A wounded animal cannot be cornered. The pressure had built for too long. The result was inevitable.

The skyline was burnt orange, with drifts of smoke rising up from pockets of the city. The evening news providing everyone with an update. A warning to stay inside. Shoot outs between cops and civilians lead the broadcast. Overturned cars set on fire, flares and debris all over the street. It looked like a warzone on the screen. The bridges had been blocked to minimize the spread. The city's heartbeat was racing.

Act II

The Disposable Hero

     Jack grabbed his best black jacket from the trunk. It matched his best black shirt and black pants. Topped off by his best black boots. He took some heat when he put his bullet proof vest under his shirt. He had hoped they wouldn't notice. They did. Jack's go bag sat shotgun in the Monte Carlo. He would need quick access, and automatic windows. He wasn't getting out of that car if he didn't have to.

     Two black vans, two black trucks. Loaded for war. Angie's security detail wouldn't be far behind. Russell King would be with Angie and at least three other security vehicles would be close by. The ember of cigarettes being lit bounced from vehicle to vehicle. They were ready.

Jack pushed play on his newfound Thunder Jeep tape and spun the dial passed ten. He planted the gas pedal and screamed out of the driveway, he slid sideways and almost took out a gargoyle on a pillar. "This should be good" snickered Mario as he followed behind. He watched Jack disappear; a cloud of dust and smoke was all that remained.

     They had mapped out a plan for when they got close, but Jack wasn't really paying attention, nor did he care about the plan. He was going to shoot the lights out and then duck out the back and go find Angie. Whoever he was meeting was obviously very important, given the current situation. It very well could be a set up by the killer. Jack's detective brain was

Act II

ctill firing on all cylinders, but the justice he strived for was personal in nature.

Jack stormed through the gated community and was well beyond the team, he wished he had asked if Nicky saw the note below Gio's feet. He must have, and it just didn't bother him.

It didn't matter now, there were a few scores to settle first.

CBPD headquarters:

"What am I looking at Bill?" asked Chief Freeman, leaning over a large table with a map of the city. They had marked out the areas where the riot had spilled into. Planning their approach for containing the chaos.

"We have special forces deployed down in these areas, and our guys are holding off the fires in here. Reports so far have no casualties, but an immense amount of damage. The goal is to shut this down before anyone gets killed." Explained Bill.

"I get that but how the fuck are we doing it? Cut the bullshit, are we shooting our way out, are we gassing them? My vote is gas, less casualties." Replied Oscar. "Len, how would you tackle this?"

Captain Len Basso sat in his chair just behind them. " I mean, I like gas for this, but if they start using firearms, I'd say we lay them out. With these types of groups, once you take a few out they turn and run."

"I tend to agree. Does anyone think this could be orchestrated by our faceless friend? Is this a huge distraction? The fact that no one has shot anyone yet is intriguing. Typically, someone has boiled over and opened fire by now."

Act II

The group nodded in agreement. This did seem out of character for the people of Crimson Bay, but then again, they had also just lived through months of terror in the streets.

"Bill, I need to run something by you" Freeman motioned to his office down the hall. The group returned to the map and continued plotting.

The door shut behind them and Freeman clicked the lock.

"What the fuck happened to your face Oscar, Jesus! Did you really think showing up at his house was going to change anything?" Bill was fuming. "So, what, we set his friend up. We needed to find out of Calvin was dirty. And guess what! He fucking was. Did it cost us another detective in the process? Yeah, so fucking what!?"

"You pushed this, you son of a bitch. This had to be don't the right way, this wasn't it." Replied Freeman. The two were in a stand off in the middle of the room.

"And you fucking signed off on it" Bill's finger had met freeman's chest.

"Get you finger off of me."

Bill was taller, he stared down at his boss. He was not afraid of this fight. Neither was Freeman.

"Jack is out there. Loaded to the teeth (guns and liquor) and he's coming. Are we just going to let our best detective go down this road? It's our fucking fault."

"The snipers will take him out"

"You didn't see the look in his eyes, Bill. That's not Jack. That's someone else, something else. He was completely off the rails. We pushed him too far with this one, Lou's death was the final nail."

Act II

Bill Taylor backed off, he knew Freeman was right. He was a massive prick, but he knew what they had asked of their detective, to go undercover in plain sight, to infiltrate the mob, as he himself, was a nearly impossible task. A window like that only opens once in a lifetime. "Look, we were presented an opportunity, and we took it. Anyone else would have made the same choice." At this point they would say anything to steer their narrative in the direction that best suited them. Freeman sat down and poured two large drinks. They were going to need them,

Bill stood with his drink for a moment. "What did you mean, he was someone else?"

Freeman had been staring at his drink. Looking for the answer at the bottom. "He wasn't in there. His eyes were grey. There was a violence about him. The composed, sharp, Jack Finn we knew wasn't there."

A knock at the door broke the uneasy air. It was Basso "Just got a call from Andy down on 5th. It was loud and abbreviated, but we believe he said "They're coming"

An empty whisky bottle rolled across the floor mat of the passenger seat. The Monte Carlo took a wide turn, if the roads weren't deserted, he would have taken half of rush hour traffic out. The engine roared, his windows were wide open, hair blowing in the wind, Thunderous Drums and Guitars at full blast. Jack's adrenaline had hit a fever pitch. He flew down the street toward the rising smoke between the buildings. The sun had just about disappeared, the night sky had crept in. Jack blew by an old hotel with a sign that had seen better days. It glowed red against the night sky, and then it smashed to the ground as Jack put two tires up on the side walk, the vibration was just enough. Trash cans caught the brunt of this move, Jack never lifted his foot.

Act II

The first sign of a crowd, a mix of barriers, cop cars and protest signs. Not much of a riot it seemed, just a lot of smoke above the buildings. The barriers held the crowd near one of the entrances to Memorial Park. As Jack got closer, he realized… The entire Park was on fire. The flames threw shadows all over the buildings, The tenants all watched from balconies as the trees burned. Beyond the park, thousands of protesters pushed back against police in riot gear. Pockets of fighting, flares, tear gas. But no bullets. The closer Jack got, the more chaos unfolded before him. He loved it.

He also knew that they would have given his description and the green light to fire a way if needed. And He knew it would be needed. The orange police barriers were wood and barely held together, they exploded as Jack blew through them, the crowd echoed with a collective scream. Terror and fear. The pressure had grown all day. This was the spark everyone had waited for. No chance they get this under control now.

Jack held on as he slid sideways into the crowd. Bodies flew over his hood, clothing, mostly shoes, flew into the air. Jack couldn't hear the screams. Just his speakers. He finally stopped near the sidewalk. Two police officers came running, they quickly bounced off the pavement as two bullets exited their skulls. Jack had wondered how that would feel. It was one thing to kill Lou and Calvin. That was life and death. He didn't even think. This was different. He didn't recognize those officers, and he didn't care. They were just in the way.

He surveyed the mess in front of him. Judging by his tire tracks, he hadn't run anyone over, which was good, he was making an attempt to minimize collateral damage. Note that it was minimize, not eliminate. More cops were coming, the shots were likely heard for miles. He jammed the gas and raced

Act II

toward a gap in the crowd. It was on now, his goal was to lead as many officers in this chase as possible. Drag them all to the slaughter.

If the entire police force was gone, then Angie would just appoint a new one. His plan was finally coming to fruition. Eliminate Freeman and his crew, and replace them all. Jack was the tip of the spear, and he played his part very well.

Flashing lights filled the streets. Jack got loose from the crowd and poured his way back toward Police headquarters. Get as close as possible, draw more of them out and let the family sort them.

Three cars, four cars, seven cars, it was on. Jack kept his head on a swivel as he burned through Crimson Bay. He knew these streets well. Every set of lights he blew through seemed to drag more patrol cars to him. He needed to create space, one hand on the wheel one blindly hung out the window trying to shoot behind him. It wasn't working. He reached into the bag and found the grenade. "Fuck it." Pulled the pin and launched it backwards. It missed the road completely and landed in a crowd of garbage cans, they exploded and sent metal shards everywhere. A power pole went with it and two cop cars took the blast from the side, flipping them both. A smile came across Jack's face, a menacing smile.

The rest of the vans were positioned by the docks. Jack was to lead them in and the vans and trucks would block everyone off, and let the fun begin. At least five dead officers now, two shot and three in the grenade explosion. That's life in prison a few times over.

Two more blocks until the dockyard.

Act II

All units responding. The chase was huge now. Even the tank had been deployed. Jack's old buddy Danny Flores was in that group. If it came to it. Danny would die as well.

The gates were open. The parking lot was empty, except a few vans hiding under the trees.

The Monte Carlo roared down the street, cops behind him and cops flying toward him. The race to the gate was on. He know found himself in a game of chicken with three cop cars bearing down on him and about fifteen more behind him.

  Jack watched the needle push and push. He reached for one of the automatics, everything slowed down. He spun the wheel, aimed into the headlights and unloaded as fast as it would go. Sliding sideways into the open gate as bullets sprayed the windshields. Tires popped and glass shattered, Jack narrowly missed the three cars as he slid into the parking lot. The screaming of tires and brakes filled the air as the three cops' cars continued into the path of the tailing pursuit. Steel bending around steel and the heavy impact of cars crushing each other was all everyone heard.

  The Monte Carlo was still in decent shape considering. Jack came to a stop and waited to see if any of the police cars even made it into the lot. He didn't waste time though, popped his trunk, jumped out and hid behind the car. He was ready with the automatics. The SWAT van flew through the gate first, followed by a line of police cars. Another van came flying through the fence to the right side. The lighting in the docks parking lot wasn't great, this was on purpose. Visibility wasn't great for anyone; they were almost shooting into the dark. Fires from the crash provided some light but it mostly just smoked everyone out.

Act II

Chaos ensued. Bullets, flash bombs, flares, tear gas, fist fights, knives, a chainsaw (bugsy). This was an all out parking lot brawl. The police cars got blindsided as they drove in, sprayed with bullets from both sides. The family was outnumbered, so the element of surprise leveled the playing field.

Both sides had manufactured cover behind destroyed cars. They needed a plan quickly.

Enter: Jack Finn. They grouped behind one of the vans, everyone was still whole, somehow. "Nice Fucking work Jackie, that was fucking impressive," said Mario. It was a genuine compliment. "I've got one more trick up my sleeve boys. I'll fire my car up and storm out through the gate. Whatever happens, happens. Once they turn to take me, you guys move in and light them up"

Mario and Nicky both looked a bit surprised, "Jack, that's suicide. You'll be dead before the road"

"No. I won't. Look at them. Every one of them hates this. The only guys who want this are the SWAT guys. And they have huge weapons, which they wont use this close to their own officers, they'll want them to let me through. And then bang! You guys put them down"

"Jesus that might actually work"

"If it does, you owe me. If it doesn't. well, then it was nice knowing you guys" Jack put on his best insane person smile and loaded his gun. "Showtime" and he disappeared toward his car.

Cross fire rang out. Time slowed to a crawl. Jack dove into the Monte Carlo. The family provided cover so he could start it up. He could barely see above the steering wheel as he planted his foot. The police braced for impact and the SWAT teams

Act II

loaded their weapons. Danny Flores sat with a mounted rocket launcher armed and ready. Cries of "Let him through" repeated. Jack was right. They backed off, other than a few rounds into his rear panel. He screamed through the crowd at the gate, he landed directly in the crosshairs of Danny's weapon.

"Target is locked. Stand by." Danny said into his headset. Jack made the turn as the family opened fire on the rest of the cops. It had worked, Jack was flying down the road and now the fight with the cops was swinging toward the De Luca's favour. One problem, Danny Flores had already activated his weapon. Jack was right in the sweet spot.

10:23pm

The sky that night lit up with an orange fireball. It was said to be seen blocks away, even on the other side of the bridge. Everyone on the docks landed on the pavement. The explosion felt much larger than expected, no one noticed the three propane tanks on the other side of the road. An eerie calm came about the scene. It had happened so fast that no one really knew what had taken place. Vehicles, debris, buildings, all strewn about the road. The parking lot was a disaster. The police had formed a makeshift camp on one side and what was left of the De Luca's found themselves at a standstill. Everyone was low on ammo and the will to continue.

Over the loudspeaker, the negotiation started: "Mario, this is Police Chief Freeman. We demand you surrender to our forces, we have you boxed in. There is no escape. This can end peacefully if you let it."

Act II

"When the fuck, did he get here?" asked Mario, under the cover of an overturned van. The top brass had slid into a sheltered position further down the street. After the explosion they moved closer to try and settle this once and for all.

"Did Jackie make it out? I can't see the car?" asked Joey Barras.

"I don't know. It looked bad. Really bad."

An oddly concerned look came over Joey's face. "I really liked him. He was one of us"

Mario sat down beside Joey. He patted him on the shoulder. "I know Joe, I know" The sound of magazines loading broke the tender moment. Bugsy and Sid were both bleeding through their shirts and down their faces, but that wasn't going to slow them down. "Where's Tommy and Nicky?"

"The other van" said Mario, he pointed to his right. They all turned, the van was on fire and upside down. One shoe lay on the ground beside the van. Glass shattered all around. Time completely froze. Bugsy ran through the broken glass, Sid followed. Nicky was their leader, their mentor, he was everything to them. They loved Tommy too, just like a brother. The last thing that went through Bugsy's mind was a sniper's bullet as he collapsed to the ground. Sid was in mid stride, one foot hit the ground, the other foot went limp, and he landed face down. The sniper was two for two.

The van exploded at 10:31pm. The De Luca Family lost everyone that night. Nicky and Tommy in the van. Bugsy and Sid met the sniper. Mario, Joey and Big Kev took the brunt of the explosion. They didn't stand a chance. The other officers rounded the corner of the flipped over vehicles to find the gruesome scene. Bodies everywhere. A crime family blown apart. Flaming debris raining down on everyone.

Act II

Freeman stood at the gates; he waited for word on the bodies. His stomach sat directly in his throat. Jack was with them, and he was likely gone. Unbeknownst to Freeman and Bill Taylor, they had arrived after the first explosion, Jack was already long gone. Graham Morgan was the first one back to Freeman. "They're all gone Chief. We can't even identify a few of them. It's highly likely Jack was in that mix"

"Hey Morons!" came a voice from above. The brass looked to see Danny Flores on top of the Riot Van. "He's over there. In that mess" Danny motioned to the industrial yard across the street, where vehicles and now the building where in flames. The scene was just as bad. More vehicle parts were scattered everywhere. A large hole in the ground. One of the flaming vehicles was Jacks.

Freeman and Bill Taylor stood in silence. Captain Basso emerged from their truck along with the rest of the taskforce. Freeman just slowly shook his head, signaling to the team that the worst outcome had been realized. Jack was one of them, whether he was a friend, foe, or other, he was one hell of a detective.

The fire department took over as they handled the blaze. The scene was filled with flashing lights, smoke, fire, and ambulances. Everything you could think of. The rest of the police force were still out diffusing the crowds, but after a fire fight and large explosions, most of the protestors deemed it a little too dangerous even for their taste.

Barricades kept the crowds back as all the crime scene teams filtered in. Oscar could only stare off into the distance. "We did the right thing" assured Taylor. "Everyone knew this might happen"

Act II

11:32pm

The clean up of this mess would take hours, this would turn into a backshift for everyone, with the reporters and journalists waiting for them in the morning light. A voice from the command truck cut through the noise "Chief, phone call. Its urgent!"

"What the fuck else could happen tonight" thought Oscar to himself as he pushed through the ever growing crowd. He stepped inside, was handed a phone. He listened for a few seconds and hung up the phone. One of the men inside the truck asked "Chief, who was that?"

A stunned Chief Freeman took out a cigarette and lit it. He turned and walked back outside "Chief? Anything we should know about?" asked the guys in the truck. He waved them off. He made a direct path to his team. Bill Taylor saw him coming, "What is it?" Freeman kept walking.

"Chief?! What is it?" exclaimed Bill. He followed his boss out onto the road. "Oscar, what the fuck is it? Who was on the phone?"

The chief hauled on his cigarette; his hand was visibly shaking at this point. He exhaled and with as much vim and vigor as he could muster, he said "Angie De Luca was murdered"

Act III

Present Day

"Wait, so you're telling us, that legally they declared you dead?"

Jack stirred his coffee. "I mean, technically I was. Everyone saw me explode into a ball of fire and everything around me destroyed. How much more proof did anyone need back then?"

Sam and Chris stared dumbfounded at this revelation.

"I can tell by your dumb faces that you don't understand"

"Clearly, I didn't die. The rocket missed my car, but it did hit the fence and all the cars I had just passed. The explosion pushed me even further down the street and I had that thing floored. I was gone, out of sight."

Sam was completely emersed in this story. They had sat there for hours listening to it. "Ok, not dead, where did you go?"

"To fucking find Angie. That was the whole point, I wasn't there to help the De Lucas kill all the cops, Christ, I had to save my own ass and keep Angie alive. If I did that, I knew I had a chance to catch the piece of shit behind that whole mess"

Act III

"There was this old gothic looking church that overlooked the water down on the east side. It's gone now, mysterious fire or something (Jack openly laughed to himself). Anyway, I knew that Angie had been married there, and that place was his hideout when shit went sideways. (Thanks, Gio for that tidbit) It made sense for him to do business deals there. Now remember, this was a total hunch, I could have been walking into an empty church and made to look like a fool."

Sam was writing down key notes as they went, "Ok, So the old church, you go in, Angie's there, then what happens?"

"Nope. Wrong. I pull up and vehicles are leaving. Four town car looking ones. I figured I missed everything, so I pulled around back and jumped out. Luckily there was a door at the back, and it was unlocked. I've got no idea what I'm walking into, so I'm armed and ready. No noise, it's calm and quiet. A set of steps at the end of the hall went to rooms above I assumed, so I followed it. The stairs opened into a large sitting room, no signs of anyone. A set of double doors had cracked open, so I dropped the shoulder into them and poked my head through. It's an old stone set of steps up to the bell tower. Now I can hear voices at the top. I climbed my way up. Theres this hallway to the main part of the bell tower, it's all shaped in arches, every five feet or so there's a big arch that goes from one side to another. I tuck myself behind one of these arches and wait. Sure, enough I see a guy in black boots, black pants and a black sweater pulled up over his head. At his feet, is Angie. Bloody, beaten but still alive. He tried to talk but blood was bubbling out of his mouth. I knew I had him, this was it. But before I could do anything, he pulled out his knife and stabbed Angie in the heart. He was gone."

Sam and Chris ate every word, they hung on to them, this was the most insane thing they had ever heard in their

Act III

lives. "How did you not catch this guy?! Blurted Chris. Jack gave a stern look. "He fucking turned and threw his blade at me. He knew I was there. Got me right in the shoulder too" Jack pulled his shirt down to reveal the old scar. "I fell back and hit my head on the stone wall. Guy was gone. And that was it. I went home. I found out I was dead the next day."

    Sam sat for a second, he didn't write anything down. "How have you been paying for stuff? You know? If you're dead?" asked Detective Davis, with the most childlike delivery ever attached to a question. Still nothing from Sam. His mind was searching for something. Jack's eyes shifted from the table to the window and back to his cup. "Davis, can you grab my other notebook from the car? This one's full. Davis stood up, slightly confused but eager to follow the order. "Yeah, sure, no problem"

"Sit down son" boomed Jack. "There's nothing else to tell, so there's no reason to get another notebook." Davis stood in limbo between his partner/boss/hero and the scary man who has definitely killed people sitting across from him. "Now, if you two don't mind. I am hungry, so unless you're about to make me some food, get ah the fuck out of my house." Jack had slipped back into his defensive grumpy demeanor. There was no hope of a continuation of this elaborate and incredibly detailed story he just told.

    Sam stood up beside Davis. "I just wanted to say thank you. We appreciate you finally letting us in. This will hopefully steer us in the right direction with our investigation."

Sam gave a half smile. Even though he didn't buy that bullshit he just said. Jack reached over to his pistol, which he had left conveniently on the table. He kept his eyes fixed on the detectives as he placed his hand around the handle. They both

Act III

slowly backed away "Alright, Alright. We'll be in touch once we have more questions."

"No, you won't," said Jack. He pulled the gun closer to him, turned it towards the detectives. His other hand grabbed his trusty whisky bottle and poured some into his coffee cup. He still hadn't broken eye contact. The barrel had found its home, pointing directly at Sam. "If you call me. Write to me. Show up at my door. Or if I hear my name on the six o'clock news. I will chop you up into pieces and use you as firewood."

"That's swell Jack. You are a gracious host. We..umm..we enjoyed our time" Sam was sputtering. He had let his guard down during story time and now he was caught off guard. He trusted Jack. Big Mistake.

They left in a haste, almost negating the last few hours. It felt like they were dealing with an elderly relative suffering from dementia, one that had suddenly become lucid and remembered everyone in the room. "Did you record all of that?" asked Sam. "I think I got most of it, it was tricky to not draw any attention to myself once he started talking." Davis replied as they approached his car. "Good, I wrote down as much as I could, I'll have to listen to that to fill in the blanks"

"Wait!" announced Davis. He came around to the driver's side. He pushed Sam back from the door and got down on the road to look under the car.

"Seriously? No one knows we are here, what are you doing?" asked Sam.

"You never know. Didn't you listen to that story? The guy is still out there and the only one who came close to catching him has been found. It makes sense to take us out. Kill the story, and the people who know about it." Explained Davis, he

Act III

almost had a point. Davis stood up "I don't even know what I'm looking for to be honest"

"Yeah, I kinda figured. Look, if it makes you feel better, fire it up and you can drive. Theres nothing strapped to the bottom of it." Sam tossed the keys to his new partner. A sign of trust that Davis thought he would never see. He opened the door and jumped into the driver's seat, with one turn of the wrist the engine fired up. The '66 sounded fantastic. The roar of the engine bounced off the old buildings down the street.

Three days later, Sam woke to the sound of something beeping. His alarm? Did he have an alarm? Where was he? His vision was blurred. His head was pounding. Likely a nasty hangover. He rubbed his eyes and pain shot through his shoulder. All he could think of was "what the hell is going on?". His vision cleared and he realized what that beeping was. His own heart monitor, next to his IV bag, next to his hospital bed. He had been unconscious for Three days.

The room was private. No one else around. Sam stared at the ceiling for a long while before anyone came to check on him. Finally, a nurse poked her head in, an older nurse with short grey hair. She had the demeanor of someone that ran the show. She hadn't noticed that Sam was awake yet as she wrote notes on a chart. Sam tried to make some noise, only a gurgle came from his throat. It was enough though; she finally turned his way and wore a surprised look on her face "About fucking time detective" she blurted out. It caught them both by surprise. "Oh Mr. Cole I wouldn't try to speak. You took in a lot of smoke; your throat and lungs were heavily affected." Sam's face asked why he was there?

The nurse took a deep breath. Her face told most of the story "Car bomb. Three days ago. And I am very sorry to tell you this, but your partner did not survive." The nurse

Act III

excused herself, but as she went to close the door, she seemed to be speaking to someone in the hall. Motioning for them to go into the room.

Sam's face twisted with fear. This was not the person he expected, he really didn't know who to expect, if anyone at all. "Nice little vacation you got yourself here kid" The man, clad in a leather jacket, a jean shirt, and black shirt underneath it, old torn up jeans, black boots, multiple gold chains around his neck, more rings than most people wear, looked like the child of a motorcycle gang and an 80's metal band. With perfect hair.

"You owe me a new door and front window, asshole." Jack Finn had emerged from his self-imposed exile and was now standing in front of Detective Sam Cole. Jack pulled out his cigarettes and grabbed a chair. Sam tried to speak but still couldn't make much noise. Jack noticed and leaned forward; he pushed the glass of water closer to Sam. "Drink that kid"

It took a minute, but finally Sam could get a few words out. "You can't smoke in here, Jack, this isn't the seventies" Jack laughed and kept smoking. "Don't worry about me kid"

"I'm not, it's the sprinkler system I'm worried about" Jacked smiled. He didn't care.

"What happened to me?"

"Well, I believe you got blown to kingdom come by a car bomb, and landed on my front step, again"

"Davis?"

"Dead, very, very dead"

"My car?"

Act III

"Also, very, very Dead. Your front fender went through my window. That'll be $2500 bucks please"

Sam just laid there and took it all in. Davis was right. "He told me there might be a bomb, I brushed it off and he took the brunt of it"

Jack laughed "Oh. He didn't take the brunt of it, he took everything, the bomb was tucked under your seat, not under the car. I think one of his legs landed on my roof. Lucky me though, great entertainment for the last three days, except for the cops crawling around. Slimy fucks."

Sam shook his head, he had no memory of anything, just tossing the keys to Davis. Suddenly it all snapped back to him "You fucking lied to me, Jack". Jack grinned and took a sip from his flask.

"I wondered if you would pick up on that"

"There's no way you would just end the story with "He threw a knife at me and ran away. You drove your car into a warzone and killed cops, and God knows who else and then went on a suicide mission through the streets. That story doesn't just end with "he ran away". Also…" Sam broke out in a coughing fit. He drank the rest of the water and tried to regain his composure.

"Also, who throws a knife? They stab you; this guy wasn't some ninja; he didn't hit you with a metal ninja star. That scar is from someone stabbing you."

"You're good, kid, I'll give you that. But no one knows the real story. And your partners phone was obliterated so everything he recorded is gone"

"You knew?"

Act III

"I would ask if the question would be "do I look like an idiot?" but I already know the answer is fuck no. Of course I knew, that's why I changed the ending"

"Did you plant that fucking bomb in my car! To get rid of that recording?" Sam's heart monitor was starting to beep faster. Jack laughed again "Seriously, kid? I didn't know you were coming, and I never left your sight. How the fuck would I pull that off?"

That made complete sense. Sam was on pain meds, and nothing really made sense at this point.

Sam's mind was swirling. No thoughts were landing, just fleeting. He would snap back into reality every few minutes. Concussions will do that for a person.

"Why are you here?" Sam finally asked. Jack was a ghost. He didn't exist, showing up at the hospital was exposing himself, it didn't really make sense.

"Weren't you listening, kid. You owe me $2500 dollars. I am here to collect."

Sam didn't laugh nearly as much as Jack. He was in a good mood for some reason.

Jack sat up, took one more sip from his flask and prepared himself. "You and I are pretty similar. It's almost scary how much. I'm sure Freeman had his eyes on you much more than you know.

Actually, I know he did, because he told me."

That revelation brought Sam to sit up, slowly, and grimacing in pain. "What do you mean...?"

Oscar and I have been friends for years. I'll miss that crazy bastard, that's for sure. You see, there was a little more to our

Act III

plan for the De Luca's. The real ending was I was supposed to "die" (air quotes). All part of the plan. It didn't matter how it all played out; we were faking my death. If I succeeded, I was dead, If I failed, I was dead. I had no way out."

"What about the fight with Freeman?" asked Sam confused.

"Oh, that was real," Laughed Jack. "Very real, he deserved that beating. I was all for faking my

Death, but Jesus, he almost got me killed for real. And Lou was not supposed to die. That was Oscars fucking fault. So, I kicked his ass."

"But… You made it sound like you had totally lost it?"

"Oh, I lost it and never found it. The pressure I was under back then drove me to drink, smoke, throw up, make bad decisions, it was so much fun. I wouldn't trade it for the world, except the Lou stuff. Fuck that, he didn't deserve to get caught up in that shit."

"So, what am I missing from that story, besides the real ending?"

"Ahh..well, they faked my death and paid me out for the rest of my days. Hence why I live where I live. But the Mayor and a bunch of other city officials are in it too. They keep that part of town empty on purpose. No one knows what I look like now, it's been thirty years. The first few were tough, I grew a beard, longer hair, fake ID's. Everything. I just disappeared into the void."

"Did you have a Funeral Service?"

Jack grinned "I sure did, and I was at it. How fucked up is that? It was about three weeks after everything settled down. I had the beard grown. I wore a wig and heavier clothes. What a trip to watch your own funeral."

Act III

"Alright, wow, umm..Who all knows about you?"

"Oscar, Bill, the mayor, well the old mayor, this new guy might not, don't care. And one other person"

"Kelly?" asked Sam. It made sense, she seemed to almost be his girlfriend. "Nope, that sucked, couldn't even tell her. Lawyers can't be trusted anyway. But that leads me to the point of all of this. The other person who knows that I am still alive, also disappeared."

"Huh?" typical response required for a mysterious twist in Jack's story. "The killer?"

"Yup. The Crimson Mask Killer himself. The one who got away. The legend, the lore, the folktales, everything. All a lie." Jack was enjoying this part. Watching Sam's mind try to lock down on what was happening. "A lie?" Sam asked "Ok, just rip the band aid off Jack."

"I did see who killed Angie. I stood there, he turned around and before I could say anything he said, "Call it in Jackie". I almost shit myself right there. The voice. That Voice! Are you serious. All of this and this is the guy who has been causing all this pain and grief. I was shaking. I looked at him and said "Why? Why is it you?...is it you?" I was so confused."

Sam was enthralled; this was the part he wanted now for months "Who?! Who was it?"

"Nicky"

Both men just sat there in silence. Sam couldn't find any words.

"Turns out, he hated the life. Hated what they had become, which explains all the greed and corruption signs he left with the bodies. He killed his own Father, his uncle, his best friends. He cleaned up the city from within. There was no way I was

Act III

calling it in. The city we know today, the fact that we no longer have an organized crime family running our city, is all from Nicky. He slaughtered his own family out of disgust for his own bloodline." Jack paused and collected himself. This was a bit of a therapy session for him.

"We stood across from each other. I said I wouldn't do it. He nodded. He understood. I told him he had to disappear, and he told me one of the most chilling things I have ever heard."

He said "Jackie, do you know why I followed my father out here? I knew who he was meeting with. I let him have that final meeting and when I confronted him about it, he said I would never understand. Because there's so much more to this than any of us knew". Angie ran the city, so we thought. But apparently, he was meeting with a group that actually ran the city. That's all I got out of Nicky before he left."

"I have been chasing that down from the shadows for the last thirty years. Who was Angie involved with? Are they still around? Did they get spooked by the murder of an entire crime family? I don't know. I just don't know."

Sam had to physically pick his jaw up off the floor. It dropped cartoon style on his bed and rolled to the vinyl below. "That is… completely.. insane..Jack. Are you fucking with me?"

"Look kid, I'm smart but that's a story I couldn't even write, anyone who could come up with a twist like that would have to be a genius."

Sam Agreed. It was a very intriguing twist in his little adventure. Angie wasn't the be all end all.

Both men sat there in silence. Brief moments of clarity followed by more confusion as they tried to wrap their minds around this new development.

Act III

"So, let me get this all straight. You have been declared dead. Financed by the government. Lurking in the shadows apparently tracking a secret group of people who run the city. And have nothing to show for it after thirty years?"

Jack's face gave away his answer "Fuck off kid."

"Theres more to it than that. These guys are untraceable. Nicky was my only connection and now it looks like he's resurfaced all these years later. That fucker. I should have shot him right then and there."

"But you just let him walk. And now more people are dead. I'm starting to see why no one wants to talk about this case anymore."

Jack leaned forward in his chair. Set his elbows to his knees and lowered his voice. "I'm going to chalk all that up to the drugs, son. Because you clearly don't get it do you?" Jack stood up and placed a card on the table next to Sam's bed.

"When you stop pissing in a bag. Call that number. We're not fucking done here" The icy stare had returned to Jack's face. Trying to be cooperative and somewhat nice was hurting him inside.

The heavy door almost came to a close as Jack made his exit. The nurse caught it with her foot as she returned to check on her patient. "It's always nice when family is there for you, isn't it" she said as she looked over a chart and made notes.

"Yeah, that was not family. That was a giant pain in my….butt" Sam hesitated to swear in front of the nurse. She was clearly his elder. She set down her chart and turned towards Sam. Crossed her arms and sternly stared at him. "Really? You think a little swear word is going to hurt my fucking feelings? Try me. I am well aware of who you are and

Act III

what you're trying to accomplish. Mopping up the past. And If I'm not mistaken, that ghost you were talking to looked a lot like Jack Finn. You know, if he were alive" she winked at Sam.

The blood drained from Sam's face. "What did you just say?" she knew Jack? She knew him. "Who are you?" he asked, almost scared of the answer. The elder nurse stood bedside and picked up the card Jack had left. "My boy, you're going to need some rest. When you wake up, call this number. Theres more at stake than you realize" That was the last think Sam saw, as she pushed the morphine in. "Goodnight Sam".

Act III

Heavy is the Head

    Crimson Bay was a shapeshifter. The view from one side of the bridge looked like an industrial dumpster fire. The view from another angle showed a more gothic run-down part of town. And of course, the view of downtown was the money maker. All for not on this day, a foot of snow covered every inch of the city. The Christmas lights strung down the streets were perfect for a scene from a made for TV movie. Only the steam rising from the sewer could be seen on the roads, nothing else.

    Sam had been home for three days at this point. The pain was subsiding, he was young, he could still bounce back. If he had of been in his forties he would have had to retire. Or old yeller'd. (taken out back and shot, it's a terrible reference about your beloved dog getting rabies and having to be put down). The card that Jack left sat on his nightstand, beside his phone. He couldn't bring himself to make that call yet. Who was that nurse? How is she connected to this? Is she real? Pain meds can do crazy things. Sam spent most of his time in his living room, looking out over his front yard and his long driveway, which was not plowed. He was stuck there.

Jacks story rung over and over in his head. His parting words, the nurse's too. What did Nicky know? What was Jack chasing all the years? None of it added up, which frustrated Sam to no

Act III

end. The pain of Davis's death was also starting to bubble to the surface. He was a good man, he was willing to learn. He didn't deserve that fate. He was Lou.

A collective that ran the city made no sense to Sam. That story painted Angie as the one pulling all the strings. There was a small amount of vindication looming in Sam's brain. He had the feeling that this city had secrets, and he was now immersed in it. Sam's only contact with the outside world was his phone, which barely worked on the outskirts of the city. He had no car and at this point it really felt like he was trapped.

Case files, pictures, old newspaper clipping, and a laptop covered Sams kitchen table. He was trying to piece together any connections from Jack's story. No dots were connecting. The same questions asked over and over in Sam's head, who was Angie meeting? Is Nicky still alive and out there?

The doorbell rang.

A younger man in a jumpsuit covered in grease with an old name tag that read "Daisy". He had longer greasy hair and large rimmed glasses.Sam opened the door "Can I help you?" he asked.

"You Sam?" came the surprisingly deep voice of Daisy.

"Depends on what your next sentence is"

Daisy watched as that one flew over his head. "Umm Mister I'm just dropping off a car and plowing your driveway"

Sam looked over the guy's shoulder. A snowplow was halfway through his driveway.

"Did you say dropping off a car?"

"Yeah, that one" He turned and pointed to the flatbed behind the plow.

Act III

The sun had peaked out and it hit the side of the car, and it gleamed.

"It's ah, a nineteen eighty-eight (checks his papers) Monte Carlo SS. According to this."

:"Jet Black. That son of a bitch" said Sam as he blindly signed for the car. "Yes, that's the one. We will unload it once the driveway is clear. It, um, it runs well, it's got a full tank of gas."

"Thanks kid" said Sam as he took the keys and went back into the house. He took a moment and realized he needed to call that number. It must have been Jacks cell on that card.

The doorbell rang again.

Daisy stood there holding something in his hand. "Hey mister, I forgot this. It's a tape, I think? It's from the old owner. He said you should play it in the car. Not sure how you play this in a car but maybe you do?"

Daisy handed Sam a black tape with red lettering. Thunder Jeep. 80's metal gods.

The card sat on Sam's bedside table for another day. He didn't want to jump into this immediately. Jack was likely waiting for a call and baited Sam with the car. Posturing at its finest. Sam stood in front of his mirror, tying his tie. Another funeral for a friend. Chritopher Davis was being laid to rest.

  The crowd was big, as it should be, mostly uniforms, a heavy active presence with a city in a state of unrest. A serial killer striking down prominent businessmen, The police chief and now one of the detectives on the case. Alarm bells started ringing in the minds of anyone who could remember the old days. Sam felt like he was living inside Jack's story. Too many details were lining up. An out of body experience could explain what Sam felt, he had seen this all in his head and now it was

Act III

right in front of him. He looked around for the outliers, the ones who stood out, but nothing was out of the ordinary. Where was Angie and his crew, lurking in the background? Sam's brain was melting fiction and fate.

    He shook hands with many and even hugged a few. One from the group was Allison Frost. Davis's "friend". They had just begun a courtship; she was visibly shaken up. As they embraced, she whispered to Sam "Tell me you'll find who did this?" Sam, nodded "I have too"

As Allison pulled away, Sam tightened his grip, she turned to him "Are you related to an Arthur Frost?" he asked. "That's my Grandfather, he was the mayor, he died before I was born." Allison waited for a response, but nothing came. Sam just moved on to the next person in line.

    Sam set his coffee into the cup holder as he waited for the lights to turn. It had been weeks since the funeral, and a month since any activity on the case. He was still on leave after the explosion, he filled his days with driving around the city, just taking it all in. He had stressed himself out, buried himself in the clues. He was burning out.

 The lights turned green, and he fed the gas to his Monte Carlo, well, Jack's Monte Carlo, he assumed. The card with the mysterious phone number still sat in the same place. Sam's brain was taking turns flipping between calling and throwing it out. The drive to find who was responsible for Davis's death and the desire to solve this huge case, had all been outweighed by the cryptic implication of another entity running the city. Sam's mind raced as fast as the car. He made the turn towards the docks, the train whistle blew long, it echoed through his ears. The red lights of the crossing flashed behind his eyes. His right foot didn't move. It was a short straightaway with no

Act III

traffic. The car started to shake with the low rumble of the train. His right foot pushed down.

Sam's mind was completely torn, he didn't know what to do, it had finally become too much to figure out. He drove this route almost every day, just listening to music, drinking coffee. Today was different, it all came to the surface. Davis, Freeman, Angie, Jack. That nurse? What was going on? The engine roared, the train did too. One mile, half a mile, a quarter, his heart was pounding.

A loud blast from the train, a warning. The arms of the crossing blocked his path. The lights flashed. Other cars from the opposite side of the track blew their horns. It was a wall of sound. A sound unlike anything Sam had heard. It carried an intensity, a rhythm. His final decision was easy and the on lookers had figured it out as they ran for cover from their cars. Grinding steel from brakes, sparks, screams from the other side.

A white light.

Silence.

Everything was slow. He could still see the train, except there was no sound. Just a ringing in his ears, a strange rhythmic tone.

His phone was ringing. He woke up.

Sam sat up in a cold sweat. *What the fuck just happened?* He thought. Meanwhile his nightstand kept ringing. He reached for it in a daze. A random number, at five am.

"What?" he abruptly answered.

A pause. More silence. Distant laughter came from the phone. A deep voice. "Kid, when I say call me. You fucking call me. We aren't messing around"

Act III

"That was a month ago Jack, didn't you get the hint? I don't want this; I just want to find out who killed Davis."

"A month! Jesus' kid, what drugs did they give you? That was a week ago! The funeral was yesterday. How drunk did you get?"

Sam sat up on the edge of his bed. "What are you talking about?"

"Also, most people say thank you when someone gives them a nice gift. Jackass."

Sam was bewildered. How vivid was his dream? "But, I.. didn't.." Sam stumbled with his words. It was early, he was fuzzy at best. He tried to collect himself before he responded again. "Yeah, is that your actual car? Or a just the same model?"

Jack laughed again "Mine is long gone. I had this one made a while back, figured I might need it down the road, you know?" His alluding to something bigger continued. He had the same delivery at the hospital. Sam was right back to trying to figure out what Jack knew. "Well, I appreciate it"

"Hurry up and get dressed. Theres an address on the card, be there in twenty minutes" Jack had cut Sam off mid-sentence. The call dropped, Jack was gone. *Fuck me sideways* he thought. Whatever that meant.

The address on the card didn't register on Sam's phone. *666 Dickenson Way*. The streets were mostly numbers and few random names. Sam sat in his driveway while the car warmed up. His brain was a fog; it was misfiring at every attempt he made to feel normal. This address wasn't even real. He would need a map, the kind he saw in old cars when he was a kid. "The glove box!"

Act III

Sure enough, an old map fell onto the seat. This was perfect. A map from the eighties showed a much different version of the city he knew today. He searched and searched until finally, right in the heart of downtown, as a small stretch between two high end neighborhoods, Dickenson Way. It looked like a street everyone forgot about. Maybe it didn't even exist anymore. *They're fucking with me. I'm going to have to drive through a magical brick wall, aren't I?* The pain medication was still fucking with Sam, clearly.

The snow had started just before Sam made it to the bridges. Traffic was light at this time of day. The drive was quicker than he expected, and smoother, who knew this old beast could still go. He crossed the water and turned down a street that was nothing but skyscrapers, billboards, restaurants and tourists (usually). At five thirty in the morning, it was just workers and steam from the sewers, mixed with the falling snow. Three blocks up, he passed Giovantas Steak house, *the* steakhouse in the city. He had never been but heard the stories. According to the map, it was a right turn at that corner. This took him between two buildings that completely blocked the sunlight. Just a dark alley with Streetlamps. A broken-down hotel sign hung above the street, just below it, the building number matched the address, so Sam pulled over to the side of the road. *I'm Here* he texted the random number from earlier.

"Room 7" showed up on his screen.

Sam tucked his gun into his holster under his arm. This place had ambush written all over it. And he was alone.

The sign and the streetlamp were the only things illuminating the front door. The hallway behind the door was dark. No footprints on the sidewalk, that Sam could see, and no signs of anything else. He pushed the heavy door open. It came with an eerie creak, as it should. The hallway was damp,

Act III

in smell and feel. A lightbulb, barely hanging on, dimly lit the end of the hall. Sam noticed the room numbers, written on sticky notes and placed on the doors. His heart pounded out of his chest. The pressure in his ears intensified, the more blood pumped into them, he tried to control his breathing, it didn't work. He pulled out his gun and put his back against the wall. He passed room six and slowly drug himself along the wall. No sound coming from Room seven, not even a light under the door. He stood next to the door; his ear pressed for any sounds. Nothing, this was a set up, he was screwed. Sam felt the surge of adrenaline; it shocked him how powerful it felt. He stepped across the hall and launched himself toward the door, his right foot connected, and the door flew off its hinges. Splinters, door hardware, dust, a mouse, all went flying as Sam crashed into the room. He dropped to one knee and aimed into the dark. The room was empty.
What the hell is happening?

Suddenly, voices came from the hallway "What the fuck is going on?" Sam readied himself in the dark. He aimed at the doorway as the footsteps got closer. He couldn't get a good view through the dust cloud, he squinted as best he could "Police" Sam yelled. A dark figure reached into the room. *Click.* The light turned on. Bill Taylor stood there staring at Sam "Yeah, no shit, so are we Cole. The fuck are you doing in here? We are in room nine"

"We? What are you doing here Chief?" asked Sam. He came to meet Jack, not the guy Jack hated. "Not everything is at it seems Cole. Follow me"

Before Sam knew it he was walking through another door. The room was well lit, tables and chairs, couches. A full wall of

Act III

newspaper clippings and a story board of every criminal in the city. Crime bosses, captains, corrupt city officials. Anything and everything. Just to the right sat Jack Finn. "Did I say seven? Yeah, I meant Nine. My mistake" he laughed to himself. He thoroughly enjoyed fucking with Sam.

Sam stood in amazement, and confusion. "What is all of this?" he asked. "In due time Kid." Replied Jack "This man to my right is Elliot Draven" sat at the table beside Jack was a tall, bearded man in a very expensive looking suit. He was thinner than Jack, but it seemed to be from a healthier lifestyle, or stress.

"He's our financial partner, accountant and main source of our funding" explained Bill. Elliot stood and shook Sam's hand "Lovely to meet you finally, Mr. Cole. I have heard a lot about your abilities"

Dumbfounded. That's the face Sam displayed. He looked at jack, who wore a mischievous grin, more so than ever. He stood up as well. Picked up his drink and took a sip. "I can see from your dumb face that maybe…just maybe.. you would want an explanation for all of this? Well, that's easy." Jack leaned on the table and propped his foot on a chair. "Turns out, some of that little story I told you, may….have not been completely accurate?"   Bill Taylor laughed, "For the love of, what did you tell this poor boy?"

Jack continued "Most of it was true. But I may have painted a few people in different lights. Such as yourself Billy boy. I may have enhanced our hatred of one another. And I may have shown old Oscar as more of a good guy and not the spineless snake he really was."

"That's all?" asked Taylor. "Well, no. I changed the ending slightly, but I did end up telling our boy here the truth. Only

241

Act III

because his partner got blown to pieces, so it didn't matter anyway"

"That's great, it was a nice story, lots of colorful anecdotes and twists. But could you kindly tell me what the fuck is this?" Sam was beyond confused.

"Eumenides, my dear boy" said Taylor, in a softer voice. A new voice Sam hadn't heard from his boss. "The goddess of vengeance. The four of us took on this moniker to try and protect the city from the underworld." Bill stood facing the wall of pictures and theories. He turned to Sam, with his hands clasped behind him, like a professor. "Not the underworld they show you on television, Sam. That is merely the tip of the iceberg. All this talk about a city ridden of organized crime, a city that only smiles, it's always sunny. Nothing bad ever happens. It's all smoke and mirrors. Propaganda portrayed through the media. Puppet strings from above." Bill turned to observe Sam's response. "Did you say four?" he asked.

"Yes. There is a fourth. Someone you may have heard of."

Footsteps from the other room, a door creaked open and in walked an older man, slicked back hair, medium build, taller than most. He stood next to Jack and smiled at Sam "I hear you've been asking the right questions, young man."

Sam tried to place this man. He couldn't find a home in his brain, dead ends. "Who is he?"

The new entrant took a step forward and extended his hand, it was heavily tattooed, and a fair number of rings. "Nicholas, Nicholas De Luca, it's great to finally meet you Sam"

The room broke into laughter behind Sam; he was shaking hands with a ghost. A serial killer ghost.

"What?" was all Sam could get out. This was a joke, right?

Act III

"You're a serial killer? How is this even happening?"

"Hey now, I did was had to be done. These guys weren't going to do anything" Nicky motioned to the others. "My family did horrible things. I did horrible things. I just couldn't continue that way, so I made it right. The only way I knew how. I couldn't just call the cops and have everyone arrested. I'd go down too. I had to eliminate them. One by one." Nicky's eyes glinted slightly, almost as if they changed color. There was hate and rage behind them. It was terrifying.

Jack handed Sam a drink, "sit down, we'll explain"

"Can it be the truth this time?"

"I mean, that story was mostly true, to my recollection"

Bill half smiled "Alcohol may have killed a few memories for Jack"

The four men sat around the table in the middle of the room. They began to explain how Jack and Bill were secretly working against Oscar. They had their suspicions about Oscars ties to another group, but they couldn't prove it. Freeman was aligned with Angie, Nicky confirmed it.

"Alright, wait. Let me say this out loud so it makes sense. You two don't hate each other (Jack and Bill)?"

"I mean a little, but not as much as that story led you too believe" added Jack.

"Ok, and you were working together against Freeman? And somehow Nicky was involved?"

Jack took another drink. "Yeah, you see, when I saw it was Nicky who killed the old man, we stood there and made a deal. He would disappear and I wouldn't say shit to anyone. And

Act III

that's the way it's been for thirty years. The only people who know are in this room."

"Well, how did you find out Bill?"

Bill was in the middle of a cigar. "I knew fifteen minutes after it happened. Jack didn't even have to say it. But we couldn't do anything. "

"Yeah, you three keep saying you couldn't do anything, or that's just how it went. That sounds like bullshit to me" Sam could sense there was something else at play. Nicky obliged the youth of the room "My father was tied to another group. The ones we believe were actually running the city. The so-called Black Flame Order. I tried to explain it that day to Jack. It was bigger than all of us."

Jack interjected "So we have spent the last three decades trying to keep them from turning this city into the cesspool I told you about. Nicky started the crusade against the corruption; he did more in those few months than any of us could have in years. He's a hero in my eyes."

Sam turned to Bill again, "why didn't you arrest him? He's a serial Killer?"

The other three laughed. "Cause he's dead (points to Nicky) and he's dead (points to Jack) and he's dead (point to Elliot). This group doesn't exist. This building doesn't exist. Everything is completely off the grid. We are the faceless entity fighting for the good in this city, against an enemy that we don't even have real proof exists. Until now."

"Three decades?"

"Yeah, mostly off the book's investigations. Which is all funded by Elliot. Also, Elliot died in the shoot out with Jack and his life insurance payout was huge and his police pension

Act III

was the best of the group. He invested under an alias and made millions. He is the money behind all of this."

"He's dead?"

Another group laugh. Elliot finally spoke up "Bill and Jack had started planning this long before, I was the numbers guy, so we put me in harms way "air quotes" and fudged a few documents and paid a few people off. Certified dead."

Bill drug the conversation back on track "We chase the lead's that seem too farfetched, the dead ends, the obvious losers. They usually lead somewhere good. And we deal with it on our own. No protocol, no rules. Sam was in disbelief "Bill you're the Chief of Police. How does this even happen?"

"I am now. Oscar was blind to our whole operation. We knew he was tied to Angie, and after his death, Oscar seemed to mellow out, but there was always something off. His decisions just seemed to be coming from somewhere else"

"Ok. Let me get this straight then. Thirty years, right, and you are just now getting to the black flame order? What else have you guys been doing?"

"Piss off kid" Jack was awake "This was all done secretly. We meet here when we have something to meet about. We have taken down other crime families that no one even knew about. We shut down corruption and greed. We all know where it leads back to, we just needed proof. It's been a long, long haul. Which is why you are here, kid. Cause I am fucking old and tired."

Sam tried to take it all in. That feeling he had, the one that ate at him. It was this. There were real secrets this city held, and he was finally getting close to them. "Wait, how did you guys get in the building? Theres no cars out there?"

Act III

"Secret underground parking. We will show you" said Jack, pouring another glass. "You mean like a secret liar? Kind of like a cave?" asked Sam with an air of sarcasm.

"Shut the fuck up"

"It's literally a parking garage. Elliot's alter ego owns the building. We are the only tenant." Jack regretted his choice, slightly.

Bill cut through the bullshit, "Look, if you're in, then we can get to the main point of this."

Sam didn't hesitate "I'm assuming from all the information you just gave me, That I have to be in or I'm likely not walking out of here?" Elliot chimed in "Smart kid".

"Yeah, pretty much. You're Jack's retirement plan."

"I thought Jack was just a myth that lived in his bathrobe, yelling at clouds? How can he retire?"

Asked Sam. Bill leaned back, he looked at Jack "Kid, what car did you drive here?"

"Monte Carlo, the one Jack gave me, ……oh, I get it."

"This isn't undercover. This is hiding in plain sight. Invisible. That car struck fear in the underworld for years. It's your turn now"

Sam nodded. "I'm ready"

I think. Thought Sam. What was he ready for? They still hadn't really explained what this group was or stood for. We fight crime?

Sam's hands trembled. "I'm…I'm lost. Bill, you said this is called Eumenides. The goddess of Vengeance. So, what exactly am I doing in this situation? Am I just Sam Cole,

Act III

Detective slash underground vigilante for justice?" Sam's face took on a childlike wonder " Did Jack have a cool nickname?"

Jack watched from his chair. He side eyed Nicky. They were both grinning at this point. "Please tell me it was something like Jack the ripper. Dr. Jekyll Mr. Finn. Please."

"We called Nicky, the Butcher," said Jack. He looked over at his old friend. "Maybe a few guys ended up chopped to bits." Nicky laughed to as he leaned back to blow cigar smoke, "Yeah, just a few" the smirk from Nicky gave it all away. They were ruthless.

Bill walked over to Sam with a newspaper in his hand. It was old. The headline was nothing, local sports team does good. Bill pointed to the bottom corner. An article piece. *The Bay City Executioner. The man and the myth.* "The Bay City Executioner" mumbled Sam under his breath.

"Civil unrest encompasses the hollow blackened corners of our blood-stained city.

> *The criminal underworld that our corrupt government claims to not exist, has reared its ugly head once again. The local authorities, the news outlets, anyone with a voice, will claim everything you hear is nonsense and to continue the status quo. Well, this journalist has witnessed firsthand the power struggle beyond the camera lens of our nightly news. The one below the streets, the one that is only referred to in whispers. The rats serve their overlords, the ones whose faces you regularly see, but there's one force working in the opposite direction. The only one working toward cleaning up this mess we call a city. Referred to in circles as the black mass and feared among the streets as the Bay City Executioner. Will this shadow ever be revealed? Or will they be overrun like the rest?*
>
> *Time will tell."*

Act III

The Hounds of Hell

Sam finished reading the article. He was intrigued by the notion of a secret society existing in plain sight. The criminals co-existing with the civilians but working in two different worlds. Ships passing in the night as they say. All being controlled by one unknown entity. Sam being handed the task of taking down this group was no small gesture.

Sam's whole world had spun out of control. From the day he stepped into the role of detective, finding out about a serial killer he had never heard of, and now learning of a secret society that rivals something that only an expert fiction writer could come up with. Myth and legend, all coming true right before his eyes. "I had these feelings, when I worked on cases, certain things wouldn't add up. There was always something more, but I could never place it."

"That's our world, kid. All that shit that people can't explain." Said Jack, "When you showed up at my door and wouldn't back down. I knew we had something to work with. We just needed a bit of time to figure all of that out."

Act III

"Well, I'm right here. Just tell me when and where." Replied Sam as he waited for the rundown of his new role. The room went quiet. Bill stood there, arms crossed, pondering to himself. "I think you're overlooking something here Cole." Bill pointed at Jack "Dead." He pointed at Nicky "Dead", and he pointed at Elliot "Super dead".

The realization that he was about to be wiped off the map didn't phase Sam. His nervous system had since shut down; he was now numb to it. That cold stare was making its way back to his eyes. The steely stare he was known for. The similarities to his predecessor checked all the boxes. Sam laid his hand on the table; he squeezed his fist into a ball. "Alright, enough fucking around. Show me what I need to see. Tell me What I need to know. Stop beating around the fucking bush."

"There he is....about fucking time Sammy" grinned Jack. All four men stood, almost in unison. "Follow us then".

Sam felt slightly confused. The room they were in felt like a true war room. Whiteboards filled with notes and diagrams, theories, tips, leads, everything they needed. They left and carried on down the hall, everything was dimly lit with old hanging bulbs. Sam didn't dare ask why they hadn't renovated or put any money into this place at all. The sounds of water running in the distance caught Sam's ear. It seemed very odd. They seemed to be walking downhill even though the hallway hadn't changed. The lights above barely illuminated the damp concrete block walls.

Finally, a large door at the end of the darkness. A quick wave of the hand from Bill and the door cracked open, he dropped a shoulder into it to help it along. Sam entered the real war room. His entire definition of the term immediately changed. The ceilings didn't seem to exist, they were so high. It was clearly a parking garage converted to into some

Act III

underground bunker. Three cars parked off to the right. A few offices to the left. A giant round table with an evil-looking light hanging above it, a war room.

Sam looked around "Ah, that explains the parking." They walked into the first office, the words "Black Flame Order" written across the top of the whiteboard. Sam looked at the faces taped below. "Motherfucker" was all he could get out.

Michael Grey – Mayor

Carson Hill – District Attorney

Oliver Reeves – Chief Justice

Charlie Banks – City Financial Director

John Oak – Housing Authority

Rory Mann – Infrastructure & Developments

~~Oscar Freeman~~ – Police Chief

Bill Taylor took his seat behind a large wood desk. "That's it. Right there. For the last thirtysome years. The names change, the titles change, but they all swear in to that society.

"We started to grow suspicious of Oscar, like we said, he just wasn't himself. So, of course, we followed him. That led us to Angie, which led us to the mayor (Arthur Frost)"

"I thought he was in the dark? Jack said he was new to that life"

"Nope, that was probably a slightly hazy version you heard. Too many knocks to the head, right Jackie?"

Act III

"Eat a dick Bill. A giant bag of dicks"

"Sometimes you say sweet things to me. It warms my heart. Anyway, kid, we have books, notes and leads on this, as far as the eye can see. It took us awhile to put it all together, to figure out who was pulling the strings. The Mayor has the final say, everyone else has their sections. They meet when they have to. Everything is in code. It's taken us decades to break it all down. Angie was allowed to be who he was because they said he could be. That's real power. And now we finally have the break we have worked for."

"Yeah? What finally did it?"

"Jack threw out a hunch that if the old crimson Mask killer resurfaced, that maybe, just maybe, it would shake everyone up enough for someone to make a mistake."

"What was the mistake?"

"There wasn't one. We knew that Freeman was connected. But we also knew that he was starting to lose it. He was the weak link of the group. He couldn't keep his mouth shut. He had also grown tired of the life and the secrets. Thirty years is a lot of secrets my friend."

"What did Freeman do to tip you guys off?"

Bill reached into his desk and grabbed a folder. He laid it in front of Sam. Pictures of Oscar Freeman and Angie De Luca. Shaking hands, making deals. Handing off cash and drugs. More pictures of Freeman with everyone on that list.

"Who gave these to you?" asked Sam as he sifted through the pile.

"Oscar did." Said Jack from the corner. "He had them in safe with instructions for them to be sent if he got murdered."

Act III

"He wanted out. He needed out."

"I still don't quite follow"

"We killed Vic. We set it up as a copycat from the Crimson Mask. That's where you landed on our radar. Turns out it worked too well. Oscar took the heat before he could spill everything. He didn't want to go through that again, not at his age. So, they made him disappear. But good old Oscar had a back up plan. And these landed in my hands the next day." Sam took it all in, "Why were you such an asshole then? Why not just tell me?" Bill's face strained sarcastically. "Because

I'm an asshole, Sam. This shouldn't come as a surprise. Jack knows it, Elliot definitely knows it, and I wasn't giving anything away until we knew you were the guy." Sam understood, it made sense now. "This is a secret society of our most wealthy and powerful, running our city. And we

are the only ones who know, and the only ones who can do anything about it. They killed Oscar to keep their secrets."

"You guys killed Victor De Luca… to draw out this society?" Sam stood, arms crossed, memorizing the names on the board. "And they bit on it?"

"It was a long shot, but we are getting old, and this shit needs to end. Our city deserves it. These people need something to cheer for. They think organized crime is gone, but they are just being manipulated to believe they are safe from harm. While these assholes puppet everything from behind closed doors."

Sam's face wasn't doing a great job of hiding his uneasiness about the whole situation. He verbalized a desire to jump right in and learn everything but the reveal of who they were hunting hit him like a ton of bricks. This isn't just some small-time group of nobodies. This is the top of the food chain, kill or be killed.

Act III

"Let's take a ride kid, follow me" said jack, walking out the door. Sam quickly followed. "Where are we going?" he asked. "For a ride. Are you deaf?" Jack walked across the large parking garage to the four cars parked at the foot of a long ramp. Two black SUV's, one black Mercedes and one 1976 Dodge Challenger. Jet Black. Jack jumped into the challenger; Sam was in awe of that car. "The Black Ghost, they call it on the streets"

"This thing is incredible. It's no monty, but it's pretty nice."

Jack scoffed at the comment "Not on your best fucking day could you even come close in that thing. That's why I gave it to you. It's a hand-me-down. I upgraded."

"Monty would..."

"Stop calling your car Monty, for fuck sakes. You sound ridiculous."

Jack fired up and peeled up the ramp. At the top, a large garage door started to open, the snow falling was all they could see. Jack stepped on the gas and cut the wheel as they flew into the street sideways. Sam held on for his life. "Doesn't this thing have seatbelts?" he asked as he tried to keep himself inside the car. "Fuck no, it doesn't have airbags either. You're dead no matter what." Jack laughed hysterically as snow flew onto the sidewalks. He finally straightened the car out about a block down the street. Sam settled down a little, but not before swallowing hard to keep his stomach contents in place.

"You all good with this kid? You seemed up for it, but now you seem a little cold. Maybe it's too much? We need to know now, cause we gotta get one of those mind erasing sticks from that alien movie, we can't have you running your mouth about everything you saw today" Sam was very unsure about the seriousness of Jack. And mental stability.

Act III

"I think it would help if I really knew what you guys actually do?"

"What do you mean? We told you. We fucking kick everyone's ass until we find the real connection to the Black Fame. Once we can connect all those dots, we take them down. Pretty straightforward, I Think. Now… We do have to chase every whack job lead, which can take us down some fucked up paths on some fucked up adventures, don't get me wrong. This isn't exactly what I call a fancy day job. It's a lifestyle now. You're dead. You're now the bringer of darkness. A whisper, A cold shiver down the spines of criminals, A shadow that looms over the greed and corruption that this city has hidden. That same Greed and corruption that Nicky tried to eliminate all those years ago. He's a great guy to pick his brain about who you should be murdering and why."

Sam listened intently. He was almost calm now. The more Jack raved on, the more comfortable Sam became in some twisted way.

"How did you get the name? The Executioner?"

"That was the press. Once those articles started coming out, it just snowballed. I didn't go around…telling everyone to call me the Bay City Executioner. It was a headline grab back then." Jack poured out his speech with so much confidence that it gave Sam chills. Maybe Jack really was dead, at least on the inside.

"But now you're retiring? How come?" asked Sam, settling in.

"It's a lot kid, you know. I've been dead for decades, chasing this idea we had and trying to bring it all to light. And with us being so close, I felt it was time to bring in some fresh legs to get us to the finish line. I'm not going anywhere, just yet, I

Act III

gotta show you the ropes, and kill those Black Flame fucks. Then I'll retire."

Sam loosened his grip on the door handle as they slowed to a stop in front of another old building. Townhouse style. All brick façades. The street was lined with them. Sam searched the landscape for something he recognized. The falling snow made it more difficult to get his bearings after having his eyes closed for most of the ride. "What's this?" asked Sam. Jack was already halfway out the door. "Jack? Who lives here?" Jack kicked the snow as he landed on the sidewalk, two steps later he was through the big wooden door, a large gargoyle sat on the concrete step. Sam rushed to catch up, he felt almost childish around Jack.

"Do I need my gun?" asked Sam as he pushed the door open. "You always need your gun, idiot." Came the voice from the darkened hallway. Sam closed the door and pulled out his gun "Right" he mumbled as he tried to fumble his way down the hallway. A light finally turned on half down, Sam could see Jack turn into a room and motion for him to follow. He made his way down and quickly ducked into the room. The next thing Sam could remember was the cold concrete floor against his face and a ringing in his ears. His consciousness was returning, as was the pain in his jaw. He could taste iron. The familiar sting of blood in his mouth.

"What the fuck is wrong with you kid? Where is he?"

Sam could sense someone standing over him.

"Where is he?" "Where is that cold blooded, no bull shit, borderline psychopath that we plucked to be the next one?"

Sam tried to gather his thoughts, but the blood was pouring from his mouth. Did someone hurl a brick at him? "You beat a man half to death, for some inside information about a few

Act III

petty thefts. They all pegged you as calm, cool and collected but we knew better. And now! You're asking if you need a gun? Is it your first day!? Jesus Cole, get it together. You'll be dead in a week with this attitude. Go the fuck home, figure your shit out. The only article anyone's going to write about you is your fucking obituary.

Act III

Welcome to the Family

An old white mail truck stumbled its way down a back road. The trees sat heavy with snow cover, drooping branches hovered over the road. A red mailbox stuck out from one of the trees beside an unplowed driveway. This led To Sam Cole's home. The box was full. No footsteps had tarnished the clean blanket of snow left from multiple storms. A dead man once lived there.

Weeks rolled on, Holidays passed. More cold, more snow. A new year began. The spotlight faded on the resurgence of a nightmare. The folk tales of thirty years ago began to disappear, gone with the cold wind. The city began to glow again; the streets filled with life and laughter. The pain and anguish shoved down deep where it belonged. Everyone was moving on.

"How's life as the chief?"

Chief Taylor, looked up from his phone. The new version of the morning paper. He gave a little chuckle and took a sip of coffee "It's been everything I've always wanted. I am living the dream"

"The dream? So, all this shit is your fucking fault? This shit is a nightmare"

"C'mon Jackie, It's not that bad."

Jack Finn placed his fork on his now empty plate. The quiet months had been kind to his health. Less stress, less headaches.

Act III

Meeting Bill was his only connection to the outside world. The leads they had were growing as cold as the nights. "You know…I really thought we had it. I really thought that plan would work. But what do I know Bill! I'm just a crazy old man living in my bathrobe."

"Thank you, for not wearing that, by the way."

"I wanted to, so bad"

The sound of coffee being poured into their empty cups brought them back to reality. Both men acknowledged the top up. Jack eagerly poked and prodded at Bill. "So…anything?" Bill lifted one eye from his phone. "Nothing, not a peep. Not a subtle mention. Not a step out of place."

Jacks face gave him away, he still couldn't believe how far away they were. "They knew we were looking. They planted a fucking…"

Bill quickly interrupted. "Shut it. Shut your mouth. Crazy old man. This isn't the place." His hushed voice had some gravel behind it. Even he didn't trust that someone wasn't listening.

    The two men finished their coffees and went their separate ways. They only met sporadically now; the leads they were chasing were gone. Square one had come again, only this time, their first-round draft pick had gone missing.

    City hall was crawling that morning. The announcement of a new budget, whispers of tax cuts, help for the helpless, voices for the voiceless. All these ideas had wound the good people into a small frenzy. The good kind, not the gunfights with the police kind.

City Hall – 9:43am

Act III

Beloved Mayor Michael Grey shuffled a stack of papers on his desk and slid them into a folder. That folder fit perfectly in his laptop bag. He hung the bag over his shoulder as he made his way downstairs. A hum of electricity filled the air; the crowds below were growing by the minute as everyone awaited the new budget announcement and what some were calling a new life for the people of Crimson Bay. The grapevine spoke of funding for schools, Hospitals, large donations and help for public housing, which was greatly needed. An easy win for a political figure. Building for the future and saving lives.

Live streams and cable outlets flooded the city with the breaking news. The mayor stood in front of a room of journalists and fellow politicians and all the members of the board. Every name from the whiteboard sat present in the room as well.

The speech he gave that morning set in motion a domino effect so well planned out that no one realized what they were even cheering for. He spoke of millions being pushed through education, medical, housing, infrastructure, even the district attorney's office was getting a piece.

The room erupted with cheers; elation flooded through the streets as everyone soaked in the new day for the city. The darkness had passed and the light at the end of the tunnel was shining. Unbeknownst to everyone…That light was a freight train.

Crimson Bay Waterfront – 11:03 am

Act III

John Oak, a larger-than-life gentleman to say the least. He was adorned in a long expensive coat, slicked back dark hair, a three, maybe four-piece suit. How many pieces can suits even have? Gold rings, chains and a cigar was always nearby. His old white Cadillac sat parked outside the main entrance to Ocean towers. One of the biggest office buildings in the Crimson Bay Skyline.

The housing office occupied three floors. Yes, he was aware the image of the public housing office being in a fancy high rise pervaded. He did not care, one bit. The grin on John's face told the whole story. His best buddy, the mayor, had signed over truck loads of money to his organization. John was a master of the loophole. A real knight in shining armor to most, and a slimy scumbag to a few others. He walked through the front lobby and took the elevator up to his floor. A long corridor, a few turns later, he entered the large glass corner office that overlooked the water. His briefcase hit the desk and popped open; he quickly filled it with yellow folders and snapped it shut. John waved goodbye to his team "See you next week"

"Have fun on your trip"

"Enjoy the beach!"

(insert generic vacation wishes from staff members who secretly hate you)

Packing up and leaving was the theme of the day. All city officials had been summoned to a retreat north of the bright lights, beyond the trees, to an old farmhouse-style resort full of log cabins and sleighrides. Very picturesque indeed. It was a yearly tradition after the budgets were released, to take a group trip and prepare for the year. Among those packing up, Bill Taylor.

Act III

He neglected to mention anything to Jack that morning. He needed to see all of this up close with no outside noise in his head. *Is this where they all meet? Is this where the Black Flame Order makes their deals?* Jack would have crashed the party. Too much of a distraction. But Nicky De Luca, a master of being invisible. Was the perfect candidate for some spy work.

The plan was using Bill as the pawn. He would go along with whatever was presented to him, all while being wired. Everyone knew that if he got the invitation to the real party, that they would check for bugs. Nicky devised a recording device that was actually a button on Bills shirt. It recorded audio and video. The washroom jokes were made early to get them out of the way.

Bill followed the convoy upstate. Nicky was already there hiding, even Bill was unaware of his whereabouts, for safety.

The main hall of the resort resembled every hallmark movie ever made. Perfectly decorated in the small-town winter wonderland theme. There was an hour long social before the meal, a meet and greet that Bill despised. A large sign hung above welcoming everyone to the retreat. Familiar

faces blurred together as Bill made his way through the crowd. He tried his best to keep his chest up, for recording reasons.

All the main characters were present. Mayor Grey floated from group to group, shaking hands and fake laughing. Close behind was the DA Carson Hill, the Mayors right hand who took up residence in Mr. Grey's back pocket. Bill caught the stare of Justice Reeves, someone Bill had many dealings with, on and off the record. The hatred was built in already. Two steadfast, stubborn, bull in a China shop types.

Oliver Reeves made the first move "Bill, welcome aboard." He extended a hand, which Bill politely shook. "A shame it's

Act III

under these circumstances, but it was going to be yours someday either way"

"Thanks Oliver. I still hate you"

Oliver grinned "Oh, most people in here hate me. I get nervous when someone doesn't."

They shared a laugh and moved on. Neither one really wanted to continue the façade. The social wound down into the meal, followed by speeches and political bullshit that everyone thoroughly enjoyed (they didn't).

    Bill became more and more frustrated with how normal everything seemed. This might have been a waste of time. He spent the remainder of the night trying to slide into conversations and pick up as much dirt as possible, but to his disappointment, there was none. He retired to his

cabin through the snow, slightly intoxicated, which was the only enjoyment he got from the whole thing.

Bill's phone vibrating by his head, woke him early. The dark still covered the grounds. "How did it look?" he asked. "This was probably a waste my friend" came through the phone. Nicky was camping out in an auxiliary building on the grounds. The rich mobster kid (adult child) wasn't fazed by uncomfortable surroundings. What's the plan for the morning?" he asked.

"I'm grabbing coffee and food and then I am out of here."

"It looks like your compadres are also heading for the highways. Half of them have packed and left"

Bill checked the time, it was only 6:30 in the morning, why was everyone leaving so fast? It seemed strange to him.

Act III

"Well, I'll be out of here soon, follow me back and we can meet up"

"10-4"

A light snowfall had started as Bill cleared the forest and made for the main road. He followed a few other vehicles in a small pack and listened to the radio. His phone buzzed in the cup holder, it was a text from the mayor offer his appreciation for Bill's attendance. This perked Bill's ears. He sent a text to Nicky *"Keep close"*.

Bill's gut knew there was something else behind this random string of words on his screen. He was right.

"Little breakfast meeting with a few of the board members. Meet us at 214 Lagan Lane. Last house on the left."

"Just got the invite, here we go"

"Are you carrying?"

"No, they'll check for it. No need to ring any alarms just yet"

Bill punched in the directions and followed the GPS. A quick 10-minute drive through a few small communities led him to a heavily tree lined drive. The trees towered over the road and one gate at the end on the left. Longmore Estate, read the wooden sign mounted on the gate pillar. Bill pulled up to the gate and reached for the red button on the intercom, the gates opened before he could make contact. They're watching.

    A long-paved driveway carved between the pines; it was almost haunting in its beauty. The driveway dropped down a hill that overlooked the hundred-year-old estate home. The asphalt seemed darker than usual in contrast to the snow. The light snowfall was struggling to make its way through the forest. Bill approached slowly and took his place behind the handful of other cars in the courtyard. He surveyed his

Act III

surroundings for anything suspicious. He took a deep breath and tried to remember that he was the Chief of Police. That thought filled him back up with the confidence and arrogance he was known for. His tiny hidden earpiece slid in nicely. He tested it, Nicky came in loud and clear.

"Alright, sit tight, this could be a shitshow"

"I have eyes on the entrance; I'll pop in if anyone else shows up. Other than that, I'll keep the interference to a minimum."

Bill opened his door "Nick, if this ends up being what we think it is. Can I trust you won't go full cowboy and make an absolute mess" The silence in his ear gave the full answer, which he expected anyway.

The door to the courtyard swung open, Big John Oak welcomed Bill "This way Chief, there's coffee and food in the kitchen" Bill shook hands with all the names he was hunting. A surreal moment. The objects of their pursuit, for so many years, sitting in front of him, eating eggs and bacon. "The long arm of the law. Finally come to visit. Please Bill, take a seat and enjoy yourself. We are merely chatting about the future, one with our newest seat holder, you." The mayor had turned on his best politician's voice. Rehearsed and dripping with condescension.

The kitchen led to a long table in a dining hall. Bill took the remaining seat, observing the pictures on the walls. All of them seemed to be of a type of bird.

Bill knew this was the first real meeting of the new board of directors for the city. He felt a small sense of accomplishment, which was quickly diminished by a focused anger. Michael Grey

Act III

sat at the head of the table, "Everyone, let's welcome Chief Taylor to our ranks. A long-standing member of our beloved police force, a fine gentleman, a known asshole, and our newest member of the board." They all raised their cups and gave an honor to Bill. He nodded in respect.

"Gentleman, as you all know, we are beginning a new year and a new regime. Out with the old and in with the new, or in this case, the less old." They all laughed. "We have a lot to look

forward to this year, and a lot of thanks to be had for us getting through the year. We lost friends and loved ones. We buried more people than we ever have. I for one have grown tired of the continuing violence we endure daily. Most of us fear for our lives every time we step out of our vehicles, Christ, even sometimes when we are in the fucking things." Laughter erupted throughout the room. Bill surveyed the table, everyone was here, as expected. This was the meeting. He could feel it. "Now as all of you know, we have lost a key member of our team, the great Oscar Freeman. A man that stood in our ranks for decades. He served all the previous orders, all the way back to the beginning."

Bill's ears perked up *Orders?*. He didn't dare show any reactions. He was sure now. They didn't even search him coming through the door. He could have unloaded on all of them and ended this, mind you he wouldn't have any answers, just a room of bodies, but maybe that was all the city needed.

"Oscar will be missed; he was a crucial cog in this wheel of justice. We welcome Bill Taylor as his replacement. I am sure he will meet and surpass Oscars lofty standards."

Bill's earpiece lit up his brain "We've got company. Three black SUV's." Chief Taylor smiled and raised his coffee cup, "I

Act III

intend on taking this role to new heights, such as my predecessor did in his prime"

Bill kept a sharp eye on all of the movements in the room. Nothing was stirring, just yet.

"You've got six suits, all big, all mean."

Sweat started to appear just below Bills hairline. Nothing noticeable, just the response of a rapid heartrate and increased body temperature.

The creak of a door opening and the clamoring of bodies entering the kitchen behind him caught a few eyes, but he pushed forward. "You have my full allegiance; you will all be held in esteem amongst our ranks. Consider yourselves the untouchables of our society" The group clapped in approval; Bill was winning them over.

The mayor stood to address the room "Ah, yes, our security team has arrived. Bill, these men are the reason we are who we are. They are highly skilled, highly trained mercenaries who do our bidding. They are ghosts to society. Your label of untouchable only meshes with our ability to be untouchable, thanks to this team."

Bill had no choice but to go along with everything presented to him. "Well, that makes my job even easier" he joked. A large hand grabbed his shoulder and pinned him to his chair. Another hand did the same on the opposite side. "Now, sit tight Chief Taylor. You are in for quite a show.

There's a lot more to our little city than meets the eye. Young Oscar was the only one privy to this information you are about to receive. He took it to his grave and thus you shall as well."

Bill faked his confusion, but only slightly. His anticipation was boiling into a panic attack. This was broken

Act III

up by the site of two men passing the table, enter a back room and emerging with another chair. A larger chair, grey in color. Bill waited for the men to turn it around. It wasn't painted grey. It appeared to be manmade, cut from a rock face. They turned it around, A throne.

A fucking throne?!

Bills face turned to real confusion. He lurched forward and was immediately pulled back.

"Don't" was all he heard from above.

Nicky's voice rang in his ear "What is happening? Is that a throne. Is this some biblical shit?"

Mayor Grey pulled his chair to the side of the table, he kept upright. "Now, Bill, I will introduce to you, our legacy, Ms. Allison Frost."

Did he just say Frost? Was all Bill heard in his ear, as a taller blonde woman in a long fur coat, likely made from household pets, one would assume, emerged from the back room. Allison wore sharp features, cheek bones, piercing eyes, almost a greenish grey. A steely cold appearance, one that would give any blood sucking lawyer a run for their money.

"Officer Frost?" was all Bill could get out.

"Oh Bill, you bought into it all. Oscars pawn, making you do his bidding, making you be the asshole that we have all come to know. Well now it's your turn to sit at the table and enjoy the fruits of your labor." Allison placed both hands on the wooden table and stared Bill down. "I can tell by your face that you are...somewhat confused? Am I right in saying that?"

Bill nodded yes.

Act III

"Of course. What am I thinking. You know nothing about us, do you? Your little pal Jack kept this little secret from you for all these years. And he took a protégé under his wing, that feisty detective

Cole. Those two, well, I guess just one now" Allison laughed maniacally. Bill's eyes widened. This alerted Allison, she grinned as she paced the room. "Oh..you didn't know that either did you. Young Sam went rouge, as they say, and he found out the hard way that bodies don't bounce on concrete."

"But, back to your friend Mr. Finn. The thorn in our sides for many years now. Oscar could never deliver on his promises of eliminating him, that useless fuck. But you, Bill, will deliver. As you can see, just Like Oscar, you belong to us now. And there is only one door out, and it's made of wood, and they close it on top of you and lower you six feet down."

Bill didn't blink. His heart rate was alarmingly high. He barely had time to focus on Sam's death, while fearing is own. "Now, back to my little story. Jack didn't tell you about a little group of friends called the Black Flame Order, now did he?"

Bill shook his head no, sweat starting to drip down his forehead. "Why would he? He hates you; he wants all the glory for himself. Taking us down would be his final swan song." Allison returned to her throne. An image burned into Bill's brain. The maniacal queen, overseeing her staff. Allsion lowered her head as she continued to speak "My grandfather, Arthur Frost, sat in this seat many years ago. He organized this society for the betterment of Crimson Bay. The number of lives we have changed are unmeasurable. Our work is the only thing keeping this city from crumbling, and we will continue until our time comes to pass along this legacy."

She's a fucking lunatic! Said Nicky in Bill's ear.

Act III

She raised her head to the table, but her eyes remained on the floor. "Jack Finn is responsible for my grandfather's death." Her eyes rose up, a rage burned behind them. "He is responsible for my Father's death (we aren't sure if that's true). And I will be responsible for his."

Bill played along. He nodded and agreed to everything Allison lay in front of them. She detailed the pursuit of Jack as if it were something they were very close to achieving.

"We took care of the other one, the Davis character. He was easy to manipulate. I batted one eye, and he was gone"

They fucking killed the other kid! Sam's partner.

"Oscar was a call I didn't want to make but he was slipping out of our control"

They killed Oscar, too.

Bill tried to speak up "Oscar? That was you, that was us? I mean"

A smirk creased across Allisons face. Her eyes seemingly made of stone stared through the top of her eyelids. A menace. "They are all us William. Not a single move is made in this city that doesn't have our hand sign off on it."

Chills ran down Bill's spine. This was much larger than he had expected. An object caught his eye, he turned to see the orange glow of what seemed to be an iron, the room turned upside down and he found himself on the floor unable to move. His shirt was pulled down; a searing hot iron pressed into his chest. He screamed in agony; the white-hot pain surged through his chest. He succumbed to the pain and lost consciousness. It was official, he was in.

Act III

Winds of Change

Knocking, continuous noise, a constant pounding of fist on wood. "Jack, open the fucking door" Rain poured down on Nicky De Luca as he hid underneath a hooded cloak, more like a large trench coat. Dead men always move in disguise; the rain helps too. A voice from the other side of the door mumbled "Why do you always show up in the middle of the night?"

"Just open the fucking door, it's pouring out here." Nicky slid through the ever so slightly opened door and shook off his soaked raincoat. "This better be good" mumbled Jack, adorned in his best robe and slippers.

"We've got them. All of them on video." A barely awake Jack poured old coffee in his cup and popped it in the microwave. "Who? Did I miss something?"

"The Order! Bill is in, also he might be dead, or missing, but he did it. He got the invite; we saw it all"

The Microwave beeped. "Come again? He's dead? Maybe?"

"Probably not. We would have heard about it by now. You have to watch this. I can't even put into words what you are about to see" Nicky was almost giddy with excitement. This

Act III

made Jack uncomfortable. "Stop it. Whatever you're doing. Just don't"

"Piss off Jack. Where's your computer?" The two of them sat at jack's kitchen table and waited for the video to load. Nicky watched as Jack took in all the reveals. Everything they had assumed and believed was true. This group was behind it all.

"That little blonde bitch is running the show? Fuck her." Jacks surly review of the video meant that he overlooked a few key points.

"Did you hear what she said though?'

"Not really, she's just some young fucking kid who got here cause her of her family. I'm not letting some nepobaby tell me anything"

"Jack, first off, where did you learn that word?"

"I watch television, idiot."

Nicky couldn't deal with a hungover, half-awake Jack. This timing was truly a mistake on his part. He grew frustrated with Jack's lack of response to the deaths of their friends.

"So, nothing? Sam? Davis? Oscar? This group is behind it all. And many more. These are the people my father spoke of. And if they scared him, then I can only imagine what they are capable of. Those six men that came in at the end, they are terrifying humans."

Jack sat back in his chair, sipped on his gross reheated coffee, and just stared at the screen. "I don't know what to tell you Nick. I guess I really never cared for the kid, that's all"

"Good riddance I say, you know?" Jack's face was telling a different story. He was starting to realize the weight of the situation. His cold-blooded, murderous side was starting to

Act III

awaken. The death of Sam Cole was starting sink in. Jack was lying to himself, and Nicky knew it, but he played along.

"Right, yeah, he was just your retirement plan. I guess you're stuck with me instead, old pal."

"You know I hate you too?" replied Jack.

"I wouldn't want it any other way. Now let's go kill these motherfuckers"

"Fine, but let me get something to eat first, my stomach is growling at me, and you know how I get when I haven't eaten. All murdery and such." Jack's voice trailed off as he mumbled to himself about being hungry and murder. Nicky laughed and poured some gross coffee for himself.

"What a psycho".

As the sun broke on the day, the local garbage pickup started. House after house, the same thing, the truck pulled down another long tree lined street, gated driveways are all they could see. They approached an opening in the tree line; a set of tire tracks pushed through the snow and into a small

field. A black vehicle sat idle in the field, smoke emerging from the hood. The windows were fogged as if someone was still in the vehicle. The worker on the back of the truck yelled for them to stop. He ran through the wooded section into the clearing. The vehicle was still on. The windshield wipers seemed to be on too. The worker looked inside to see Bill Taylor slumped over the steering wheel. The man quickly opened the door, and the powerful smell of alcohol flooded his senses. Bill fell out of the vehicle into the snow. He had no shirt on and seemed to be unconscious.

"Hey! Dave, this guy's fucking dead!"

"Yeah? Check his wallet!"

Act III

The opportunistic garbage man searched Bill for his wallet. He looked back at his partner who had exited the truck and was walking over. "Nothing on him, he reeks of booze"

"Should we call it in? He's in bad shape" The two men looked at each other and shrugged. "Did you check for a pulse? Is he actually dead?" asked the driver.

The first on scene sanitation official felt for a pulse on Bill's wrist. "Yeah, I got nothing, Dave. Holy shit, I've never touched a dead guy before."

"Jesus, Tony. You just felt the top of his wrist. The pulse is underneath by the palm."

"Oh, ah, yeah, right. Let me just… Yeah ok, I feel something. Good, cause I didn't wanna touch no dead guy."

Dave shook his head "You're an idiot".

"What are we gonna do?" asked Tony.

"Easy, throw him in the back of the truck and come back for the car. Whoever he is, he's a waste"

click

The sound echoed off the trees on the still morning. Cold steel pressed into the back of Daves skull. "Wrong, fellas. It looks like you two are riding in the back of the truck" Dave made a quick turn and lunge but met the butt end of a gun, he went out. Tony didn't move. The gun turned on him.

"Pick him up" the man demanded. His voice was deep and muffled by the bandana covering the lower half of his face.

Tony just stood there. Terrified. His brain was frozen; he couldn't get it to tell his legs to move. Tears welled up in his eyes.

Act III

"Count of Three, Tony." Tony shook, but he still couldn't move. He was completely gripped with fear. A gun pointed at you for the first time will have that effect.

"Three". Two shots rang out through the forest. One for Tony. One for Dave.

The call came in early to the police department about gunshots upstate, a garbage truck on fire, and two trails of blood. Not a word about a car or a police chief. The first responders and onlookers described the scene as perplexing and strange. There seemed to be more activity than

what was in front of them. Tire tracks lead to nothing, blood-stained snow, bullet casings, a burnt-out garbage truck with two bodies inside. No one could make heads or tails of what they were looking at.

The old police radio in Jack's kitchen told the story. "You know they have updated versions of these?" Nicky nodded toward the dusty radio; he turned to gauge Jack's reaction. "Yeah… I know. Fuck off."

"Well, this changes things." Jack was starting to come around and his mind started spinning.

"Alright, I have questions. First, why didn't Bill tell me. Second, why didn't you tell me and three, why am I the last to know about these assholes. These assholes, (Jack stood up) who killed our friends. They killed Sam. They killed little baby Davis; he was just a boy. They killed that old fuck, Freeman. I mean I'm not mad, we kind of put him in that spot, but still. Fuck them." Jack was pacing around his kitchen in his robe, ranting and mumbling.

Nicky sensed that Jack was slipping. "it's not just that they killed our friends. They've likely killed hundreds. Made people disappear. They've secretly shaped the city for their

Act III

benefit. The city deserves better, and it doesn't even know it. My family was the driving force and the face, and they hid in the shadows and pulled the strings. Everything I grew to hate about my own lineage was because of them. And for that, I will kill every last one of them."

Jack had come to a stop, he was listening. His old eyes had that spark again. He started to grin as Nicky reignited that fire within. The doorbell took them by surprise, as it does.

Both men reached for their guns. Nicky from his holster, Jack from his waist band. They both peered through the front window, Bill's car sat running in the driveway, it was in bad shape.

"Oh, shit that's him" They both raced to the sidewalk. Bill slumped over in the driver's seat, again.

They drug him back into the house, he was a mess.

"This isn't how I left him. They did this" said Nicky as they propped Bill up on a chair in the living room. He had blood splatter on his pants, his shirt was half on this time, but he was still barely conscious.

"He took one hell of a beating. Look at his eyes, he almost looks…lumpy, you know? Like he was pummeled." Jack looked over Bill again and added "Did they drop him off?"

"I doubt it" Nicky splashed a cup of water on Bill's face. He barely reacted. "From the end of that video, it looks like they held him down and beat him after they branded him"

"What a strange party ritual"

"These guys aren't normal Jackie. This is a whole new level. They are above the law, above the government, above everyone. Untouchable."

Act III

Jack held his coffee cup under Bills nose "You really believe that shit? All these years hunting these fools and we finally put it all together and now they're untouchable?"

"Not really what I meant"

"Sounded like it…. Sounded like a scared whittle baby"

"You done?"

"I could go on"

"This is why we don't tell you things, Jack. You're unhinged at the best of times"

"That's Bay City Executioner .. to you, good sir. Need I remind you of my long… long list of arrests?

The long list of lowlife wannabe crime bosses who didn't stand a chance?"

Nicky made the face of someone who had heard all of this before. Because he had, many times. A dialed in Jack was unstoppable. He haunted the dark corners of Crimson Bay and was the ultimate thorn in organized crime for decades. It wasn't even an undercover gig, he didn't hide it, he just looked like a madman with great hair who lived life at one hundred miles per hour.

      But, like every hall of fame career, the golden boy was retiring. Or so he had hoped until the death of his protégé. Now his retirement tour had turned into a revenge party.

"You're both idiots" came the groggy voice of the Police Chief. "I need water, and pain meds, coffee, food and my gun."

"Nice little shopping list, Chief, how are you feeling?" asked Jack, with full intrigue.

Act III

"Exactly how I look. Like someone who was beaten, branded and left in a field to die" Nicky surveyed the damage again "Why would bring you in, tell you everything, brand you and then leave you for dead?"

Jack came back with another coffee, "Makes total sense to me, soak him in booze, give him a concussion, all kinds of reasons for people to doubt anything he says. If he survives, no one will believe him, if he dies, they move on"

"And if two garbage men find him and then they get killed?" asked Nicky.

Bill was confused "what garbage men?" Nicky pulled out his phone and ran the clip again. Bill was shocked. He had no memory of any of that. "They found me?" he asked.

"Bill, we watched the whole meeting that you recorded, but there was something at the end of the tape that you need to hear"

      A long silence in the video, Nicky fast forwarded to the end. Voices in the distant. A guy named Tony, another named Dave, they searched Bill for money. And then they heard it. A third voice. Gun shots and then nothing. "Who was that!?" remarked Bill, Jack and Nicky both shrugged slightly, "We don't know".

Act III

The Shadow of Death

Days passed, minutes, hours, seconds. They ticked in the brain of all three men. This was the final shot for Eumenides. The three amigos would ride off into the sunset. Jack had wound himself up into a bloodlust. Nicky was carefully planning and scheming from the dark, and Bill, he was sitting in meetings with the men who tried to kill him and all he could do was smile and shake hands with them.

The plan had been devised. Jack's Wildside mixed with Nicky's focused hatred and skill had produced a seemingly foolproof plan to topple the Black flame. It was direct and left them all wondering why they hadn't thought of it before: Kill them all. One by fucking one.

The underground parking lot of Elliots Building filled up quickly. All four spaces were taken; the fifth empty spot had been crudely scratched off. The war room had one name written on it, that was Charlie Banks. The financial director for Crimson Bay, and the Black Flame Order.

Elliot was in a great mood "Start with their money. Make Chuck squeal and then dismantle their finances." The other three agreed, "and cut him limb from limb, drop the body parts at Allison Frosts front door."

Act III

"Yeah, you know what. I'm with Jack on this one... let's make a mess of this. We didn't come all this way, through the years of chasing to play it safe."

Guns. Check

Knives. Check

Various explosive devices. Check.

Hand grenade. Check.

Chewing tobacco. Check

Bag of sour candy. Check.

"Gentleman, it's been fun. But I'm too old for this shit now. So, lets fucking end this." Said Jack as he stepped into the ghost. His '76 dodge challenger was made for days like this.

The plan was to ambush Charlie at home. Elliot had done his homework and Charlie's wife was away. They didn't have children which made him an easier pick to get slaughtered first. The rotten scumbags who also had children created a juxtaposition that even the most cruel and cold-blooded would find tough to follow through on. The plan would hopefully only need a few sacrifices before it got Allisons attention and then they could focus on taking her down.

"Head of the snake" was written on the whiteboard. The head, being Allison Frost.

Rain bounced off the windshield as Jack stormed through the streets. The old streetlamps blurred as he passed. Charlie lived downtown in a high rise, easy picking for Jack. The traffic was light, no one blocking his path. The challenger turned the heads of everyone on the sidewalk. Normally, jack would take a less direct approach, but this was the final ride. The buildings started to get closer and closer together, taller as

Act III

they reached for the sky. Some seemed to disappear into the clouds, lost beyond the rain.

A text came through from Nicky. *I'm inside. Hurry up.* "This fucking guy" said Jack to himself. Nicky had a knack for leaving last and showing up first. The engine roared and Jack slid around the corner on the wet pavement. He put it in park at the front entrance, kicked open his own door, walked up the steps, punched out the door man and headed up to the fifty third floor. The faces of the bystanders in the lobby would only be described as disbelief. No one moved or said anything. A large man with flowing hair, long black coat, cut up jeans, big black boots and many gold chains walked into their lobby, knocked a guy out and kept moving without breaking stride. Not a cell phone recording in sight, that was part of Jack's skillset, he was gone before anyone knew what happened.

The elevator opened on the fifty third floor to Nicky leaning against a cold tile wall. The hallway had the warmth of an ice storm. Both men pulled their firearms and readied themselves down the ultra rich corridor.

"Second last on the right."

"Any signs of anyone else?"

"Nothing, no movement, did you punch out the security guard?"

"Doesn't sound like me. I'm a lover"

"Right."

Nicky paused beside Charlie's door. They both stood still and listened for any sounds of life. After a long silence, Nicky stepped in front of the door and kicked it in. Not exactly the best way to keep a low profile, but that wasn't their goal anymore.

Act III

The door surprisingly flew off its hinges with ease, it smashed into a table and sent furniture flying. No response from inside. They entered the front room and cleared it; they went all through the large lavish apartment. Nothing. No signs of anyone even living there. It was perfect inside. Jack leaned on the large quartz island "Does this guy exist? Because... this place looks staged."

Nicky pulled on drawers, tipped over anything he could move, opened every closet. "We had good intel on this one. Elliot never messes up. "Well, skip, he fucked this up." Said Jack as he opened a beer from the fridge. "You think he was tipped off? Or worse, they know what we are doing, and we are basically fucking dead?" He tossed Nicky a beer, "we are off to a great fucking start. Go look out that window and tell me if the cops are here. Someone punched the security guard and he's probably pretty mad by now."

Nicky laughed and walked to the sliding patio door "Oh fuck!" Nicky opened the door and rushed out on to the deck. Jack didn't move.

"He's still alive!" yelled Nicky from the deck. Jack slowly sauntered outside. He turned to see Nicky overtop of what looked to be a human, in a puddle of blood. Jack finished his beer and cracked another one. "Fuck, they took out one of their own."

"I don't think so Jack. He's still here, let's get him inside"

"That's a lot of blood Nick. This jacket is a family heirloom; I can't get blood on it."

Nicky picked up Charlies' arms and walked him backwards into the apartment. He propped him up against the wall and tried to clean up his bloodied face. "Charlie? Can.. you.. hear..me? Who did this to you?"

Act III

Jack re-entered the room and slid the door shut. "yeah, we got to make this quick, Billy boy and his blue friends are down there now"

Charlie mumbled through the blood in his mouth, something about a hood. Something about a figure in a hood. He passed out again before they could get any more words from him. Jack stood at the door, watching for the elevator "Time to go, Nicholas" he made a face that said hurry the fuck up. Nicky followed him out the door and down the hall, they took the service elevator and narrowly missed the crusade of officers going up the adjacent elevator. An easy walk through the staff quarters and they landed in the back alley. Gone with the wind.

Banks is dead. Read the text on Jacks phone. It vibrated in the cup holder as he blew through a stop sign. Nicky picked up the phone and read it aloud. "Old Bill, always a couple steps behind. Text him back, ask him how the security guard is doing" Jack laughed. He pulled a pocket beer he stole from the apartment and cracked it open. Nicky didn't bat an eye. He laughed too as he sent the text. They had to keep Bill in and out of the loop for all their safety. Burner phones were always their thing until Elliot bought them ones that were untraceable. No one asked how or why. They just put them in their pockets.

The bell above the door at the 6th street deli seemed to ring nonstop, the lunch rush for the city's best sandwiches. Between the bells, the television in the corner was tuned to the news. Channel 5's Laura Snow sat above the ticker that read "Breaking News" She tried her best to give a recount of the gruesome murder of Charlie Banks, a city official. No one in the Deli paid much attention. Charlie wasn't a prominent figure; he kept a lower profile on purpose. The money behind the Black Flame Order depended on it. Allison would surely be

Act III

furious with the news. The target on Jack's back grew with every second he was still breathing. Unbeknownst to her, he had nothing to do with it.

"Holy shit they got Oakes too!" shouted an older patron from the back of the Deli. A few people turned toward the small television in curiosity. "They did what now?" mumbled a few others. The ticker at the bottom of the screen had changed. *Serial Killer on the loose, city officials targeted.*

City officials Charlie Banks and Housing official John Oak were both found dead in their respective downtown high-rise apartments earlier today. Police Chief Bill Taylor briefs the crowd of reporters outside his office only moments ago:

"We are saddened to report the deaths of these two beloved individuals. The investigation into their deaths will be extensive and we will bring their killers to justice"

Reporter:" So you are saying their deaths are related?"

Bill: "I can't comment at this time"

Reporter: "You are saying they were murdered, for sure? You are suspecting foul play? Do you think these men deserved it?"

A flustered Bill:" Look, I didn't say, would you get that out of my face. These men have families, you arrogant little prick. How would you react to hearing the news that your family members were slaughtered by a serial killer"

The only way to covey what happened next, would be to take a can of gasoline, stand outside a fireworks factory, pour a long line on the ground, light a match, throw it, and watch the show.

The Deli erupted.

The laundromat next door erupted.

Act III

Every lunch place in the city.

Everyone downtown looking up at the giant ad screens.

Thousands of people in Crimson Bay just heard the words they were hiding from for decades.

A serial Killer, targeting high profile individuals in Crimson Bay. Cue the city-wide Panic Attack.

Bill walked back to his office, through the crowd, he ignored everyone. He shut the door behind him, locked it and sat down behind the big oak desk that Oscar had once occupied. The bottom drawer slid open, the bottle of liquor looked up at him. He obliged.

His two phones sat on the desk. One started ringing, it was the mayor. The other one rang as well. It was Elliot. Bill grinned as he sipped from his cup. Both phones wanted the same thing from him, and he chose to let them ring.

"No Answer"

"What do you expect, he's probably hiding in his office, half shit faced, probably with his gun in his mouth crying like a little bitch."

Elliot and Nicky looked at Jack with a concerned expression "I want to ask what is wrong with you but I'm constantly just answer my own questions"

"Me? Guy fucking sends the city over the edge and I'm the messed up one? Give me a break."

"They want you dead. Like now. I'm not sure how you're walking right now to be honest "added Elliot. He was furiously searching his computer for something.

"When you guys arrived at John's place. Where there any similarities to Charlies?"

Act III

Nicky detailed John's apartment. "Pretty clean. Quiet, very similar feel to Charlie's. John was in the kitchen, beaten half to death. Charlie was out on the deck. Other than that, I can't think of anything."

Elliot spun his computer around to a photo of a hooded figure, almost skeletal. Grim reaper looking. "Hooded figure?"

"Yeah, yeah, both of them mumbled that shit before they died" Jack was in full storyteller mode.

"Maybe that's what you see right before you die"

The three of them sat in silence in the war room. The only safe place they had left in the city.

Elliots phone rang, it was Bill.

"They want to meet"

Elliot asked" Who? Them, them?"

"Yeah. The meeting is set for tomorrow night at the church. That's all I know"

"You want to burn this one down too Billy boy?" yelled Jack from the other side of the room, he had started pacing about.

"Just give me a heads up so I can get the fuck out of there."

"Fuck, I was joking, but that's not a bad idea." Jack's face lit up, as much as it could. "That's it Bill, we burn these fuckers alive in the church were Nicky killed his own father at! It's almost beautiful and poetic."

Nicky sighed. "Jack, you burnt that church down twenty years ago. This is the new one. It's made of concrete."

"So, I can't…?"

"No, likely won't work."

Act III

"Guns?"

"Gun's will work, yes."

"Fuck it, I'm still bringing the gas."

Elliot was still furiously typing. He was trying to find any ties to this death figure that both men had breathed as their last breath. "There must be some connection. Did the hooded figure kill them or did they just see it flash before them?"

"Here it is! The Shadow of Death. The final moments of someone's life before it is all taken away. The character is an overlord type, a myth in fact. Something to be experienced, not so much to be seen. Not exactly the grim reaper, but more a vigilante of death, crossing names from a long list. The innocent are not disturbed by this hooded figure, only the dark souls are summoned to meet him"

Both men had froze in their tracks. Jack set his beer down. "Did you just say there's a ghost killing people?"

Elliot and Nicky both stared at Jack. "No."

"You absolute moron"

"Fuck you both and your fancy computer. I know what I heard" Jack went back to his beer. Nicky leaned over to Elliott and whispered "I mean he is kinda right"

"You can shut up too. It's a mythological creature that haunts the evil in our city. It's clear as day"

"Are you on Mushrooms?"

Elliot shook his head " No, this is a completely logical hypothesis, based on our current information."

"The information being two dead guys who just happened to mumble the same shit"

Act III

"Then who killed Charlie and John, Nicholas?!" shouted Elliot.

Nicky and Jack now both had beers. "I don't know, it wasn't us."

"Good luck convincing Allison of that." Elliot was frustrated with his team's lack of belief in mythological creatures. He wouldn't accept the coincidence theory that Nicky had presented, no matter how logical it seemed.

The three of them set out devising a plan for the following night. Gathering as much ammunition as they could get their hands on, without drawing attention to themselves. Guns, bullets, bombs, automatic everything, armor, grenades, more grenades, gasoline. The trucks were loaded up, same as Jacks Challenger. The whole going out on his sword mentality had taken over the group. They were dead either way, which is how they saw it. The most powerful, violent and corrupt group wanted them torn limb from limb. Running wasn't an option, it never was. The only option now was full speed ahead. Straight into a brick wall.

The rest of the day was one that historians would refer to as "The day before the end" After news broke, the fear mongering started. The news outlets, the social media platforms, everything that held the city's limited attention span. The government hates you, rise, take the power back, the police aren't protecting you, they are just letting violent serial killers run loose. All of the nonsense from the basement dwellers at their keyboards. But it slowly worked. It built and built as the hours ticked on. A police chief, clearly frustrated. The mayor held his briefing and assured everyone that it was being dealt with and not to look to the past for future solutions.

Act III

But all the crowds heard was "Copycat killer from decades ago! The Crimson Mask killer is back! Run to the hills!"

A frenzy grew. As night fell, the protesters emerged. Signs, torches, chanting. Large groups formed at city hall, at the police stations. Anywhere someone might listen. Demonstrations on every corner. Effigies burned in parks. Fear and anger filled the city. The temperature rose that night. As the sun came up, it also brought the city to a boil. And it didn't take long for the pot to spill over, burning everything in sight.

Act III

My Only Friend. The End.

Every household in the city watched the same image from the night before. Crowds everywhere. Violence, Vandalism, Protests. The city was unsafe. Schools were cancelled; workplaces were halted. The day had been taken hostage by a city that would no longer be lied too. It wanted answers. Another serial killer. With no one ever arrested. No suspects. It screamed cover-up. How could this happen again? The kids raised in homes where crimson mask wasn't spoken. The fear they all felt. The families of these slain humans. The police officers who lost their lives hunting these monsters in the dark. A black eye on the city hat was never to be repeated. Was about to be repeated.

The proverbial dark cloud hung above the skyscrapers. The bridges seemed empty, the wind freely pushed loose trash down the streets. The distance rumble of protest groups at the city centre. The streets were either deserted or unsafe to walk down, all depending on their proximity to a public office.

News vans roamed the city, interviewing anyone who would talk to them. The questions were vague, meant to steer the narrative away from what was really happening. An uprising, from the underworld. The puppet masters were preparing to step into the light after decades hidden from sight.

The police headquarters was a frenzy of activity. Task forces formed at every turn; they were preparing for the worst. Everyone has memories of thirty years ago, whether it is first

Act III

or secondhand accounts. The streets filled with armored vehicles, tanks, everything to control the riots.

"I won't accept anything less than a sweeping defeat of these mobs. They may as well have torches and pitchforks at this point" Chief Taylor announced as he stood before his officers in the bullpen. He was torn but kept it inside. His phone was flooded with messages from unknown numbers. The meeting was set at the church; he was to attend or else. He was also meant to set his team up for failure, a failure so catastrophic, it would crumble the very structure in which the policing system was built on. Anarchy would rule and drive the city into disrepair. The Black Flame Order would take it's rightful seat, with the Mayor, out in the open, no longer a hidden entity. Allison Frost would have her day, her coronation if you will, for she was the only member who wasn't already set in place. This would be her masterpiece, her legacy. The city adored the Mayor, and he would endorse her as the rightful leader of the new world.

"She's Batshit crazy if she thinks this is going to work. Like, really, Fuck her and the fucking horse she fucking rode in on. If this little bitch thinks she can run my life, shes got another thing coming, oh boy, does she ever."

Nicky's face, mostly his eyebrows, furrowed in a concerned look. He stared at Jack, as he normally did, during these rants, and he digested what just came from his partner's mouth. "It's a wonder you were never married. Women must have just lined up around the block for any tiny minuscule chance to even breathe the air in which you inhabited."

Jack looked back at Nicky. "What the fuck do those words even mean Nick?"

Act III

"It means you are just as batshit as she is, maybe….maybe you two will hit it off"

"Oh, we are hitting it off. Her head is going to hit… off this fucking bat"

Jack and Nicky sat high above the downtown core, overlooking the river, the bridges and a few blocks over, the church. They sat on top of one of the office buildings that Elliots secret money owned. Watching and waiting.

"That's a beautiful sentiment, Jack. It's almost schoolyard crush-esque. You two are so similar, yet neither can see it. And then you bash her skull in with a bat. Tale as old as time"

"My mother always said I was a lover"

"She did?"

"No. She left me outside a fire station. I was put up for adoption."

"That's terrible, how can someone do that to a baby"

"None of that's true Nicky. You know how I get"

"The love of a parent. I killed mine, so really what do I know."

"I think this is why we are friends Nick. I keep forgetting that you are the actual cold-blooded killer. You are so much more fucked up than me, and that's why we get along so well."

Jack took a bite from his apple and pondered as he sat looking at the huge screens in the square below. They continued to show highlight reels of the rioting, which had devolved into looting as well. Riot gear clad police officers fighting with civilians was the main character for the next few hours. The live updates were accompanied by the soundtrack of the city. Car horns, sirens, gun shots, screaming, smooth Jazz, all the scary sounds.

Act III

The first round of vehicles pulled up to the church. Black SUV's pulled down the alleyway and a few minutes later they exited on the opposite side. A secret rear entrance, obviously. The meeting was set for nine o'clock. Bill had gotten the message to them earlier. The henchmen from the video arrived as well, only this time there were a few more than the six. Jack counted fifteen men in sight.

"Yeah, I get it. They're large humans, but that just gives more target to shoot at. Although, on closer inspection, they may be made of steel."

Something down the street, a flash, caught their attention, both men stood at the parapet to get a better look. A fire had broken out two blocks down. The crowd had made its way closer and now they could see a police car on fire.

"That's not good. It's full anarchy out there now." Said Nicky as he lowered his binoculars. The sound of a tank rolling down the other end of the street took them by surprise. "I'd say we picked the right spot for a show" added Jack. He had started checking his weapons to make sure everything was locked and loaded.

"This is what she wants. The city crumbles in on itself and she steps up to rebuild it in her own likeness. Condemns the judicial structure and inserts her own rules and justice."

Jack didn't even look up "You have had way too much time to think about this"

"Can you fuck off, I need your head in the game when this goes sideways, which it will. Very fucking quickly"

"You want to see how serious I am about this?"

Jack stood up, put his rifle to his shoulder, his eye to the scope, pointed it at the crowd the next block over. He picked the first

Act III

person he could find that was looting a store. A woman threw a Molotov cocktail through a plate glass window and ran. Jack shot her in the head. One shot, done.

Jack turned around and walked over to his fold up chair. He sat down, kicked open his cooler and grabbed a beer. The screams from below were ear piercing. According to the screams, that women was named Karen, unfortunately.

"For fuck sakes Jack. Why her?!" Nicky was beside himself.

"Fucking…. Lou's ex-wife Karen. She was the worst. I've wanted her dead for thirty years"

"That was a woman in her twenties. Dickhead."

"Oh really? Shit, I should probably clean this scope. Could have sworn that was Lou's ex-wife."

Nicky was as cold-blooded as they came, but even he had a small amount of moral code when it came to murder. He only killed people who deserved it, like his own father.

"You've gone soft De Luca. Remember? That's your last name. That's the name that struck fear into the hearts of everyone. The name that held a room hostage in silence when you entered. The crown prince of Crimson Bay." Jack was getting under Nicky's skin, and he knew it.

"What would the old man think. His boy went soft and .."

Jack couldn't finish his sentence. The blood in his mouth mixed with the pain of having someone sucker punch you in the side of the jaw, had made it difficult to talk. Not to mention he was now face down in the snow pile beside his chair.

Act III

"Don't forget, Jackie" Nicky crouched down beside he old pal. "I killed my father." Nicky stood up and walked to the edge of the building. More snow had started to fall.

"and my mother" he said into the night. Jack had made it back up to his feet. Bloodied and snow covered. "What did you say?" asked Jack. It was more of a mumble.

They looked at each other but nothing was said. No one knew the other part of the story. The part where Rebecca was so depressed after the murderous rampage that took her husband and friends away from her that she decided to see what the front of a subway train looked like at full speed.

"I really didn't think the pain it would bring to my own family. All I focused on was relieving the city of the long tenured grip of greed and corruption."

"And that's all we are doing now. Just saving the city. Again. Because Bill's team of idiots can't get their shit together"

The two men stood staring at the chaos below. The mayors face on a giant screen telling everyone to remain calm. The riot police trying to round up crowds of protesters. Violence on every street corner. The downtown core had become a warzone in a few short hours. The snow had accumulated enough to warrant the snowplows to act, but they all refused.

The large doors of the church slammed shut, the noise brought Nicky and Jack back to reality. Jack is still leaking blood. A line of vans and SUVs had arrived. The meeting was about to begin.

The group entered the cathedral. The room at the back of the church had a set of stairs that's lead to a basement meeting room. Security had every door blocked. Getting to that basement would be almost impossible, unless they killed

Act III

everyone. Which was the plan. Jack would attempt to spare Bill, but if it came down to it, well, then it came down to it.

A long narrow room was used for the meeting of the Order. A large wooden table with old wooden chairs sat before the throne. This was not their typical meeting. They were reeling from the deaths of their own. Allison held court, her tone was neither subtle nor calm. The tension in the room was palpable. A legacy takeover of a city that they already ran from the shadows. The bringing of the light, as Allison put it, The black flame order.

"Tonight, we solidify ourselves as the ultimate society of justice and order in this city. We will finally step into full view. The city will understand who really has all the power. We will be there to guide them into the next decade. All while reaping the proper benefits and adulation we so rightfully deserve." The room agreed. They drank every drop from Allison's cup. She promised more money, more power, fame and fortune as they ran the city in their own mold. No more sneaking around.

Jack and Nicky loaded into the Challenger. The plan was to come around the corner at full speed and take out as many people as they could. Open fire and rush through the front doors. If they made it that far, then the grenades would get them passed the second wave. By the time they reached the basement, they would eliminate anyone in their path. Elliot was waiting in the building next door with his arsenal, so when the order members fled out the back door, he could pick them off, one by one. Or all at once, he wasn't picky.

"This sounds like a great plan Jack. It really does. Just a few holes in it. But I'm sure we will patch them up as we go" Nicky had his hand wrapped around the handle above the door and one foot pushing down on the floor mat, trying to keep

Act III

himself in the car as Jack hammered through the snow and slid wildly around the corner.

"Yeah.. well.. fuck it.. here we go!" Jack dropped both windows. An impressive feat while drifting through the snow. The scene broke down in slow motion. The car slammed into the first group of security guards; shots rang out through the air. The windshield cracked as bullets deflected into the snow. Bodies flew through the air. The suits of the security guards made it look like someone threw a bowling ball at a group of penguins. And opened fire on them.

Nicky hung from the open window and held his finger on the trigger until the clip emptied. Jack attempted the same, but he couldn't keep the car moving and shoot everyone he wanted to. The car finally stopped just past the front doors. They bounced off three SUV's and seven guards. Bodies spread across the steps; The first phase of the plan was going well. Jack jumped out and grabbed one of the remaining guards. Neither had bullets left so they squared off in an old school fist fight. Nicky ran to the door; he gave it a full dropkick. It didn't move. Nicky pulled himself back up, the door hit him with full force, sending him down the steps, three more guards came spilling out. They jumped on Nick and drug him inside. Jack didn't even notice, the fight had taken a turn for the worst. The three guards returned to help; jack didn't stand a chance. They drug him inside too. Phase one almost worked. Phase two was a little different than they planned.

"Get him up" is all Jack heard as he started to regain consciousness. The lights of the cathedral were blurry. The shapes in front of him took awhile to come into focus. There they were, everyone he hated, and Bill.

Act III

"Vigilante justice is not something we take lightly in this city. The two of you have been a thorn in our sides for quite some time. Even longer than I have been alive.

It is time for us to finally rid Crimson Bay of the great Jack Finn. The Bay City Execution. The one man we have yet to cross off our list." Allison stood atop the steps overlooking the pews. The Order lined the altar. Bill included. Jack was waiting for him to make a move, if any at all.

"Must be a short list then" laughed Jack, he didn't care for any of Allison's nonsense.

"Oh, but it is. It has two names on it. Yours is the only one left. The other name I have wanted, for the murder of my family and their closets friends. The one who started this war. The one they referred to as the Crimson Mask, Nicholas De Luca. A security guard drug Nicky to the fore front.

Jack didn't waste anytime "He looks pretty alive to me, you dumb bitch"

The guard to his left broke his ribs with one punch. Jack dropped to the floor.

"This has been a long time coming, for all of us." Allison pulled out a butcher knife. She walked to Nicky, who had been knelt beside her.

"For my family" Allison carved the butcher knife just below his hairline. She carved the line across his forehead, the blood spilled down his face. The Crimson mask. Nicky screamed in agony, but the guards held him in place. He lost a staggering amount of blood in a short period of time. Right before losing consciousness, Allison grabbed his throat and forced him to look her in the eyes. There wasn't fear in Nicholas de Lucas' eye. There was relief. Allison plunged the butcher knife through his heart. He was killed instantly.

Act III

Allsion wiped her hand in Nicky's blood. He slumped to the floor. She walked down the step toward Jack. He spit at her feet. He was all class. She rubbed her hand across his face, smearing blood in his eyes. She returned the favor, spitting in Jack's face. "Bring him up to me. We will cross him off the list"

Bill stood shaking. He had no weapon. He tried to avoid eye contact with Jack while trying to figure out the next move. He saw his opening as one of the guards had Jack's arm and his machine gun was hung over one shoulder. Bill had to grab the gun, open fire and really hope for the best or all of his friends were dead. Bill knew Elliot was close by, but he had no way to reach him.

One swift movement, Bill summoned all his courage and lunged at the guard. The commotion caused everyone to turn. Bill had the gun, and it was pointed at Allisons skull.

"Nobody fucking move!" he yelled. Every gun in the place drew and locked on him.

"Nope, no way. I'll blow her head clean off. Let him go, or she eats every bullet in the chamber"

Bill was doing his best, but his nerves from the years of police work were shot.

"You don't have it in you Taylor. You never did; you're just like Oscar. Useless." Allison had nailed her retort.

The next few moments felt like an eternity.

The sound of tires squealing outside, a scream from outside, the explosion of wood, the shards blown across the room. Guards' dove for cover as a black car smashed through the doors and pushed its way to the front of the church. "Elliot!" yelled Bill. Elliot had come through, he knew his old friend

Act III

would finally step into action. The door kicked open and before anyone could see through the debris clouds, bullets rang out and guards dropped in every direction. Elliot jumped onto the hood and walked toward Allsion and Jack.

"What an entrance," laughed jack. "Holy shit man, nice car"

Allison stood her ground. She held the knife to Jack. Bill held the gun to her.

"Put it down Allison, you're fucking done" said Bill with every ounce of rage he could muster.

Jack looked up at his friend, standing on the front of the car. A black hood and a long black coat, and a bandana covering the lower half of his face, with a skeleton's lower jaw on it. He could only see his eyes.

"What the fuck" gasped Jack. Allsion turned in confusion. The dark figure lowered his hood. Just at that moment, a guard, from behind the altar, shot Bill in the leg, Bill screamed and fell. Allison drew back the knife. The hooded figure shot the guard and Allison, right between the eyes.

Jack gathered himself as he continued to stare at the man on the hood. He looked at the car again. A jet-black Monte Carlo SS.

The man's eyes were cold. He stared back, nodded, and leapt to the floor. Jack stood to greet the man, but he jumped into the car and slammed it in reverse before anyone else arrived. Jack turned to help Bill.

"Holy shit Jack, Elliots a wild man. Where did he learn to drive and shoot like that"

Jack attended to Bills wound, which wasn't nearly as severe as his screamed let on. Jack didn't respond.

Act III

"Nicky didn't deserve that" said Bill quietly.

"Yeah, he did, Theres a price for this life, and he paid it."

A voice from the back of the church sounded familiar "What the fuck is this?" it was Elliot.

He tucked his gun away and started climbing over the rubble. He surveyed the damage, bodies piled up in every direction. He finally spotted a familiar face in the wreckage. His face told the story. Sadness overtook Elliot. He lowered himself beside his friend. In a soft voice "Nick. No… you fucking menace. You're at peace now. I will miss you."

Elliot stood up, "Of course Bill got shot" The others laughed, even Bill.

"Jack what the fuck is this?"

Before Jack could respond, Bill jumped in "wasn't that you in the car?"

"The fucking car with a death wish? It definitely looked familiar. But it wasn't me"

Elliot gave a look to Jack. They both recognized that car

Bill looked over at Jack, "Jack, who was that?"

"I really don't know Billy boy. A guardian angel?" they both laughed.

" Or maybe just the shadow of death watching over us."

Act III

Two months Later

      The city was slowly grieving. The death toll from the riots had hit triple digits. The Crimson Bay cemetery was running out of plot and looking to expand. The Black Flame order had been extinguished; a line that Jack used many times after the shootout.

      A new Mayor, A new team of city officials, all sworn in, not a bad apple in the bunch. The right people for the jobs, finally. Warmer weather finally setting in, but only slightly warmer. The rainy spring season would wash away all the old snow and leave a clean slate.

Jack: Still cranky, starting to accept Nick's death.

Bill: Limping, still the Chief of Police.

Elliot: Still dead on paper, richer than ever.

Jack had ventured out of his house on a rare stroll down by the water, under the bridges. A coffee, slightly on the Irish side, accompanied him as he found a bench in the little park that overlooked the boat launch.

      Retirement was supposed to be at the forefront for Jack. He had held many secrets, for too long, fought the good fight in the dark. The weight he felt was crushing him, even

Act III

with the relief they found eliminating the Order. Someone else would rise up, they always do. The history buffs would lead you to believe that the city was safe and had very low crime rates for the past decades. They would also be very wrong, there was always a danger, it just operated at a level no one could see or hear.

Jack stared out into the water, just contemplating life.

"You didn't shed one single tear" came a voice from over his shoulder.

"I didn't have to" said Jack, he didn't move a muscle. "I wasn't fooled for a second"

"The look on your face said different"

"I was just shocked you even showed up"

"Aren't you going to ask about the others?"

"I don't have to. I knew it was you. How many others were there?"

"Enough. Once I hit the right nerve, it led me to the Order. They know how to hide in plain sight"

Jack finished his coffee and tossed the cup. He didn't dare turn around. "How bad was it?"

"Just an Elevator shaft. Nothing I can't handle"

"Fair enough… so what do you need from me?"

"You gave me enough; I needed to find my own"

"I named you the Shadow of Death. Hope it fits on your calling card" Jack laughed.

"Theres an uprising Jack. A storm"

Act III

"Yeah, well you enjoy that. Cause I'm old and broken and tired and hungry and I don't wanna do this shit anymore and I never wanted to do it in the first place and I...." Jack finally turned around.

He was alone.

The End.

Act III

Manufactured by Amazon.ca
Acheson, AB